AMISH
CHRISTMAS
SLEIGH

The
AMISH
CHRISTMAS
SLEIGH

KELLY LONG
AMY LILLARD
MOLLY JEBBER

KENSINGTON BOOKS
www.kensingtonbooks.com

KENSINGTON BOOKS are published by

Kensington Publishing Corp.
119 West 40th Street
New York, NY 10018

All Kensington titles, imprints, and distributed lines are available at special quantity discounts for bulk purchases for sales promotion, premiums, fund-raising, and educational or institutional use.

Special book excerpts or customized printings can also be created to fit specific needs. For details, write or phone the office of the Kensington Sales Manager: Kensington Publishing Corp., 119 West 40th Street, New York, NY 10018. Attn. Sales Department. Phone: 1-800-221-2647.

ISBN-13: 978-1-4967-0015-5
ISBN-10: 1-4967-0015-5
First Kensington Trade Paperback Printing: October 2015
First Kensington Mass Market Edition: October 2016

eISBN-13: 978-1-4967-0014-8
eISBN-10: 1-4967-0014-7
First Kensington Electronic Edition: October 2015

10 9 8 7 6 5 4 3 2 1

Printed in the United States of America

CONTENTS

A SLEIGH RIDE ON ICE MOUNTAIN

KELLY LONG

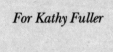

For Kathy Fuller

PROLOGUE

Christmas Eve, Ice Mountain, Pennsylvania,
One Year Ago

The heavy tread of his black boots barely made an impression in the hard-blowing snow, but he loved a roaring gale of a storm, especially on this, the most holy of *nachts*. He'd nearly gained the porch of the small cabin when he pulled the wooden *boppli* sled from his thick bag. His blue eyes shone beneath the blur of white as he felt the just-right weight of the sled, meant to pull a baby on fun-filled jaunts.

Then his steps slowed as he caught sight of the scene inside. He peered in the lighted cabin window at Fran Zook, her head bent in her hands while her husband, Daniel, attempted to comfort her.

Seeing the grieving couple shook him as he stood holding the sled in the snow. He whispered a soft prayer, and the sudden light of a single star pierced the whipping snow surrounding him. He knew he'd been both heard and answered. He mounted the steps and gently laid the sled down on the porch. With a deep breath, he gave a muffled knock to the thick wooden door and then backed away.

When Daniel Zook opened the door, the blustering cold slammed into him. He shivered hard as he bent to pick up the sled.

"What is it?" Fran asked wearily, and he saw her gaze straying with tear-reddened eyes to the empty cradle in the corner.

"A *boppli* sled," Dan answered. His voice shook on the reply.

Fran sobbed aloud. "*Ach,* how could he do this to us? What a cruel gift, and after the funeral today, too . . . she looked so small."

"I know," Daniel said, but he didn't put the small sled down. He turned to his grieving wife. "Yet maybe, maybe, Fran, there is promise in the gift—"

"*Nee.*" She choked on her tears and stared at him with an angry glare. "There is not. Burn that sled. I don't care." She glanced listlessly at the cradle again.

Dan looked at the sled in his hands. He understood his wife's pain. He shared it with her. Only time would heal his wife's heart . . . and his.

Instead of following her wishes, though, he crept through the storm to the shed. He went inside to the back corner, behind a wooden shelf filled with tools. He set the sled down, found an old tarp, and covered the gift carefully.

CHAPTER 1

Present Day, Ice Mountain, December

The mountain snow was dazzling to the eyes and the senses, and thirty-four-year-old Sebastian Christner still had child enough in his heart to enjoy the brisk intake of breath that filled his big lungs and made him dig his hands deeper into the pockets of his heavy black wool coat.

"Give us a push, *Herr* Christner!" one of the Mast *buwes* called to him in ringing tones from the top of the hill. Sebastian broke into a smile. Growing up, he'd been the eldest of a whole brood of children, and sledding held wonderful memories for him.

He waded through the knee-deep snow and started up the sledding path where many of the *kinner* were playing, rosy-cheeked, against the background of a bright blue sky. Sebastian caught hold of the back of the big runner sled loaded with three boys in all manner of bent elbows and knees and gave an easy push. The sled was off, and exultant whoops of joy echoed back up the hill. Sebastian swept his gaze across the tilt of the land for another sled. Then he saw a single child, a young *buwe*, sitting on a tree stump, cheering as wildly as his feeble limbs would allow as each sled took off.

Sebastian plowed through the snow to the child's side and sank down on his haunches. He searched the pale little face that turned to him with its gaptoothed smile.

"Hiya, *Herr* Christner." Nine-year-old Ben Zook's voice was high and thin, but his dark brown eyes were steady.

"Be you cold, child?" Sebastian asked, noticing the faint tremor of the boy's arms and mittened hands where he held his crutches.

"Only a bit. My sister brought me up here to watch the sledding while she does the wash. She said she'd be no more than an hour."

Sebastian quickly unbuttoned his coat and slung it over the child's frail shoulders. "Sisters forget sometimes."

"*Ach, nee*," Ben replied, visibly luxuriating in the new warmth as he snuggled deeper into the folds of the coat. "Kate never forgets me. She says I'm in her heart."

Sebastian smiled and thought of the kind girl, though he couldn't seem to bring to mind her features at that moment. Rather, he had a mental impression of quick, able-bodied movement, a sturdy build, and dark brown hair. He half-shook his head—what Kate Zook did or did not look like was of no matter to him.

"Would you like a ride?" Sebastian asked, pushing aside his idle thoughts of little Ben's sister.

The child's face flushed a rosy red and his eyes shone. "*Ach, jah.* But Kate said not to go down with anyone. I might get hurt."

"I'm sure she meant the bigger *buwes* . . . I'm an *auld* hand at sledding, and I'll make sure you're safe." Sebastian got to his feet and easily swept Ben and his crutches up into his arms.

"*Kumme,* we'll borrow the runner sled." Sebastian laughed, his heart full, as the child snuggled against his chest.

He hailed the Mast *buwes,* who gladly loaned their sled. With Ben still in his arms, he dropped down on the solid wooden slats and carefully positioned the child between his legs, minding the crutches, and grasping the lead rope.

"Ready?" he said to Ben.

"*Jah!*"

Sebastian leaned his weight forward a bit and they were off, skimming down the path, until the trees became one big, thrilling blur.

Ben squealed in excitement, and Sebastian couldn't contain a hearty laugh as the sled dipped and flew. He held the lead rope easily but had to give a sudden tug to the right when a girl with her hands on her hips suddenly stepped into the path in front of them.

A spray of snow flew into the air as the runner blades cut hard. By sheer will Sebastian was able to keep the sled from tipping. Even so, he lost his black-brimmed hat in the process and was wiping snow from his eyes when a soft voice carried to him with vigor in the cold air.

"Benjamin Zook! Do you know you might have been hurt or worse? What were you thinking?"

Sebastian smiled upward as a flurry of skirt approached. "It was my fault, truly. I encouraged him to have a go."

"*Jah,* well . . ."

Sebastian looked up as Kate Zook's voice suddenly trailed off. He froze, caught by the intensity of her jewel-blue eyes as she stared down at him.

At twenty-six, Kate Zook knew she was not only approaching spinsterhood by her community's standards, but that she had more worries to deal with than she could handle. Yet, at that moment, all she could think of was the fact that she'd never been this close to Sebastian Christner before. Sure, there'd been a time she'd served him lemonade at a summer picnic and his shoulder had accidentally grazed her breast . . . her heart thumped now at the memory she'd nursed, spinning it into a fair yarn in which he'd turned, apologized, and asked her to marry him. But he'd done no such thing, and his shoulders were so broad and strong that he probably hadn't noticed the incidental touch in the first place. *But I did . . .*

"Uh . . . Kate?" Sebastian's deep voice cut into her thoughts. "I think Ben might be getting cold."

She moved with alacrity, feeling her face flush with remembrance as she bent to lift her younger *bruder* from the sled, the boy still clad in Sebastian's heavy black coat. She noticed the manly scent of pine soaping that clung to it, sending her senses into a slow simmer.

He rose to his feet to tower over her as she held Ben. Sebastian's auburn hair had a faint curl to it and his blue eyes seemed to glow with some secret merriment as he stood, coatless in the cold, his red shirt and black wool pants making him stand out with a cardinal's beauty against the white of the snow.

But she couldn't focus on Sebastian, although she wished she could let her gaze linger on his fine form a little longer. She needed to get Ben inside, and she gave Sebastian a brief nod as she turned to go, almost staggering in the snow under the additional weight of the man's coat that swallowed her brother's thin frame.

Sebastian stepped in front of her, his arms—strong arms, she noticed—outstretched. "Here, let me carry him inside, *sei se gut.*"

She turned slowly as Sebastian reached out large hands to scoop Ben from her arms. It was a relief in more ways than one, she thought ruefully. She'd been both literally and figuratively carrying Ben since the buggy accident that took their parents' lives—leaving her unscathed but Ben permanently disabled at the age of two. She hadn't known what to do until her cousin Daniel and his wife had invited her to come and live on their property on Ice Mountain in a small abandoned cabin. But even now, with the community's help, she often found she had little money to plan for Ben's future . . . Yet, still, surely *Gott* had a plan . . .

"Your thoughts run deep this morning?"

Kate snapped her head up at the question from the tall man beside her who was moving easily through the snow.

"Kate's always thinking hard," Ben explained.

"Ben, I . . ." She swallowed, unsure how to respond.

"Don't tease your sister," Sebastian whispered

sotto voce with a sidelong glance at her that set her heart thumping.

"I wasn't." Ben smiled. "Kate's smart."

Sebastian nodded politely. "I'm sure she is."

Kate longed for some clever retort to come to her tongue or some flirting manner to suddenly enchant her, but she was what she was and she could only mumble a vague invitation for tea and cookies. To her immense surprise, Sebastian accepted.

CHAPTER 2

He wondered vaguely why he'd agreed to sit at the small table and drink lukewarm tea, but then she served giant sugar cookies and the moment was redeemed for him. He loved cookies—plain and simple.

"*Herr* Christner, do you want to see my marble run?" Ben asked when they'd finished eating. Kate continued to putter about the tiny kitchen.

Sebastian glanced at her. He was probably interfering with her housework and should leave, but he couldn't resist a look at Ben's toy. Everyone on the mountain knew Sebastian was a renowned toy maker. Bishop Umble had even allowed him a computer and Internet access in a shed near his *haus* so that he might take orders from all over the region, not just locally on Ice Mountain. Sebastian had been surprised, but the bishop said that bringing joy to a child's face was worth a little bending of the *Ordnung*.

"Sure, Ben." He smiled. "I'll look for a minute. Then I've got to go."

Ben swung ably across the floor on his crutches and gestured to a carved wooden series of levels in a rectangular frame that sat in a place of honor on a small side table.

"Watch!" Ben called, then dropped a single marble into the top of the run. The marble made its way quickly down the simple slats and shoots, then shot out the bottom in seconds.

Sebastian crossed the room and picked up the simple toy. It was obviously inexpensive and meant to hold a younger child's interest but he held it with gentle hands. "Where did you get it, Ben? It's a beauty."

Ben pointed with his crutch across the room. "Kate got it for me a long time ago when we lived in Lancaster."

Sebastian glanced over at Kate as she was doing the dishes, then let his gaze sweep the corners of the neat but relatively bare room. "Then it's surely special, seeing as it was a gift from your *schwester*. Is it one of your favorite toys, Ben?"

The child shrugged matter-of-factly. "It's my only one."

Sebastian hid his surprise. *Only one toy?*

"But that's okay. I'm getting older now. I don't need another toy."

Sebastian nodded as he carefully replaced the marble run, making sure to keep his tone even, although his heart ached for the child. "True, you are growing up. But we never are too *auld* for toys, *sohn*."

"Please don't give him ideas, *Herr* Christner," Kate said, moving to stand nearby as she dried her hands on her apron. "I—uh—mean no disrespect to you, but Ben knows that money is short and we can't always afford—"

Sebastian held up a placating hand. "I understand. Please forgive me. I meant no harm."

She nodded, and he was about to leave when an idea came to him. He paused, and dismissed the thought. But it had hit him so hard, his head hurt. He looked at Ben's lone toy, at the clean but nearly empty cabin, and Kate's insistence on being independent. Could he walk out of this house and not extend help?

Yet to do so would put everything he'd built at risk . . .

He shook his head. *Nee,* he couldn't do it. He turned to Ben and was about to tell him good-bye when different words came out of his mouth, words that nearly horrified him with their simple intensity. "I've been thinking lately that I'm in need of two people in my life—an apprentice for my toy making and a *hauskeeper." Have I completely lost my mind? What is she going to think I want, and worse yet, how can I have someone nosing about the place on a regular basis?* But even those doubts didn't stop him from uttering the question. "What would you and Ben say to helping fill those roles?"

He froze, wondering what he'd done. He looked from Ben's excited face to Kate's shocked one, and couldn't begin to understand how he'd gotten himself into such a painful predicament.

"Say *jah,* Kate! *Sei se gut,* Katie?" Ben was pulling at her skirt and balancing on one crutch while Sebastian stood, looking flushed and anxious, and still impossibly handsome, all at the same time.

She wet her lips. *It's like a dream* . . . But then her practicality took over—there were no such things as dreams, not real ones anyway. *Yet maybe Gott* . . .

"Ben, hold on. I need to talk with *Herr* Christner a moment about this. Will you go to our room and read for a bit—with the door closed, please."

She waited anxiously while her *bruder* hobbled away, casting one last pleading look over his shoulder before he went into the bedroom and closed the door.

She indicated the table with a quick gesture of her hand. "May we sit again?"

"Of course." He moved past her to resume the seat he had been in earlier.

Kate did the same, trying to think of what to say.

"You wonder how this came up so suddenly, maybe?" he asked.

She grabbed on to his words like a lifeline. "*Jah*—I—have you been thinking about it?"

She watched him exhale slowly, then he shrugged and gave her a quick smile, a flash of even, white teeth. *He's so handsome* . . . She quickly refocused when he cleared his throat.

"I—um—you may not know it, but I fear I'm the object of . . . talk . . . in the community at times— among the womenfolk." He flushed a bit and she hid a smile.

Ach, *do I know* . . . Sebastian Christner was one of the most eligible bachelors on Ice Mountain, and he was often the subject of giggling chatter by women both young and *auld* . . . especially the single ones, but she was surprised that he knew of it.

"And?" she asked, wondering where he was headed with the conversation.

He bent his head a bit so that his thick lashes lay

against his high cheekbones for a moment, and she shifted in her chair.

"I—I think, Kate Zook, that you might—keep the women at bay—as it were, especially now." He looked up and spread his hands helplessly. "The holiday season is very busy for a toy maker."

She felt her heart sink. *So I'm a guard dog, a tough* auld *bird who will . . .*

He reached across the table and brushed at her hand with the whisper of a touch. She stilled her thoughts and looked at him.

"Forgive me," he said slowly. "I put that badly. I need help and perhaps you do, too. And Ben—he has a *gut* mind and could learn a trade despite his disability."

She nodded. "That's true—but the, um, *haus-keeping . . .* how often would that be? Only for December?"

She told herself that she imagined the relief in his sky-blue eyes when he nodded his head. "*Jah . . .* for December, say, every weekday and then maybe once a week after that. And Ben can *kumme* as often as school allows."

Then he named a sum for wages that made her eyebrows shoot up in surprise. *I'd be able to save something for the first time in years and maybe get a few gifts for Ben for Second Christmas.*

"When would I, er, we start?" she asked, trying to rein in her excitement at the possibility of actually being in his home on a brief, though regular basis.

"How about Monday?" he asked, and she thought he suddenly seemed restless. No doubt having made his decision, he wanted to be gone, so she got to her feet and extended her hand.

"*Danki, Herr* Christner. I accept."

He slid back his chair and got to his feet, his hand immediately engulfing hers. "Sebastian, *sei se gut.* Just call me Sebastian."

She nodded, secretly savoring the taste of his given name on the tip of her tongue while she watched him put on his coat and hat. Then she saw him to the door with a tentative smile. She realized she was watching the play of his lean hips beneath his long coat as he descended the snow-dusted steps, when he half-turned to wave a hand good-bye. She quickly closed the door and turned to press against it for a moment as she closed her eyes in a brief prayer of thanksgiving for the provision of work. Then she opened her eyes and set her chin. If she was going to be a good *hauskeeper,* she might as well start with keeping herself away from him, along with every other interested woman on the mountain . . .

CHAPTER 3

"No siree, I got plenty of time ta sit and listen 'bout how you're screwin' up yer life."

Sebastian sighed and leaned a hip against a workbench full of tools and wood shavings. He probably shouldn't have told his *Englischer* best friend, Tim Garland, about hiring Kate, but as he glanced around the workshop, he grimaced at the mess. He was a master toymaker, but lousy at cleaning up.

He frowned at his best friend and knew the older man wasn't likely to let the matter go easily. Tim Garland was as irascible as a timber rattler, but he was a *gut* man who saw that Sebastian's toys never failed to reach the post on time.

"She fed me cookies."

"Lord, have mercy . . . I know yer weakness for cookies."

"Tim, *kumme* on. If you think this workshop is cluttered, you must not have seen inside my cabin lately—it's a mess, to say the least." Sebastian picked up a small lathe and ran a practiced finger down its length.

"The mess never bothered you before." Tim harrumphed. "You're woman-hungry, boy, that's what." He squared his spry shoulders. "I knows it when I see it."

Sebastian snorted. "You don't know a shirt from a skirt, my friend. I simply saw an opportunity to help a family, and I did it—that's what *Gott* expects of us."

"Aw, don't go gettin' all *Amisch* on me, Seb . . . I've knowed you too long." Tim laughed, revealing a gap of missing front teeth, and Sebastian had to smile.

"All right—I'll admit she's got pretty eyes. She's also got a hurt *buwe* . . . And a too-small house and not enough toys . . . or happiness—I couldn't let it go."

Tim got to his feet and stretched, then adjusted his ball cap and zipped up his parka. "Well, there's some truth, anyway . . . All right, boy, I'll see you Monday for another load."

The old man bagged the five brown paper–wrapped packages and opened the door, letting the snow blow inside for a moment while Sebastian waved him off.

Then Sebastian went back to his worktable, pushing aside his friend's words, and concentrating on the making of a miniature wooden Noah's ark that he needed to finish and ship to California before Christmas.

"Yep," he muttered aloud, peering at a half-formed pair of giraffes, along with all the other projects that were in various stages of completion. "I definitely have no time for romance . . ." Yet one part of his brain kept seeing Kate's jewel-blue eyes, highlighted by white snow, and he wondered uneasily if he was being entirely truthful with himself . . .

"Do you have your service satchel packed, Ben?" Kate asked, rushing as usual to get breakfast cleaned up before the community's bimonthly Sunday church meeting. She and Ben rode with her cousin Daniel and his wife, Fran, and somehow Kate always managed to be late.

"I'm too *auld* to have a satchel," Ben said, but Kate waved aside his words.

"Every *buwe* and *maedel* is allowed to bring a puzzle or coloring book to service to keep them occupied, Ben. You'd never make it through the three hours without your satchel."

"I would, too. I like to listen to the singing and to Bishop Umble's sermons or the deacons when it's their turn. I'm growing up, Katie, especially since I'm going to apprentice with *Herr* Christner. I wonder if we'll see him to talk to today?"

Kate paused in pulling her cloak off the peg near the door and felt with absent fingers around the front of her warm bonnet. What if Sebastian did speak to her? Normally, he would barely nod in her direction, or any single girl's direction, for that matter. But now she was his *hauskeeper*—she hugged the thought to herself and went to help Ben button his coat.

"I think, Ben, that *Herr* Christener is a very private man, so maybe we shouldn't tell anyone yet about our new jobs."

"A secret?" He smiled up at her. "*Wunderbaar!*"

Then a brisk knock on her front door alerted her that Daniel and Fran must be ready in the big sleigh.

Kate hurried to fling open the door and tightened her bonnet strings as a sharp wind blew inside.

"Fran's waiting," Daniel said, bending to lift Ben up and carry him outside.

Kate followed, feeling her mood dampen a bit. Fran was not always kind with her words, but Kate understood. Last Christmas, when little *boppli* Alice passed away from pneumonia, it had been almost more than Fran could bear, and she was still bitter to this day.

So Kate readied a smile as she slipped under the lap blankets and cuddled close to Ben, who loved the hot potatoes that Daniel always placed in the bottom of the sleigh for extra warmth.

"Hiya, Fran. I'm sorry to keep you waiting in the cold," Kate said clearly.

The jangle of harness as the horse set out dispelled the bleak look Fran threw in Kate's direction. "Does it really matter, Kate?" the older woman asked. "You're always late and you always will be."

And that is that . . . Kate sighed to herself, then found peace in the gumdrop-shaped bushes, mounded with a frosting of white snow, and forgot her cousin's irritation for the moment.

Sebastian was exhausted. He'd stayed up until 4 a.m., then fallen into bed for a fitful hour, only to get back up and start to get mentally ready for Sunday service. His hands had itched to do a bit of work, but he knew that the bishop wouldn't have approved, so he'd prayed instead, then gone to help set up benches in Ben Kauffman's big barn.

As he set the hard, backless benches in place, he had a sudden image of Ben Zook trying to hold any position comfortably with his crutches for the long service. It was something Sebastian hadn't considered before, and he hurried over to Bishop Umble.

"Sebastian—" The *auld* man had smiled up at him. "What do you need with such urgency?"

"It's Ben Zook," he'd blurted out. "The *buwe* should have a chair to sit on for church, something more comfortable for his legs."

Bishop Umble had smiled faintly. "A chair? I suggested it to Kate once and she told me he was fine, but I, too, would feel better if the child had better support for his back. I'll leave it to you to convince her before church starts. We'll put a chair at the end of the row where they normally sit. *Danki*, Sebastian."

As he'd watched the bishop walk away to attend to something else, Sebastian realized he was now required to somehow convince Kate to allow Ben the chair. He wanted to groan aloud; the only place he could talk with her would be outside, when Daniel Zook arrived, and the more he talked to any girl, the more it was sure to set tongues wagging in gossip. Still, he had hired her as his *hauskeeper,* so he might as well get used to it . . . But persuading Kate Zook when she had her mind set was probably not an easy task, and he turned wearily to go and watch for the family's sled to arrive in the thick snow.

* * *

Kate stared over Fran's head at the unmistakable sight of Sebastian Christner standing, apparently waiting, for Daniel's sled to arrive. He waved at her cousin with a gloved hand and caught the reins Daniel tossed down to him.

Kate was very aware of other community women arriving by sled with their families and looking in their direction, and she felt her heart begin to thump alarmingly. Even Fran gave her a sideways, suspicious glance. And Ben was practically hollering in greeting and scrambling to get to the side of the sleigh in his enthusiasm to see Sebastian.

Kate missed whatever quiet exchange happened between the two men when Daniel exited the sleigh, but somehow, after Sebastian had greeted her *bruder* and Fran, Kate found herself alone with him as the others went off into the barn. *Probably he's changed his mind about me working for him . . .* But then she moved to put her foot on the metal rung used to climb down from the sleigh and Sebastian lifted her easily and swung her to the ground as if she weighed no more than thistledown.

Kate had never thought of herself as especially feminine, certainly not dainty or one who needed caring for, but in that moment, the big man before her had made her feel every inch a woman—and one who was heated from the inside out despite the cold. She smiled uncertainly up at him and he returned the gesture, though there was something in his light blue eyes that she couldn't read.

"Uh, Kate—I, um, was setting up benches early this morning for church service . . ." He began, then seemed to lose direction.

"That's nice," she said inanely.

"And I thought of Ben."

Ben?

"*Jah,* I asked the bishop if Ben might have a chair to sit in for service and he agreed, that is, if you agree."

He spoke in a rush, as if anxious to get the words out, and she had the absurd notion to giggle. It was one thing to stand on pride with *auld* Bishop Umble and quite another to try to do it when one of the most handsome men on the mountain—not to mention her new employer—was asking the same question.

"Ben may have a chair . . . I suppose I have always tried not to let his injury stand out, and in doing so, I've been a bit prideful." *And perhaps neglectful of what Ben really needs . . .* She looked down at the white ground until Sebastian's deep voice caused her to lift her chin.

"I would imagine you've always done your best for Ben. He's blessed to have such a *gut* sister."

She nodded, too unsure to speak without tears. *No one has ever noticed my life with Ben and certainly never praised me for it . . .*

"*Danki,*" she whispered.

He nodded. "*Kumme,* take my arm. The ground is slippery. I'll walk you in."

She folded her fingertips tentatively around his bent arm, feeling the warmth of his body through his coat sleeve, and felt like an *Englisch* princess to be so escorted. Of course, she dropped her hand at the entrance to the barn, but not before many had seen and she had to slip into her place next to Ben with her eyes downcast but her heart uplifted in thanksgiving to *Gott.*

CHAPTER 4

When the service started with its usual progression of hymns, Sebastian longed to let his eyes slip closed in weary lassitude, but for some reason he couldn't fathom, his hands tingled when he remembered the firm feel of Kate's waist as he swung her down from the sleigh. He sighed inwardly—maybe Tim Garland was right—he was woman-crazy. He choked back a laugh, then thought with seriousness that not many women would have shown the courage Kate had to admit that they'd been prideful. . . . *I admire her for her gumption, that's all.*

Then he tried to focus as Bishop Umble took his place before the community to speak. The *auld*, long-bearded man paced before the group with his gnarled hands folded behind his back while his wise eyes seemed to take in everyone gathered.

"In the book of Hebrews, we read that 'Faith is being sure of what we hope for and certain of what we do not see . . .' "

Sebastian recalled the verse and thought of its

absolute truth, but knew he did not always live by it. Still, he leaned forward a bit, anxious to catch each word of the sermon despite his uneasy feeling that he had a migraine headache coming on.

He started to pray, asking *Gott* that the migraine might pass him by, because he knew how much work he needed to get done the next day, then he abandoned the petition as Bishop Umble's words struck home.

"So what do you hope for?" the bishop asked. "The rest of the world might hope for riches, freedom from sickness and disease, or even a bigger home, but you, *Amisch* men and women of Ice Mountain, what do you hope for in your secret hearts?"

The question hung in the chill air and haunted Sebastian. He knew what he wanted, but it could never be. Never. What was done was done, and though *Der Herr* might forgive his sin, he must always bear the consequences of his actions.

Sebastian gazed down at his folded hands in front of him, and the rest of the sermon slipped away from his consciousness. Hours later, he got to his feet to file out of the barn, and his head throbbed with the beginnings of pressure and pain.

Kate saw Ben ensconced at the children's table among his young friends, then went to help Ann Kauffman with the serving. In the summer months and springtime, it was much easier to have the community gather for Sunday dinner following service, but in the winter, folks had to eat in shifts but usually congregated in groups according to age and interests. The young men would stand and hold their plates while the graybeards would eat at the main table. The women would usually serve and then eat last.

Ann Kauffman smiled tiredly when she saw Kate. "*Ach,* would you go into the second pantry and get more sugar? *Danki,* Kate . . ."

The "second pantry" ran adjacent along the wall to the first pantry and was in truth simply another closet filled with kitchen supplies, though having a second pantry was of great use to many a *haus frau.*

Kate forgot to grab a lantern in her haste to help and found herself in the nearly dark pantry, looking for the sack of sugar, when she froze in mid-movement. Through the thin side wall, she heard the unmistakable sound of Sebastian's deep voice coming from the other pantry. And she found herself helplessly eavesdropping . . .

"Uh, I'm afraid I didn't bring a light, and it's impossible to know where the canned pears are with as many *gut* things as your cousin Ann puts up every year." Sebastian kept his voice level, not wanting to offend the pretty nineteen-year-old Tabitha Deitweiler, a young relative of his hostess. But the girl was, without a doubt, taking distinct advantage of the dark to touch his chest.

"I apologize, *Herr* Christner . . . I had no idea you were in here," she purred, letting her fingers rise to stroke his throat.

Yeah, right . . . He felt annoyance begin to compound the headache he had originally sought refuge from in the small, dark room and carefully caught her wrists.

"Listen . . . Tabitha. There's many a man who would no doubt love a few stolen moments with you, but I should warn you that some might try to take advantage of your willing—er, the situation."

He could envision her pout as she pulled her hands free from his, only to have another go, this time encircling his neck.

"You sound like my *fater*," she whined.

"I'm *auld* enough to be your *daed* . . ." *If I'd been as promiscuous as you probably are at your age . . .*

"But I like older men," she said, obviously straining for his mouth and hitting his chin.

He put her firmly from him and reached behind her to open the door, letting in light from the kitchen. Mercifully no one was near the pantry or he'd have been accused of philandering, and somehow, all he could think of was Kate Zook and what her reaction would be to that kind of a situation.

"Go," he commanded the petulant Tabitha.

She huffed and obeyed. "You're no fun," she hissed over her shoulder, but he was simply glad to lean against the shelf for a moment, deciding that his migraine was worsening and that he'd have to make his excuses and go home.

Kate waited with bated breath until she heard Sebastian's heavy footsteps exit the first pantry. She felt like giving Tabitha Deitweiler a firm swat on the backside for waylaying Sebastian, and she knew a certain pride in his more-than-honorable response. But it made her wonder exactly what kind of girl he would like to meet in a dark room—not that she wanted to be that kind of girl. *But still, the idea is—interesting.* She felt herself flush and happened to run her hand across the middle shelf, coming in contact with a large sack. She poked a finger inside, then tasted it, realizing she'd found the sugar. She hurriedly grabbed the sack and headed back out into the kitchen, deliberately concentrating on Ann's bustling form and feeling a little embarrassed at her eavesdropping.

"*Ach, danki,* Kate. Now, if you might go round and refill the sugar bowls, I'd be grateful," Ann said in passing.

Kate hurried to comply with her hostess's wishes, but when she happened to glance around the room, she realized Sebastian was nowhere in sight. She did notice Tabitha Deitweiler, though, making eyes at one of the King youths, and Kate wanted to wring her neck. Then she quickly sought prayer in response to her uncharitable thoughts and finished with the sugar bowls.

Kate noticed Fran sitting down alone on one of the Kauffmans' living room couches. *Now is as gut a time as any to tell her that I'm starting work tomorrow, I suppose* . . . But she felt nervous as she approached her cousin's wife and also knew why—the only "rent" she and Ben paid for their cabin was the help that Kate gave to Fran around her *haus,* and working for Sebastian would surely make that more difficult. In fact, Kate knew that many women wondered what there was for her to do for Fran, with such a small household, but Kate knew Fran still sometimes suffered from depression over the loss of her baby and found it difficult to manage now and then.

So, Kate approached the other woman with hesitation. But, to her surprise, Fran gave her a wan but welcoming smile and motioned for her to sit down.

"Is everything all right?" Kate asked cautiously.

"I'm not feeling too well, actually. I think I ate too much of that delicious ham. . . . But I've been wanting to talk to you, Kate." She lowered her voice. "You see, what Bishop Umble said today about faith and being sure of what you hope for really seemed to speak to me, to my life and the way I've been living."

"How so?" Kate wondered aloud with interest.

Fran's eyes teared up a bit. "I realized that I've been living too much in the past and have not been grateful enough for the present moment. I know that what I want is to be happy and have peace now and to let the past go. And you're part of my peace now, Katie . . . I—I haven't always been kind to you or even nice at times, but it was because I was so blanketed in my own sorrow. I want to tell you now that I'm so glad you and Ben are here, and I want you to know that I think I'm going to be able to give you more time to work in your own life because I feel ready to be a wife again to Daniel and to keep his home."

Kate stared at Fran in disbelief at *Gott*'s provision.

"What's wrong?" Fran asked rather anxiously.

Kate smiled widely. "Nothing. But I have some news to share with you, too. . . ."

CHAPTER 5

On Monday morning, Kate nervously gathered cleaning supplies in a bucket and hitched up the small cutter sled that she used to take Ben to school.

"Do I get to *kumme* to *Herr* Christner's today after school?" Ben asked eagerly as they started off.

"I'm not sure; I'll find out," Kate answered in absent tones, her mind on doing a good job.

She dropped a still-questioning Ben off at school, grateful for the Mountain *Amisch* teacher, Jude Lyons, as he came to help her *bruder* down and up the specially built ramp at the school*haus*.

Then she drove on, guiding the horse and sleigh out to Sebastian's cabin. She tied the horse to the hitching post out front, then climbed the steps, clutching her supply bucket while a moment of nerves almost prevented her from knocking on the door.

But Kate gasped when the cabin door was eased open and she saw Sebastian wince at the shaft of incoming light. He looked terribly sick, his auburn hair clinging to his forehead in damp swirls; he had dark bruise-like circles beneath his blue eyes, and his chest and feet were bare.

"*Kumme* in," he muttered hoarsely.

"Uh—*Herr*—I mean, Sebastian, are you ill? Should I go and fetch Sarah King?"

Sarah, the new young healer on Ice Mountain, had taken over for beloved *Grossmuder* May, who had passed away the previous spring.

He waved away her words weakly and widened the door an inch more. "*Nee*, it's just a migraine. I get them now and then. . . . I told you to start today and you can." He visibly shivered at the cold and she hastened inside.

She heard his grateful sigh when he closed the door on the daylight; the cabin was in darkness with the shades drawn and no lanterns lit.

She took a hesitant step forward and ran full-tilt into his bare chest. It was like touching oak covered in warm satin, and she jerked her hand back instinctively.

"Uh . . . sorry," he mumbled. "I'll light a lamp."

She waited while she sensed him move deeper into the room, and the flare of a match soon became the warm glow of a lantern. But Sebastian rubbed at his temple as if even the small circle of light was too much.

"Kate, I'm going to lie down and sleep this off. Feel free to work as little or as much as you like—you can just straighten up a bit maybe. I'm sorry things are such a mess. . . . I, uh . . . sorry—I feel dizzy. . . ."

He fled the dim circle of light and soon she heard a door close, leaving her clutching her bucket handle in indecision. *Perhaps I really should go to Sarah King; she could at least send him something to ease his pain.* . . .

Her mind made up, Kate set her cleaning supplies down and quietly slipped from the cabin.

Sarah King lived about half a mile from Sebastian in a rather secluded cabin. Kate knew she could take the horse and sleigh most of the way there but would have to hike the last hundred feet or so. She was glad she'd worn her sensible black boots, even though they only covered her up to her ankles. Still, her knitted stockings were warm and she hastily moved through the light snow falling to untie Janey, her faithful sorrel horse.

She navigated with ease through the snow on the dirt road that was crisscrossed with other sled tracks fast being filled in by the snow. She passed Ben Kauffman's general store and then the school, and soon she saw the healer's cabin perched on its rocky ledge. She got out and tied Janey's rein to some low-hanging bare branches, then began the climb upward. She slipped only once, sliding down and coming back up with a cold mouthful of snow. She sputtered, floundering, then regained her footing and soon knocked at the wooden door.

Sarah King welcomed her with a bright smile.

"Kate, *kumme* in," Sarah invited. "Would you like some hot cocoa? I hope everything's going well—Ben's not ill, is he?"

Kate shook her bonneted head, inching toward the open fire's warmth with grateful feet. "*Nee,* Ben is well. It's—it's actually Sebastian Christner. He's got a bad migraine and is feeling quite poorly."

"*Ach, nee* . . . I hate migraines." Sarah moved to the large cabinet in the kitchen that was filled with mysterious bottles and vials and dried bunches of herbs. Kate watched as the other girl began to mix various crushed herbs and dried flowers in a small wooden bowl. "Is his stomach upset, too?"

"Uh—I'm not sure, but he said he was dizzy." Kate felt herself blush, wondering if Sarah was privately questioning how she knew that Sebastian was ill, but the healer seemed to find nothing out of the ordinary and Kate began to relax.

"You'll have to brew him a tea using these herbs—I've got feverfew and butterbur here as well as some mint. Make sure he drinks a full cup and quickly—it should bring him relief in a short time." Sarah handed her a small brown bag of pungent herbs, and Kate tucked it inside her wool cloak.

"*Danki,* Sarah. I appreciate your help," Kate said, smiling.

Sarah dimpled in return. "And I appreciate that you have been granted access to the mysterious Sebastian Christner's life. I don't think he would have let you see him sick if he didn't trust you. People don't usually want to be vulnerable unless they're with someone they like."

Once more, even though Sarah's tone held no curiosity, Kate felt herself color hotly. *To think . . . he might like me.*

She bade the healer a *gut* day and felt that she fairly floated out the door, not minding that the once-light snow had now become mixed with freezing rain, making her climb back down to the sled even more difficult. Still, she managed to untie Janey and urge her back out into the slippery lane, anxious now to get to Sebastian with some relief.

* * *

The persistent striking of ice against the cabin roof only served to aggravate the pain in Sebastian's head; he felt entirely miserable. He lay, alternately shivering and sweating, on his bed, too exhausted to get another blanket from the wooden chest across the room. Instead, he wondered vaguely if it would be inappropriate to holler and ask Kate for a cup of tea—it certainly wasn't something he'd expect from a *hauskeeper,* but then the thought of actually raising his voice made him realize he was *narrisch,* and he drifted instead into a fitful sleep. . . .

It was high summer; night—replete with lightning bugs, a chorus of grasshoppers, and the baritone of a mature bullfrog echoing from the creek. The placid moonlit dark was broken only by the soft sounds of pleasure that came from the back of his throat as he kissed the Englisch *girl he'd just met at a baseball game. He was nineteen and it was his* rumspringa; *he'd stuffed his* Amisch *clothes in the back of his buggy and changed into jeans and a T-shirt for the game. Now he sat with the brown-haired girl near the age-old pond and worked his hands through her hair.*

"Take off your shirt," she whispered and he complied eagerly.

Then she was returning his kisses with hot vigor and he groaned aloud.

"Touch me," he managed to get out. "Please touch me. . . ."

When Kate got back to the cabin, she slipped off her soaking boots and longed to strip off her wet stockings but refrained. Instead, she hung up her bonnet and cloak and lifted the lantern to navigate in the direction of where she thought the kitchen might be. Truth be told, it was hard to tell because the cabin was such a wreck—clothes, half-finished toys, and drawings on large sheets of paper cluttered the place. When she got to the kitchen, it was even worse, with dirty dishes overflowing the pump sink, old food in kettles on the woodstove, and again, more drawings littering the table.

He must be so involved and focused on his work that he has no time for such things as cleaning and cooking . . . the poor man probably hasn't had a square meal in weeks. She let her thoughts drift for a few moments until she located the teakettle, then set the lantern down and got to work lighting the woodstove. It took a while to get the water boiling, and in the meantime, she rolled up her sleeves and managed to stack the dirty plates as well as gather together the silverware that was buried in the sink.

When the teakettle whistled softly, she turned with a clean mug and got out the fragrant herbs from her apron pocket. He seemed to have no tea strainer about, so she used a piece of muslin she found in a drawer, stretching it over the mouth of the mug and straining the hot water through the healing herbs. Once done, she lifted the lantern again along with the hot mug, and began to make her cautious way in the direction Sebastian had gone earlier.

She reached what she surmised to be the bedroom door, and realized she had no way to knock with her hands full. She gave the wood an experimental bump with her hip and, much to her surprise, it gave under the pressure, easing open without a sound.

"Sebastian?" she whispered, stepping deeper into the room. She almost tripped over a pair of boots and the hot tea sloshed over her hand. "Ouch!" she said, unable to contain herself.

Then she realized he'd stirred on the bed as she heard the intimate rustle of sheets moving. She swallowed hard, reminding herself that she was there to help him, and lifted the lamp higher.

Sebastian lay facedown on a massive carved oaken bed with his head pillowed on his arms. The sheets were tangled loosely around his hips, and his back was bare, well-defined musculature tapering to lean ribs and waist and then . . . She almost fled the room. . . . *What would Fran say if she knew I was in a room with a half-naked man? And what a beautiful man at that . . . He's so . . .*

"Please," Sebastian muttered suddenly from the bed.

Kate froze in midstep. *Please. Please what?*

She watched him shift his head a bit, rubbing it against his arms, and realized he must be deep in pain and speaking without thought. Bolstered by the need to help him, she approached the bed once more and set the lamp down on the floor so the light wouldn't bother him too much. Then she gently touched his shoulder, unable to control the shiver of pleasure that went through her at the sensation of his skin beneath her fingertips, before she pulled away.

"Sebastian? I have some tea here for you—it will help."

He made a choked sound against his arms and groaned. "Please . . . touch me."

Kate felt her world spin. *What is he saying?*

He moved restlessly and some instinct made her

put her hand back on his shoulder. Suddenly she became aware of the deep tension in his muscle, and she realized that he must surely be asking for help. She set the teacup on the table beside the bed and leaned over him, thinking briefly of how she'd massaged Ben's legs after the accident. Now, her capable fingers found the knots of tension in Sebastian's back and shoulders with ease and she began to apply varying degrees of pressure. His response made her swallow and silently ask *Gott* for forgiveness. . . .

Sebastian knew, in some vague part of his brain that wasn't registering pain, that he was dreaming—dreaming deeply and without restraint in a way he'd not allowed himself to do for a very long time. The feminine touch on his shoulders was fast making his headache recede and was creating in its place a feeling of abandon and wanting that he normally repressed.

He shivered when she touched his neck and couldn't help arching his back under the hypnotic pleasure, then felt her touch his hair for a moment. He turned with a groan, pulling this dream girl down to him, wanting her small and full against him. He eagerly sought her mouth with his own. Her lips were soft, unresponsive even, and he couldn't understand why she didn't give as he was desperately trying to do. He grew frantic, slanting his head and kissing her with all of the finesse that he remembered from *rumspringa* until her soft, hot sigh told him that she was enjoying his mouth.

He ran his hands down her body, and she squirmed against him, further enticing him, though he was surprised that her dress was wet and he felt frustrated by the damp barrier.

"Take this off," he ordered, feeling a smile touch his lips. It was his dream and he planned on having as much pleasure as his mind could devise.

He cupped his hands around her full, phantom breasts and a squeak of protest ricocheted through his consciousness, causing him to still, then attempt to open his eyes.

His dream fast evaporating, he realized the girl from his thoughts had become a living body that pulled away from him to scramble upright next to the bed.

He lifted his head in the mellow light and stared blankly up at Kate Zook. Her breasts strained against her dress with each rapid breath, and her rich, brown hair had worked loose from her *kapp* to tumble over her shoulders. Even in the shadows, her soft mouth appeared reddened, and he put his fingers to his own lips in both acknowledgment and confusion. He shook his head, his headache fast reappearing, and lowered his hand to the sheets.

"Kate—what? I—*dear Gott*—I'm sorry . . . Did I hurt you?"

She shook her head. "*Nee*," she whispered. "I—I brought you some tea for your headache."

Her voice shook a bit, which made him feel even worse, but he refused to let himself break his gaze with her. "Kate . . . I was dreaming and . . . Look, I—I'll marry you."

The thought terrified him, but he realized that it was the only thing he could honorably offer after what he'd done, but to his surprise, Kate sniffed, then half-smiled.

"You'll do no such thing, Sebastian Christner. It was a dream you were having, and I got tangled up in it by accident. You don't owe me anything. No one but we two will ever know, and if it makes you uncomfortable, I—I'll stop being your *hauskeeper.*"

He couldn't help the feeling of relief that surged through him at her words. It wasn't that he didn't find her attractive, but he had too dark a past for any woman to bear. . . . He expelled a slow breath.

"*Nee, sei se gut,* Kate. Please keep the job—I need the help."

She nodded, obviously glad, then turned away a bit to start to repair her hair. His eyes drifted down the curve of her back and hip, and he had to mentally shake himself in disbelief at the desire coursing through him. He sought for any diversion.

"Uh, Kate . . . is this the tea?"

CHAPTER 6

By Wednesday, Kate had found her feet at her new job. True, she had some distracting feelings whenever her mind drifted back to those moments in Sebastian's arms, but she told herself that it had been an accident—nothing more. The fact that he'd offered marriage had come from a misguided sense of honor, she reminded herself sharply, and she told herself that she was more than content to be his *hauskeeper*. Still, if he ever did choose to marry, Kate knew she wouldn't be able to go on working for him—the idea of him with another woman simply didn't bear thinking about. . . .

In truth, though, Sebastian spent most of the day in his workshop and barely paused to eat. However, he had picked Ben up from school twice now and had begun to introduce her *bruder* to the mysteries of the workshop—a place she had not been invited to see as of yet.

"Not that I need to see it," she murmured aloud now to his empty cabin. "I have more than enough to do here."

It had taken her nearly three days to thoroughly clean the kitchen, and as she got to her feet after giving a last swipe to the drying hardwood floor, she decided a nice lunch for Sebastian might be in order, and she began to poke in the cupboards with interest.

"Got a special message fer ya." Tim Garland held out a folded note and Sebastian took it absently. "'Tis from Dr. McCully down Coudersport Hospital way; he seemed a mite upset."

Sebastian turned his attention from his workbench and opened the note. Dr. McCully was a friend to the *Amisch* of Ice Mountain and many went to see him when their ills became too difficult for Sarah King to manage. If the doctor was sending a message, it was probably important. Sebastian scanned its contents, then blew out a long whistle of a breath and ran a hand through his hair.

"What's it say?" Tim asked, shrugging out of his coat and hopping onto a stool.

"The hospital's annual Holiday Hoopalooza is this Saturday, and the computer guru who was supposed to do a light show for the kids who have cancer can't make it." Sebastian sighed. "Dr. McCully wonders if I might come instead and bring some toys for the patients. There are three kids on the cancer unit—two boys and a girl."

"Well now, that oughta be easy enough—I'll get word to Mr. Ellis at the bottom of the mountain and see if he'd be willing ta drive—ya know he's always willin'—and you jest gather up some toys and go." Tim yawned.

"What'll I take?"

Tim snorted. "Ya got a workshop full of toys—take anything."

"No, these children are very ill. It'll have to be special."

"Ah, boy, here we go. You're gonna kill yerself tryin' to make jest the right toys in three days. Ya can't do it with all your holiday orders."

Sebastian grinned at his friend. "I can—if I don't sleep. . . ."

Tim just shook his grizzled head. "Ya know what yer doin', don't ya, boy?"

"What?"

"Yer avoidin' that little woman in yer cabin there."

Sebastian looked up in surprise. "What do you know about Kate?"

"Enough to know she's a fine figure of a gal." Tim crossed his arms and winked, and Sebastian felt himself flush against his will.

"See." Tim laughed. "You knows it, too . . . besides that, Seb, I've knowed you long enuf to know that ye're lonely inside."

Sebastian frowned. "I thought you said I was just woman-hungry?"

"Well, now, old Tim might not always hit it on the head the first time, but I nails it on the second . . . and I says ye're lonely. Ain't no way to live, boy."

"I'm fine with my life," Sebastian muttered but had to avoid Tim's knowing eyes.

Kate watched Sebastian enter and hang up his coat and hat. He appeared to be preoccupied, but her obvious sound of distress when he began to cross the clean kitchen floor in his large, wet boots must have penetrated because he stopped, then slipped the boots off with a smile.

She was pleased to see his smile grow as he took in the bright, cheery kitchen with its coffee cans of geraniums she'd brought from home on the windowsills. Then he looked down at the small but well-laid table, and she felt her pleasure increase when he practically smacked his lips.

"Everything looks *wunderbaar,* Kate! Especially the cookies . . . are they molasses?"

She nodded, surprised when he slid out a chair and held it, obviously waiting for her to sit down. She did so hesitantly, unsure of the propriety of a *hauskeeper* eating with her employer, but Sebastian seemed to have no such qualms.

"You forgot to set two places," he pointed out, going to the dish drainer and grabbing a clean plate and silverware and setting them before her.

"I—I thought maybe . . ." she began.

He sat down opposite her, and the chair creaked under his big frame. "You thought that you're here to serve me?" he asked with a boyish grin. "Not quite the same as working for me, I'm afraid. We're together in this"—he waved a hand in the air—"not-so-messy *haus* of a cabin."

"*Danki,*" she whispered, barely able to contain her pleasure at his words.

She watched him bow his head for a moment of silent grace and hurriedly did the same, not wanting to be caught staring.

Thank You for this man, Gott. Help me to be able to help him indeed. . . .

She lifted her head and found that he did the same. Then he looked at her with a dark, arched brow.

"May I try the cookies first?"

She almost giggled at the seriousness of his expression. "Of course, I always eat meat-loaf sandwiches for dessert."

"Great," he said, then took a large bite of one of the cookies she'd whipped up as an afterthought. She'd have to remember his fondness for sweets. . . .

While they ate, she listened as he told her about the letter from Dr. McCully, and Kate was struck by a sudden inspiration. "*Ach,* may I go and help you?" she asked, then cast her eyes down at her plate demurely, not wanting him to think she was deliberately seeking his company. But then she lifted her chin, opting for truth. "I think I might enjoy going, because when Ben was in the hospital, I had rather a good time with the children. They need cheering up."

"That would be an answer to prayer, Kate. . . . I'm worried I'll be no *gut* dealing with really ill kids. But what about Ben?"

She smiled. "He was invited to the Masts' for a taffy pull on Saturday and then to stay over *nacht,* so I was going to spend the day cleaning . . . I mean, cleaning my cabin, but I'd much rather give you a hand."

He lifted his water glass and seemed to consider the clear liquid inside. "I appreciate so much who you are, Kate," he said quietly. "You are kind and generous, you're a great cook, and you have . . . an incredible tolerance of my messes."

She felt herself blush and had to look away

again but not before she watched him drink deeply of his water with merriment shining in his light blue eyes.

As the days passed leading up to Saturday, Sebastian found himself working hard, but he was also energized from within by Kate's own hard work, turning his messy cabin into a pleasant home.

She'd somehow conquered his bedroom, and now he slept on freshly washed and ironed sheets that smelled of mountain mint. His shirts were pressed and hung on several new pegs that she'd installed. And he had even caught her dusting his dresser, which had glasses and cups on it from nighttime milk and cookies that never had made it back to the sink.

"What are you doing?" he'd asked, having to avert his gaze from the sight of her full bosom pressed against a stack of cups. He'd reached to take them from her, his fingers accidentally grazing the side of her breast. If she'd noticed, he couldn't tell, but his own hand tingled with warmth, and he'd had the unholy desire to see her in her night shift, with her full figure only lightly clad.

"You have a lot of cups," she'd remarked as he'd dumped the lot in the sink.

He'd turned around to face her, reaching down to tenderly tuck a loose strand of brown hair back behind her *kapp*. "And you"—he tapped her pert nose with a quick finger—"do not have to wash them."

She'd bustled him out of the way. "*Ach, jah,* I do, Sebastian Christner. I'm your *hauskeeper!*"

And he'd had the sudden, distinct feeling for a moment that it would be wonderful if she could be more. . . .

CHAPTER 7

On Saturday, Kate sat in the back of Mr. Ellis's station wagon, keeping only half an ear on the conversation going on in the front seat between Sebastian and their friendly *Englisch* driver. She was instead studying the note Sebastian had passed back to her from Dr. McCully, detailing the names and ages of the three patients on the small Coudersport cancer unit.

Kate wished she'd been able to gather a few small gifts of her own to bring, but she hadn't had time on such short notice. Though, she mused, now that Sebastian had paid her weekly wages, she supposed she could have gone to Ben Kauffman's store and found something. She smiled a bit to herself when she remembered her surprise the day before at finding the envelope with her name written on it in an abominable scrawl and discovering her pay. Despite all that Sebastian had to do, he still hadn't forgotten her or the importance of her salary.

She leaned back, enjoying the movement of the

car, and soon enough they turned onto the winding road that led to the hospital.

"I'll head down to the cafeteria," Mr. Ellis told them as they left the car. "They've got great vanilla pudding down there."

Sebastian laughed and Kate smiled. She noticed that Sebastian carried a bulky gray sack with him and realized it must be the presents.

They parted ways with Mr. Ellis, and then she followed Sebastian through a maze of corridors until they came to a large set of double doors labeled PEDIATRIC ONCOLOGY UNIT.

"This is it, I guess," Sebastian said, seeming hesitant, but then all trace of reticence seemed to disappear as they entered the unit.

"First stop," Sebastian said, smiling at her as they paused before a closed door. Kate consulted the list . . . Jonathan, age three.

Sebastian was about to knock when the door opened and an exhausted-looking man came out. "Hello, I'm Jonathan's father. He's finally sleeping. It was a long night."

"Well then, can you give this to him when he wakes?" Sebastian asked, reaching in the sack and handing over a baby blue–wrapped gift with strange hippos and ribbons on it.

"Thank you." The father smiled tiredly. "I surely will."

Sebastian nodded, and Kate followed him down the hall, wondering if all the children might be feeling too poorly to receive any gifts.

They entered the next room, where a television on the wall was blaring out noise. The occupant of the bed wore black sleep pants and a black T-shirt with baseball cap pulled low over green eyes that glared at them defiantly. This was sixteen-year-old Steven, and that he was angry with life was easy for Kate to see.

Sebastian switched off the TV and then went to lean a hip against the end of the bed.

"What do you want?" the teenager asked with a scowl.

"We've brought you a gift," Sebastian said easily.

"Take it back."

Kate watched helplessly as Steven leaned against the pillows and closed his eyes, but Sebastian seemed unaffected by the display of anger. He reached into his sack and pulled out a simple brown box, tied with a single green ribbon and adorned with a sprig of fresh pine.

He set it on the foot of the bed, then motioned Kate into a nearby chair, where she went and sat, grateful to have something to do. She watched Sebastian casually walk to the window and look outside.

"You here all alone?" Sebastian asked without turning.

There was silence and then Kate saw Steven grimace. "Yeah, what's it matter?"

"Your dad ran off and your mom died of the same kind of cancer you have, right?" Sebastian murmured.

Kate looked up in surprise while Steven struck the bed with a weak hand. "What have you been doing? Reading my life's story?"

Sebastian turned and came back to the bed. "I had a family once, too."

Kate listened, eager for any details about his life.

"So?" Steven asked finally.

"So . . . it makes Christmas suck when you're alone, so stop the attitude and take the gift. I spent over fourteen hours working on it."

Steven sighed. "If it'll get you outta the room, I'll open it." He heaved himself up in the bed and grabbed the box. Kate watched, pain lancing her heart for the young man when he ran a finger briefly over the pine.

"That's white pine," Steven said, staring down at the box. "I worked YCC for a summer and learned all the trees before I got this . . . cancer."

"You're right about the tree type," Sebastian said, then glanced at Kate and winked. *As if to reassure me,* she thought warmly.

She watched as Steven swallowed and carefully laid aside the fragrant pine, then undid the ribbon and opened the box. He stared down at the gift for so long that Kate wondered what was wrong until she saw the youth swipe away obvious tears with a rough hand.

Steven set his jaw and stared up at Sebastian. "My old man got me one of these—right before he left. But it was cheap plastic, not wood like this. I smashed it to bits. Then later . . . well, later, I wished I hadn't."

Sebastian nodded and Kate watched, amazed at the turn of emotion in the room over a small toy.

"Give it a try," Sebastian suggested and Kate saw Steven lift a compact wooden kaleidoscope up to point at the overhead hospital light. He turned the base of the toy and stared for long moments. Then he lowered it and held it carefully in his hands, and Kate realized that he had lost all the sixteen-year-old bravado and looked like an excited kid again.

"How'd you do the colors by hand?" Steven asked.

"Bits of broken glass," Sebastian answered with an easy smile. "You see, I always think of kaleidoscopes as being a little bit like life and faith—you can take what's broken and meld it together to bring about something new and whole, an ever-changing picture but an unchanging love of yourself and others."

Kate felt her eyes well with tears at the gentle, wise words, and Steven wiped away fresh tears, too.

"I'll think about it," the boy said finally.

"Good!" Sebastian laughed. "That's all I can ask. Merry Christmas, Steven."

Sebastian stretched out a hand to Kate, and she rose from the chair. "A happy Christmas," she murmured to Steven.

He nodded, then mumbled a thank-you.

When they went back into the hall and had gone a few doors down, Kate looked up at Sebastian. "You're amazing," she said simply, not knowing any other way to express how she felt about him. But to her surprise, a shadow of bleakness crossed his face and he shook his head.

"Things aren't always what they seem, Kate."

But she couldn't suppress her happiness and gave his hand an encouraging squeeze. "But sometimes they are." She smiled.

Kate was aware that he trod with even more silent steps into the room of the last patient. This must be Karen, age seven . . . she recalled from his note in the car. This time Kate saw a myriad of tubes and machines surrounding a frail, sleeping little girl. Her bald head was tucked against a young woman's shoulder, who looked up with a weary smile as they entered.

"Hi," the woman whispered. "I'm Karen's mom."

At her words, the child stirred and opened huge blue eyes to blink sleepily at them; then she sat straight up in bed. "Oh," she cried excitedly. "Dr. McCully said there was a special present coming today if I was a very good girl, and I have been good, haven't I, Mama?"

"Very good, love."

Sebastian was looking for a table or some place to set the gift when Karen yanked a sliding table over her lap despite the resulting beeps of the machines. "Here"—the little girl grinned—"I can open my present here."

Sebastian chuckled, a rich, full sound that made Kate smile.

"All right, little one," he said, approaching the bed. "But your present is special because it comes with a story."

"Here"—Karen's mom rose—"please sit down." She moved toward Kate. "I'd like to run to the cafeteria if you two wouldn't mind sitting with her for a few minutes? Maybe the story would occupy her?"

Kate smiled. "*Ach,* we'd love to. Please go and get some food or whatever you need."

Karen leaned her head over to receive her mom's kiss, and then the woman slipped from the room.

Sebastian pulled another chair near the bed and sat down, indicating that Kate should do the same.

"A story?" Karen fairly bounced against the white sheets. "Oh, I love stories."

"Well," Sebastian said. "Why not open the present first?" He reached into his sack and pulled out a rectangular-shaped package, gaily wrapped with teddy bears against a red background and bright ribbons twined about in gentle loops and swirls.

"It's wonderful," Karen sighed, clapping her small hands. "I love teddies. I have mine right here. See? He does treatments with me."

Kate nodded at the well-loved bear and felt a lump rise in her throat at the child's practical acceptance of her illness. But Sebastian smiled and put the package on the tray table.

Karen made quick work of the ribbons and then the paper, opening the gift with an authentic excitement and joy that was thrilling to watch.

Then Karen sucked in a breath of awe and Kate felt like doing the same when she saw what was inside.

"Oh my," Karen whispered.

Kate stared in fascination at the perfect replica of a beautiful cutter sleigh painted a rich burgundy and well trimmed in satiny black. The runners of the sleigh gleamed, real wrought metal, again coated in black. Long, miniature leather reins ran to a perfectly carved wooden horse, painted in bright white. Its long tail and flowing mane were real horsehair. But perhaps the most amazing thing about the toy were the occupants of the sleigh itself—two carved wooden teddy bears, a bride and groom, sat on the rich velvet-covered seat, each clothed in gorgeous *Englisch* wedding attire; fine satin and lace, a top hat and discreet veil. Mrs. Bear carried a flowing miniature bouquet of white Christmas roses that sparkled with some coating or glaze so that it shone like magic.

It was the most beautiful toy Kate had ever seen, and she looked at Sebastian with a mixture of pride and wonder at his skill as an artisan.

He ran a gentle finger down the length of the bride's gown and leaned closer to the entranced child. "And now your story, sweet Karen."

Kate leaned forward the better to hear, when Karen suddenly touched the toy with reverent fingers, then turned to look at Sebastian with serious eyes.

"You're Santa Claus, aren't you?" she whispered. "I mean, the real one." Her gaze moved to Kate. "And you're his wife? His helper? That's why you both dress funny, isn't it?"

Kate caught her breath, not wanting to disillusion the child but unsure of what to say. She looked helplessly at Sebastian, who seemed perfectly calm.

"Our time grows short, Karen," he said. "And I must tell you your story before your mama returns. Are you ready to hear it?"

Karen nodded once, apparently satisfied, then lifted the sleigh into her arms and leaned back against the pillows, holding the new toy close to her heart.

Kate listened, as enthralled as Karen, to the soft-spoken story of the sleigh, and knew that she'd remember it for always.

Though Mr. Ellis was more than happy to drive them anywhere, no car could make it up Ice Mountain in the winter. The snow-covered and ice-slicked roads made it impossible for car tires to gain traction, so Kate and Sebastian bid their *Englisch* friend good-bye and started on the mile hike upward through the snow and ice. Kate had made this trek several times over the years, and normally she would hurry her steps in order to get back home as soon as possible. But this time was different. She walked slower, her steps more purposefully measured. Despite the cold, she wanted to enjoy the journey with Sebastian by her side.

Their footprints from that morning had long disappeared in the wind that tossed the snow about in small whirlwinds close to the ground. A fresh coating of white began to fall when they still had more than half of their trek before them.

"Here," Sebastian said, holding out his arm. "Can't have you falling."

Kate clung to Sebastian's arm and looked up at him, his smile warming her through. After a few minutes she thought he must generate some internal heat of his own because she also felt warm and toasty where she clutched his arm. It was difficult to speak in the wind and snow, though she longed to tell him again how much she admired his gentleness and intelligence with the *kinner* at the hospital. She realized that before she'd simply been attracted to him, but now her heart felt a warm burgeoning and a jolt of realization went through her. She almost wanted to laugh at the absurdity of discovering that she was falling in love with him even as the snow fell more heavily, making the walk up the mountain more difficult than normal.

As they neared home, she also realized she wasn't ready to be separated from him. Though they'd spent the day together, they hadn't had a chance to talk. Besides, she didn't want to spend the evening alone, since Ben would be at the Masts'. She shot a glance at his handsome profile and used one mittened hand to pull her scarf down. "Do you want to *kumme* to *mei haus* for supper?"

"What?" he hollered over a blast of wind.

She opened her mouth and yelled, wanting to laugh at the ridiculousness of trying to have a conversation in a snowstorm. "*Kumme* for supper?"

He grinned down at her. "*Jah!*" he roared, and this time she did laugh, relishing the taste of the fresh snowflakes that filled her mouth, and loving that he didn't hesitate to accept her invitation.

CHAPTER 8

Sebastian entered her small cabin with gratitude for the snug warmth of the banked fire and wood-stove. He watched Kate take off her wet boots, then did the same himself, except he noticed the skirt of her dress was soaked.

Her gaze followed his to her skirt. "I need to change," she said. "I'll only be a minute; then I'll start on supper."

He nodded and watched her head for her bed-room. He tried to ignore the shadowy images of her that he recalled from his bed the day he'd kissed her. He also tried to do the polite thing and avert his gaze, but he failed. In truth, he could barely drag his eyes from the swing of her hips when she went to the small bedroom, closing the door with a soft *click*.

He went and built up the fire, glad of something to do with his hands. When she'd invited him to dinner tonight, he'd jumped at the chance. The idea of going home alone, especially after what he'd witnessed in the hospital, didn't appeal to him. Seeing the sick children had taken a toll on him. He was glad he'd been able to bring them a little cheer, and he made a promise to himself to pray for them. Yet the trip had also given him a sense of helplessness. There was so much the children needed that he couldn't give them, and their pain tugged at his heart.

Having Kate with him had been more helpful than he would have guessed. He'd sensed she would be wonderful with the children, and she was. What he hadn't expected was how right she felt by his side. How her quiet, calm presence during each visit had given him the support he needed to keep his emotions steady as he interacted with the children. They had felt like a . . . team. One that he wasn't ready to split up just yet.

The fire had started to blaze by the time Kate reentered the room, clad in a bright cherry-red dress and fresh white apron. He couldn't help but notice she'd changed her stockings, too. Just as he couldn't help noticing—appreciating—the full curve of her calves as she passed by him.

"That didn't take long," he said, pulling his gaze from her legs and reminding himself to keep his observations in check.

"I'm a fast dresser. Doesn't take any time to pull one dress off and put on another."

His eyes widened at her offhand comment. So much for keeping his thoughts pure. "*Gut,*" he muttered, trying to shove away the tempting images her innocent words conjured up in his mind. It wasn't working out too well.

"Have a seat," she invited. "I'll whip us up some supper. How do ham steaks and fried potatoes sound?"

"Great." He pulled out a nearby kitchen chair to sit on, catching her smiling at him over her shoulder before he lowered his frame on the seat. She seemed happy . . . happier than he'd ever seen her. He had to admit he was pretty happy himself. Kate was the first woman who made him feel content simply being in her presence. Watching her do the homey task of cooking supper soothed his mind and soul.

She stretched, arching the small of her back, to lift a container from a high shelf. As she strained to reach it, he jumped up from the chair and came up behind her. "I'll get it," he said, his chest nearly pressing against her back. He leaned forward—a little more than he should—and caught the scent of her. As his fingers touched the metal tin she had been trying to retrieve, he glanced down at her smooth neck and swallowed. He didn't want to move away . . . and the memory of how she had responded to his kiss slammed into him. He cleared his throat as he took a step back and handed her the tin. Then he hurried back to the table and sat down, gathering his wits about him.

"Here," she said, coming to the table, her voice matching the cheery expression on her face. If she'd been affected by their nearness a moment ago, she was hiding it well. He, on the other hand, was struggling to hide the *definite* effect she had on him. "They're something different," she said. "Russian tea cakes. I hope you like them." She pulled the lid off the tin and handed the container to him.

He breathed in the delicate scent of powdered sugar and looked down to see what looked like tiny snowballs nestled against one another. "*Ach* . . ." he murmured. "They look delicious. *Danki*, Kate."

She smiled brightly, then returned to her cooking. "There are chopped walnuts in them," she said over her shoulder. "And plenty of butter and powdered sugar."

He lifted one of the delicate cakes and popped the whole thing in his mouth. It melted delectably. "They're marvelous," he said, reaching for another. "Although I'll admit, I've never met a cookie I didn't like."

"Why do you like them so much?" Kate asked as she shook the pepper shaker over the ham.

His fingers paused halfway to the tin, and he suddenly lost his appetite at the memories her casual question provoked. He lowered his hand to the table and put down the tin. "My *mamm,* I suppose. She was a wonderful cook and an excellent baker. She loved to bake cookies for us," he said, after gathering his thoughts.

He felt Kate's eyes on him and tried to resume his former jovial air, but it was gone, evaporated like the ice in winter inside Ice Mountain's mine.

"Do you—get to see your *mamm* much?" Kate asked, angling her body away from the stove to face him.

He shook his head. "*Nee* . . ." Normally he would stop there. Whenever anyone asked him questions about the past, he dodged them. He'd become adept at avoiding revealing too much of himself. But now . . . ensconced in Kate's small, warm kitchen, with the taste of sweet powdered sugar still on his tongue, the comfort and safety he saw in the depths of Kate's eyes made him, for the first time, want to talk. He trusted Kate . . . and he never gave his trust easily. But how could he let her into the darkness he kept buried from everyone? He wasn't sure he could.

He sensed her waiting for some sort of expansion on his answer and he almost closed his eyes against the swamping pain that childhood memories of his mother brought up in him. "I—uh—my mother and I don't see each other. It's my doing. . . ." he finally managed.

Kate put a lid on the frying pan, and he saw her give him a sympathetic glance. "I'm sorry for bringing up hurtful things, Sebastian."

"No—no, you didn't know."

She put the spoon down and clasped her hands together, not looking at him. "*Jah.* But I shouldn't have pried. I know you value your privacy."

His heart pinched. In the span of a few minutes, the ease between them had grown strained . . . and it was his fault. She'd asked a simple question, and now she was the one feeling bad about it. Without thinking, he stood and walked to her. He put his hand on her shoulder and turned her to face him.

He'd meant to crack a joke and give her a wry grin to break the awkwardness between them. But as he gazed down at her, his heart—and mouth—overtook his mind. He pressed a quick kiss to her surprised lips. Her very soft, welcoming lips.

"That's for your Russian tea cakes," he said quickly, coming up with an excuse for kissing her. Still feeling the heat of her lips on his mouth, he moved away from her, not trusting himself not to kiss her again or take her into his arms. He knew that he'd found something wonderfully special with her. What he didn't know was how he was supposed to handle it.

* * *

Kate tried to be casual after his impromptu kiss, but she secretly rejoiced. *Surely he must have some feelings for me. How easy it would be to love him . . .* Love? Was that what these mixed feelings of joy, comfort, safety . . . attraction . . . were? She snuck a glance at him as he savored another cookie. Everything about him was so perfect—not just his handsome looks, but the gentle heart and giving spirit that lived beneath the surface. How could she not love him?

But . . . how could she tell him without sounding desperate or immature? They had only known each other for a short time, and while feelings couldn't be measured by the ticking of a clock, he might not agree. And she couldn't bear to ruin this evening. *I must bide my time and give him a chance to grow to know me better.* . . . And once more, as she cooked, she thanked *Gott* for her job as Sebastian's *hauskeeper.* She realized she was also thankful that Sebastian was willing to reveal some of the sadness of his life with her, and surely, she would one day understand more. She'd grieved for the loss of her own parents for years and still missed her *mamm* on certain holidays, but *Gott's* will was His own even if she couldn't understand it at times.

She brought two plates of piping hot food to the table, and Sebastian sat down with his earlier sadness seemingly passed. They prayed and then he began to gently tease her and she realized with some deep intuition that he was flirting with her. *Me . . . Kate Zook.*

"You're blushing," he said with a smile as he forked up some of the tender potatoes. "Why is that?"

"*Ach* . . . the heat from the stove is—was . . ." She broke off helplessly, a novice when it came to idle words, but he didn't seem to mind at all.

"*Jah* . . . the heat from the stove, which is over there, would surely affect a woman over here." He grinned at her, and she couldn't help smiling back at him.

"I would think you know well enough why I'm blushing," she said evenly. "I bet Tabitha Deitweiler would blush, too, if she'd been kissed by you. . . ." She clapped a hand over her mouth in abject horror and he started to laugh.

"Kate Zook, you were eavesdropping! Where were you? *Ach*, I know—the second pantry."

She dropped her head to hide her face in her hands, but he put down his fork with a *clink* and pulled her hands away. "I feel terrible," she moaned, not wanting to look him in the eye.

"Don't." His voice lowered to nearly a whisper. "I'm happy that you were interested enough in me to eavesdrop." He continued to gaze at her. "Kate," he whispered, all laughter gone from his voice.

"*Ach* . . ." she whispered, unsure what to do, then she turned to look at him and saw that his own cheeks were flushed and his pupils were dilated and she understood what he wanted, perhaps even needed. She drew a deep breath and half-closed her eyes, then tentatively pressed her mouth to his.

She gasped against his lips as he pulled her out of her chair to sit firmly on his outstretched knee. She felt his arm encircle her waist and draw her close as he deepened the kiss. She wasn't a small woman, but in his arms and pressed against his broad, lean body, she felt positively delicate. Her heart began to thump in earnest at his encircling nearness. *Yes . . . this is love.*

Sebastian was torn between sensations: the gentle softness of her bottom against his knee, the tender pressure of her hesitant kiss, and the fullness of her breast pressing on his arm. He forgot about *rumspringa* and all the other girls he'd ever kissed until time collapsed into one heated funnel of touch and taste and yearning.

He realized after a few moments that he needed to set her from him because he couldn't act on the clamorous drive of his thoughts, but she made such a sweet sound of protest between her soft lips that he groaned and kissed her even more deeply.

"Kate," he rasped, finally lifting his head. "I'm not asleep now. We cannot play at this—it's like playing with hellfire."

She stared at him, as if dazed, and he really wanted to sweep her up in his arms and carry her into the next room and . . . *Hellfire indeed.*

He stood up abruptly, and she would have probably toppled to the floor had he not caught her and set her evenly on her feet with gentle hands.

"Kate, I've got to go. *Danki* for the food and—everything else."

He watched her for a second and her jewel-blue eyes clouded as if in sadness or disappointment. "You do think me another Tabitha, I'm afraid."

He stepped close and caught her sweet face between both his hands. "Don't say that—ever. Maybe I haven't spoken it right, but it's not your kisses I want, Kate—it's all of you. Your generous heart, your tender soul, and your everlasting kindness—

you make me feel alive inside, and that's something no one's been able to do for a very long time." He kissed her once more, rough and hard, then slipped on his boots, grabbed his coat and hat, and went out into the cold evening air.

Kate left the dishes to soak in the sink and took a single lamp into the bedroom. She undressed and pulled on a flannel nightgown, then climbed quickly into the chilly bed. She hugged the quilts about her, tenderly savoring everything Sebastian had said to her after supper. *All of me . . . he wants all of me.* She smiled to herself; it seemed that *Der Herr* was making her dreams come true, and even if she didn't understand everything about Sebastian, she knew he was a *gut* man and that she'd love him for all time.

CHAPTER 9

On Sunday morning, Sebastian was up before the dawn, thanks to the first full *nacht*'s sleep he'd enjoyed in a long time. And he knew it was because of Kate and the growing feelings he had for her.

He dressed quickly, then hurried over to the dark workshop, nearly jumping out of his skin when Tim hailed him from the darkness.

"Sleep right, did ya, boy?"

Sebastian mentally tried to slow his pulse. "Do you have to do that?" he asked in exasperation as he turned on the lights.

"Do what?" Tim asked lazily.

"Skulk around in the dark . . . you know I hate that."

"And you knows I got hoot-owl eyes, boy. So, what's the problem? Land 'a mercy, anyone would think you wuz in luv, you're so jumpy. . . . Oh, now, wait jest a minute here. . . ."

"I don't want to hear it," Sebastian retorted, switching on the computer and sitting down to check for new toy orders, though he knew he couldn't work on a Sunday.

Tim poked his head in front of the screen, and Sebastian groaned. "Yer in love, ain't ya? Admit at least that much."

"All right. If you will go away and let me work— I'll tell you."

Tim withdrew his head. "All righty. Tell ol' Tim all about it."

Sebastian drew a deep breath. "I'm going to tell Kate about my past."

Tim staggered backward and collapsed into a chair. "I thought you were in love, not plumb crazy. What would you do something like that for?"

"You heard me. I finally found the woman I love, Tim. And if I'm reading her right, she loves me." He remembered the sweet innocent passion in Kate's kiss, the loving emotion she had expressed in their passionate embrace. He didn't have to hear the words from her to know how she felt. She'd shown him. And now, he'd have to show her . . . by telling her the truth. "I'm not going to lose her. I want to marry her. She deserves to know."

"When you gonna do it?" Tim asked with the ominous tone that implied Sebastian was facing sure execution.

"I don't know for sure, but soon."

Tim bowed his head and Sebastian frowned. "Now what are you doing?"

"Shut up, boy. Can't ya tell when a body's prayin'?"

Sebastian turned back to the screen with a sigh and discovered himself mentally praying, as well.

*   *   *

On Sunday, Kate rose early and set about making some gingerbread to take to the Masts' when she picked up Ben. She felt so alive in her spirit that her fingers seemed to fly at their task, and she soon had a basket filled with fresh gingerbread squares topped with a dusting of powdered sugar.

She went out into the cold and harnessed Janey to the sled, then set out with a smile on her face to the Mast home. She thought the morning had never seemed so bright and once or twice had to shield her eyes from the snow glare but she still couldn't keep from smiling.

When she arrived at the Mast home, Ben was, of course, unhappy at having to leave his friends, but the promise of gingerbread and the possibility of making snow angels on the way home were enough to persuade him, so they bade good-bye cheerily to their friends.

Once they'd come to a clearing between two large pines, Kate drew rein and got out, going around the side of the sled to lift Ben into her arms. It was a favorite tradition between the two of them, ever since Ben's accident, that they would make snow angels despite the difficulty with Ben's legs.

"Hurry up, Katie," he urged while she brushed a crumb of gingerbread away from the corner of his mouth.

"All right," she replied, then carefully laid him down in the fresh, unmarked snow on his back. He immediately began to flap his arms, and Kate moved to help him slide his legs back and forth to make the angel's skirt. She laughed at the pleasure in his brown eyes as he stared up at the bright blue sky and barely noticed that they weren't alone until someone gave a loud whoop behind her, which made her jump and turn.

"*Ach,* Bishop Umble," she gasped. "You gave me quite a fright."

"Sorry," the *auld* man said with a smile. "But I simply love making snow angels." He promptly proved this love by dropping backward into the snow next to Ben, and they all three laughed out loud like children. Kate wished everyone might have the unusual privilege of seeing their aged leader so enjoying flailing about in the snow, but eventually he sat up with care, so as not to disturb his angel's body.

"*Ach.*" He smiled. "That does a soul *gut!* You know, sometimes my life is like making a snow angel—I want everything to be kept neat and perfect with nothing to mar the plans I've outlined, but then *Gott* sweeps in and turns everything upside down."

"Then what do you do?" Ben asked seriously, struggling to sit up until Kate helped him.

"Why, *sohn,* that's when I've got a decision to make. Am I going to accept the change *Gott* has brought, or am I going to fight Him until things look and go the way I expect and want?"

"But isn't it easier to accept than to fight?" Ben asked as Kate lifted him carefully into her arms. She looked down at the less-than-perfect images in the snow.

"Some prefer the fight, my *buwe,* but never know the freedom in surrender and acceptance," Bishop Umble said. He smiled at Kate. "Gotta get home to the missus. A *gut* day to you both."

Kate looked down at Ben in her arms, noting a new freckle on the bridge of his nose. She hugged him tight and he wriggled in her arms. "The bishop is funny, isn't he, Kate?"

She walked with him back to the sled. "Sometimes, but he's also very wise. Now, let's go home and have some cookies."

"Gingerbread and cookies? *Ach,* boy," Ben cheered. "What are we celebrating?"

Kate smiled. "Just being alive . . ." *And in love!*

On Monday morning, Kate squared her shoulders when she entered Sebastian's cabin and decided to tackle the gloomy and piled-up living area. She first surveyed the vague shapes of furniture buried under clothes and papers. There appeared to be a comfortable cushioned couch and an old chair and a massive desk. She decided to start with the desk and possibly try to organize some of the papers that protruded from drawers and cubbyholes in the beautiful old piece of furniture.

She was an hour into organizing things into piles when she realized she kept bumping her arm on the stuffed middle drawer. She gave it a hesitant pull and realized it was stuck. She sighed and gave one more tug and the wood gave, leaving her on her backside with the drawer full of papers. She had to laugh at herself. She had gotten to her knees to replace things when a crumpled sheet of light blue paper caught her eye in the back of the drawer space. For some strange reason, she felt her heart begin to pound as she reached for the paper, but she felt drawn to it nonetheless.

So far, she'd organized things by brief glances but when she touched the blue paper, she felt the urge to read it and pulled it hesitantly toward her. She reached up and adjusted the lamp, then felt a hesitation in her spirit, a sense that she should leave the crumpled page alone, but she rationalized that one look could not hurt. She unfolded the page and realized that a newspaper clipping was crumpled inside the official-looking print of the paper.

To her great surprise, she realized that it was a parole letter for one Sebastian C. Christner. . . . Her eyes skimmed the document, and she felt a sickening in her stomach when she saw the words "speeding" and "involuntary manslaughter." Then she turned her attention to the newspaper piece. The faded headline seemed to glare menacingly up at her—"Amish Man Kills Amish Woman."

"What are you doing?"

Sebastian's voice was low and confused, and she looked up hastily to see him standing near the desk in his hat and coat, his long dark pants covered with a dusting of snow.

"I—I was cleaning and found this. I'm sorry . . ." She held the papers up to him and swallowed.

He stared down at her outstretched hand, then took the papers from her. "I was just coming in to tell you the truth about this, Kate."

She rose to her feet and hugged her arms about herself. "I guess I find that hard to believe."

"Why? Because now you think I'm a murderer?"

She shivered in spite of herself. "Are you?"

He glared at her, his normally light eyes darkened with pent-up emotion. "I need to explain."

"All right," she said slowly.

He sighed and took off his hat, running his hand through his hair. "I was nineteen and it was my *rum-*

springa. I had been drinking a bit at an *Englisch* party . . . wearing *Englisch* clothes . . . Someone offered to let me take their sports car for a ride. I remember that the roads were icy—but I didn't care. I thought I could handle the vehicle. I came around a sharp turn too fast and hit an *Amisch* buggy head-on. . . . I remember hearing a child scream, and then I got out and went to the buggy. The horse was dead, but the buggy . . . the buggy. Well, the mother had been killed instantly by the collision, and the children with her—there were two of them—they'd been bumped around but were all right. I—I knew them. They were from my own community. My family and the church forgave me, but I had to get away and start over. I haven't seen them since." He drew a harsh breath. "I spent six years in prison and then was on parole. It was in prison that I learned how to carve toys. . . ."

Kate's mind telescoped back to the buggy accident that she'd been in when her parents died. . . . "It was the same," she said, feeling curiously disembodied from the words.

"What was the same?"

She lifted her head, knowing that tears streamed down her face, but she didn't care. "A car was going too fast and hit our buggy. I was all right, but my *mamm* and *daed* were . . . and Ben was hurt. It was the same as you. . . . It could have been you driving and destroying my family." Her voice rose, becoming shrill.

"Kate, I . . ." He held out his empty hand in obvious supplication, but she shook her head.

"You tricked Ben and me, and I don't know why," she cried.

"*Nee*," he ground out, lowering his arm. "I did not."

"Ben trusted you—he loves you like a father. And I . . . How could you?"

"Kate, I did wrong. I know I did. I can never forget it, but we could build a new life together and . . ."

"*Nee*," she sobbed, running forward to push past him blindly and get to the front door. "I quit this job, Sebastian, and you need never pick up Ben again!" She opened the door and ran out into the snow, leaving her cloak and bonnet behind.

Sebastian squeezed the papers in his hand, then slowly stumbled forward to stroke the warmth of her cloak. He swallowed hard as tears burned the backs of his eyes.

"It didn't go well, boy?" Tim asked softly from somewhere behind him.

"*Nee*," he choked, bowing his head.

"'Tis sorry I am, Seb. Truly."

He nodded and half-glanced at his friend. "It's no more than I deserve."

Tim shuffled forward and tugged at his coat sleeve. "That ain't the truth, boy. God wants you to forgive yerself, to have an abundant life."

Sebastian dragged in a harsh breath. "*Gott* wants me to pay penance and I will. I'll keep up with the toys, but after Christmas . . . after Christmas, I'll move on to some other community—and try to forget her and the *buwe*." He turned from the door and laid a weary hand on Tim's shoulder, then dropped the papers on the neatened desk, walking away and not looking back.

* * *

Kate fell facedown in the wet snow halfway home from Sebastian's cabin, but she didn't bother to get up. Instead, she turned her cheek to the coldness and let the sobs shake her body. She cried with all of the grief that she had kept pent up for so long, realizing she'd never taken or even had the time to do it before. She'd gone from nurtured child to practically being Ben's mother, and it was so hard to be a full-time caregiver sometimes. . . . Then as her tears slowed, she realized that she was crying for Sebastian and the pain he'd endured, as well as the pain she'd heaped upon him, denying him any grace, and only being consumed with herself. It was a striking enough thought that she got her hands and knees in the snow, and suddenly, with clarity and insight, she remembered the snow angels and Bishop Umble's words about fighting *Gott*. She understood that she'd been fighting for a long time and it was Sebastian's pain that had finally allowed her the release she needed. And she realized that she was not about to let him suffer any more. Getting to her feet, she hastily swiped her sleeve across her face and knew she had to go back and tell him she'd been wrong. She decided to race home and change first since she was soaking wet and freezing cold, and she slogged through the snow, praying all the while.

CHAPTER 10

Kate hurriedly changed her dress and undercloth-
ing and bundled up in her Sunday cloak to head
back to Sebastian's. She had just tied her bonnet
strings when a knock sounded at the door and her
heart leapt. *Maybe it's Sebastian—though why he
should come after the way I behaved is beyond me. . . .* All
of this went through her mind in a flash as she hastened to open the door. To her surprise, Fran
stood there, looking radiantly happy.

"Kate, do you have a few minutes? I'm sorry
you're going out, but I simply have to talk to you."

Kate caught the suppressed excitement of her
cousin's posture and reluctantly widened the door.
"All right. *Kumme* in."

She chafed at the delay but tried to focus on
Fran all the same. She didn't remove her cloak or
bonnet, though, hoping it might be a clue that her
leaving was urgent.

But Fran sank down onto the living room couch
as if she had all the time in the world. "*Ach,* Kate—
it's so *wunderbaar.*"

"What is it?" Kate asked, trying to conceal the impatience in her voice.

"I'm pregnant. We went to see Dr. McCully to double-check, but I'm about two months along."

Kate felt her anxiousness slip away as genuine happiness filled her heart for the other woman. She rose and then bent to catch Fran close in a gentle embrace.

"Fran, that's such *gut* news. I have prayed for you."

Fran pulled back and looked up into Kate's face. "I know. *Danki.* And now I'll let you go, but is everything all right? You seem a bit upset."

Kate straightened and smiled. "Everything will be fine." *I hope and pray . . .* "But I do need to *geh.*"

Fran got to her feet and Kate saw her to the door, deciding at the last moment that she might bring the tin of peanut butter kiss cookies she'd baked as a love offering to Sebastian. She raced back to the cupboard, grabbed the tin, and was two steps from the door when she heard another knock.

She groaned silently. *It must be Fran again. . . .* She flung open the door in mute exasperation to stare blankly at Bishop Umble.

"Kate, I heard you're not working at Sebastian Christner's anymore. Martha had a bad fall this morning and sprained her ankle. I hoped you would *kumme* and work for us for a bit to give her an extra hand."

"I would love to, Bishop, but I . . ."

"I'm afraid I can't take no for an answer. I've got my sled right here, and I'll pick Ben up after school and send word to Fran and Daniel. We really need your help."

Kate was quelled by the semi-stern eye the *auld* leader cast upon her and knew she had to give in for the moment. *A body just doesn't tell Bishop Umble nee . . . and I can always go to Sebastian's later on in the day once I get Martha Umble settled. . . .*

She held the door open and drew in a deep breath. "*Sei se gut, kumme* in. I—I'll go pack a light bag. . . ."

"*Danki,* Kate." The bishop smiled and she had to blink twice to make sure she was wrong about the twinkle that seemed to shine in his eyes.

She turned back to the bedroom and decided that loving Sebastian was making her *narrisch. . . .*

Sebastian bent over the workbench and tried to scrape a dull edge into precision; the tool slipped in his usually capable hands and he cut his thumb.

"Here's a hankie, boy." Tim offered a red checkered cloth and Sebastian gave it a doubtful glance, then took it anyway, using it to staunch the flow of blood.

"Thanks," he muttered to his friend.

"Look, Seb, I knows yer torn up inside, but are ya really gonna let that woman go so easy like?" Tim questioned.

"Don't pick your nose," Sebastian said absently, thinking about Tim's query. *What am I really going to do about Kate . . . and Ben? Can I let go of this shame and regret and try to face her again?*

"If ya were up fer another try, I gots an idea," Tim offered.

"What is it?"

Tim leaned close and began detailing a plan that would involve plenty of labor but might well be the way to win Kate's heart. Sebastian knew he had to try—he couldn't stand the thought of Kate believing he was like the man who'd killed her parents and hurt Ben.

"All right," he said after a bleak moment's reflection. "I'll try."

Tim whooped and clapped his hands, but Sebastian remained sober, praying that Kate would give him a chance and let go of the past.

"There's an elephant in my shoe," Martha Umble declared upon seeing Kate.

Kate paused in undoing her cloak and stared at the older woman. "Did she hit her head when she fell?" Kate asked in an undertone to the bishop.

"*Nee,* I forgot to tell you that the tea Sarah King brewed her for pain seemed a mite potent and didn't really agree with the missus. Sarah said the oddities would wear off in a few hours."

"Okay," Kate said, hanging up her cloak and slipping off her boots. *At least it should be an entertaining few hours. . . . Maybe it will make the time pass more quickly.*

"I've got several sick calls to make," Bishop Umble announced. "A few of the community are down with the flu. I'll leave you here, Kate, and I'll make sure to be back in time to swing past the school and get Ben."

He was gone before Kate could reply, so she went over to Martha Umble, who was sitting in a cozy kitchen chair with her right foot elevated on a square stool.

"Can I get you anything, Martha?" Kate asked.

"The Christmas tree needs decorating, and there's a beaver in the closet. Move the beaver first." Martha indicated the kitchen pantry with a wrinkled finger, and Kate sighed to herself as she went to remove the imaginary pest. "Now, that's not the way," Martha chirped as Kate bent and tried to judge how big a beaver would be with the span of her empty arms. "You left his tail there. Pick it up!"

Kate obeyed, thinking that surely *Der Herr* must have a sense of humor. She disposed of the invisible pest outside, then came back to the kitchen, wondering where the bread dough decorations were for the nice little fir that had been set up on a living room side table. The Mountain *Amisch* usually kept the same simple ornaments made of bread or applesauce and cinnamon dough from year to year. The women would form simple shapes or twists with the dough and then apply several layers of shellac to the finished pieces to keep the mice away and to put a sheen on the ornament.

She found herself realizing that Christmas was not that far away, and though her community didn't usually exchange gifts until Second Christmas, she always wrote a special card out for Ben for First Christmas. *Now I might be able to write one out for Sebastian, as well, if . . .*

"Stampede!" Martha bellowed and Kate glanced over in time to discover where the Umbles' ornaments were; Martha had the tin open and was apparently shattering the simple ornaments in an

effort to combat oncoming cows. Kate rushed to
her side and tried to take the tin from her without
getting hit in the head by the fast-disappearing flying dough.

"Martha, please! We'll have to make all new ornaments. . . ." A pretzel-shaped piece of hardened
dough klonked Kate in the forehead and she gave
up, moving out of the line of fire to take a look in
the kitchen cabinets for dough ingredients. The
Umbles seemed to have only a little of the glue that
was usually mixed with the applesauce and cinnamon, and Kate wondered if she dared to run over to
Ben Kauffman's store for some, but one look at
Martha's wild eyes convinced her otherwise.

The bishop returned with Ben around three
o'clock, but not before Martha Umble had lived
through a zoo breakout and an attacking flock of
seagulls. It was enough to have emotionally exhausted Kate, except for the fact that she was too
keyed up at the thought of seeing Sebastian as
soon as possible.

But Ben seemed to have other ideas. "Kate, can
I talk to you in the other room?" he asked as soon
as he'd crossed the floor with his crutches.

Kate put a finger to her lips, indicating they
should whisper as Martha was finally resting comfortably in the chair. She walked with Ben to the
guest bedroom once the bishop had waved them
off.

"Ben, what is it? I've got to go to the store to get
some glue and I have to . . ."

"Bishop Umble told me you aren't working for

Sebastian anymore. Does that mean that I can't go to the workshop?" His wide brown eyes were serious, and Kate swallowed hard, remembering her cruel words to Sebastian about his not needing to see Ben again.

"*Nee,* Ben . . . I mean, maybe for today you shouldn't go over. I have to talk to Sebastian. You see, I owe him an apology, and I haven't yet had the chance to offer it because of *Frau* Umble's ankle."

"I'm going over anyway, even if I have to take the sled myself," he announced.

"Ben," Kate exclaimed in shock. It was completely unlike her *bruder* to ever be disagreeable, let alone outright defiant. "What are you saying?"

His gaze was stormy for a moment and then it seemed to pass. "Kate, I'm sorry. I guess I was disappointed about what the bishop said, that's all."

She bent and gave him a quick hug. "It's okay. I will make things right again. Do you think you can wait for one day? I'm going to try to go to Sebastian's right now."

He nodded, but there was something about his posture that made her uneasy. She dismissed the thought, deciding it was her imagination, and quickly left the room, only to realize she had no sleigh of her own to drive.

"Bishop Umble," she whispered when she entered the kitchen. "Do you think I can use your sled for a bit?"

"The right runner's a bit wobbly. I need to check it after I have a nap."

Then I'll walk. . . . Kate thought with determination. *If I cut through the fields, I can make it in probably less than half an hour. And if I'm freezing, I'll convince Sebastian to warm me up—if he'll accept my apology.* . . .

The thought propelled her as she dressed to go outside and into the wet snow.

CHAPTER 11

"We got company comin'; I'd better get on," Tim said, causing Sebastian to get to his feet as his friend departed.

Moments later the door to the workshop burst open. Kate straggled in, gasping slightly. He stared at her, loving every part of her, even the one piece of her heart that was angry and hurt.

"Sebastian—" Her teeth chattered as she spoke. "I hiked over here—to tell you that I'm sorry. I behaved like a foolish woman, throwing away happiness with both hands." She paused for breath, and he slowly moved around the workbench to approach her.

She smelled like wet wool, but her own sweet fragrance still rose to his nostrils and he had a hard time not taking her into his arms. But he knew instinctively that she had more she wanted to say.

She looked down for a moment, then lifted her gaze to meet his eyes. "Sebastian, what I said—I'm not normally like that, but I realized that I had so much grief pent up inside and I took it all out on you. Can you please, please forgive me?"

He smiled at her a bit. "Can you forgive me? Can I forgive myself? The answer is yes to all because I know that *Gott* brought you into my life to change it, to lift the past out of its ruins and to build something new. I realize that I have no business telling kids like Steven about the kaleidoscope and new life without actually living it out myself." He took a step closer to her. "Kate, will you help me live out a new life?"

He watched the color rise prettily in her cheeks. "*Jah,*" she whispered.

And then he did bend to take her in his arms, melding her sturdy frame to him, loving her gentle curves. He reached sure fingers to find the damp ties of her bonnet and slipped it off, then he undid her cloak. "Kiss me," he commanded in a whisper, and she complied until he could no longer think, only feel and taste and want.

Kate was awash in sensation. Of their own accord, her fingers found one of the pins that held his shirt together and she tugged it free. He groaned in response, his eyes half-closed in pleasure. Her fingertips found the hot, satiny feel of his bare skin and she wanted more, moving on to the next pin down. She slipped it out, momentarily letting her finger run along the pointed edge, enjoying the prick of sensation before dropping the pin to the floor.

"*Ach,* Sebastian . . ." she whispered, spreading the blue cloth of his shirt. "You're beautiful."

"*Nee.*" He shook his head and stared down at her with a hot light in his blue eyes. "You are beautiful, and soon you will be my *frau* and we can finish what we only play at now."

His words sent a fever pulse rushing through her blood, and she stretched to kiss his mouth when a faint sound stopped her.

"What is that?" she asked, noting that he, too, had raised his head to listen.

"It's the school bell. I haven't heard it rung like that in years." He gently put her from him. "I'd better go and check. Something must be wrong."

Kate snatched up her cloak from the floor. "I'm going with you."

He nodded his assent, then took her arm in his to go outside and hurriedly harness the cutter sled. Soon they were off across the darkening white fields, and Kate found herself praying that whatever was wrong would soon be righted.

They soon arrived at the school, where many other folks had already gathered. Kate saw that the bishop had been standing on the snowy steps, but he hurried down and through the small crowd when he saw Sebastian and her arrive.

"Kate," Bishop Umble puffed, clearly distraught. "You're all right? I was so afraid after you took my sled that you'd had an accident."

"What?" she asked blankly. "I didn't take your sled. I walked to Sebastian's."

Bishop Umble stepped back with a frown. "Then who . . . ?"

A bolt of intuition caused Kate's heart to pound with sudden fear. "Where's Ben? Is he at your *haus?*"

"*Nee.*" The bishop shook his head. "Martha and I thought he'd surely gone with you, but that sled wasn't safe."

Kate sat, frozen in horror as all manner of images of Ben being hurt rushed through her mind. "The workshop," she said slowly. "We had words about him going to Sebastian's workshop. He must have somehow gotten into the sleigh and taken it alone."

"Then we need to search the distance between," Joseph King, a tall, dark-haired man, said briefly. "The dark will soon be against us."

"*Jah,*" Sebastian agreed. "Some on sleds; some on foot. We need lanterns."

"I want to go," Kate said.

"*Nee,* sweetheart, please. I cannot worry about both of you. . . ." He paused and Kate shuddered as she felt the first drops of a freezing rain begin to pelt the area.

"*Ach,* Sebastian . . . what if . . ." She could not finish, and he squeezed her hand tightly.

"*Nee,*" he whispered. "Don't think. Pray."

Jude Lyons, the schoolmaster, had opened the school and was handing out lanterns as more men came. Soon women brought steaming pots of coffee, and the rain made dull clinking sounds against the metal, seeming to grate on Kate's nerves despite her gratitude for everyone's help. But night was coming, and she could only wait.

"Tim!" Sebastian called wearily into the dark hollow of trees, holding his lantern high, after an hour of fruitless search.

"Now, what in tarnation are ya hollerin' fer, boy? I gots the little fella, back in an old cabin here, safe and sound. 'Course he was pert' near frozen before I got him in front of the fire, but . . ."

"You found him . . . praise *Gott!*"

"That's who to praise, if I don't say so myself. You wanna come and carry the lad out?"

Sebastian caught his friend in a backbreaking hug, then put him down. "*Jah!*"

Sebastian followed Tim Garland back under the long, snow-crusted limbs of some heavy pine. There stood one of several deserted cabins on the mountain, lit up now by a cozy fire in the fireplace, shining through the window.

"Here we go," Tim said, letting Sebastian in the rickety door ahead of him.

"Sebastian!" Ben cried merrily. "I'm having hot chocolate."

Sebastian swept a sidelong glance at Tim, who shrugged innocently. "Ya knows I always carry a supply of chocolate on me."

"This is Tim," Ben said, wiggling his bare toes near the fire, where he sat under a pile of old quilts.

"I suppose you conjured up the quilts, too." Sebastian smiled at his friend as he spoke in an undertone.

"I does what I can, boy," Tim said humbly.

Sebastian moved to kneel down close to Ben and to catch the *buwe* in a close hug. "You gave your sister quite a scare, Ben. And I'm afraid there'll be consequences for running off like that. . . ."

"That's all right, Sebastian. I know what I did was wrong, and I did get very scared when the runner gave way and the horse took off back toward the bishop's. It was so cold in the snow, but then Tim . . ." Ben yawned hugely. "Wait, where is Tim?"

Sebastian shrugged. "Hard to say. *Kumme,* let's

get you back to your sister and call off the man-hunt."

Ben wriggled in his arms as he swept him up, quilts and all, and Sebastian knew how very much he'd come to care for the *buwe*.

"What about the fire?" Ben asked, glancing toward the flames.

"Tim will see to it," Sebastian said with assurance, then stretched to pick up his lantern and headed out into the night with his arms gladly burdened.

Kate promptly burst into tears when they began to ring the school bell again, indicating Ben had been found, and Sebastian walked in carrying her *bruder*.

"Don't cry, Katie," Ben said, waking with a mournful sigh. "You can punish me because I know what I did was wrong."

"Why did you do it?" she asked, feeling for him through the quilts, to reassure herself that he was real.

"I knew *Gott* didn't want me to, but I wanted to be grown-up and try to prove that I could manage a sled. Tim told me that a real man listens and obeys and doesn't run off plumb-crazy. . . ."

"Did he hit his head? Who's Tim?" Kate looked up at Sebastian worriedly.

"Ben's fine. Probably exhausted, that's all. Let me help you get him home to bed."

Kate nodded, then thanked the bishop and all those she passed as Sebastian carried Ben to his sleigh. They rode back to Kate's in happy silence and then tucked Ben comfortably in bed, with several hot potatoes beneath the covers to keep his feet warm.

"I'd like to tuck you in, too," Sebastian murmured suggestively, running his hands down her back when they'd closed Ben's door.

She stood stock-still, sensation drugging her with funny feelings up and down her arms and legs.

Sebastian sighed. "But I won't. There'll be plenty of time for that once we marry."

Kate nodded, half-regretful.

But then he bent and brushed his lips across hers, pulling back for a heated second to murmur in her ear. "I wonder if I could have the pleasure of your company for a sleigh ride on Christmas Eve?" he asked.

She looked up at him in surprise. "But Ben . . ."

"Will be fine and fast asleep when we *geh*." He smiled.

"*Ach* . . . all right. I'd love to."

"*Gut*," he whispered, bending to kiss her once more and then quickly leaving.

She stood for long minutes in the kitchen after he'd left, praising *Gott* for Ben's safety and looking forward with pleasure to the gift of a sleigh ride on the eve of the Christ Child's birth.

A few days later, Sebastian watched Tim button his parka.

"Well, boy, I expect this is the last run, bein' that Christmas is so close and all."

"I know." Sebastian sighed.

"Oh, now, don't you fret none—I'll be back next year, same as always." Tim lifted the satchel of toys, and Sebastian held out his hand to his friend.

Tim shook it with a rough swallow, and Sebastian had to smile.

"You behave, old man."

"Naw, you behave with that little lady. I look forward to deliverin' toys to your kids someday." Tim grinned and Sebastian laughed.

"Give me some time."

"Here now, don't take much a'tall when yous think on it. . . ."

"Never mind!" Sebastian opened the front door of the workshop, and Tim walked out into the north wind. Sebastian watched for a moment, then turned back inside to continue preparations for Christmas Eve with Kate.

CHAPTER 12

On Christmas Eve, Kate tucked Ben into bed, then bent close to his face. "Do you mind if I kiss you gut nacht, Ben, now that you're growing up?"

He smiled up at her, but his brown eyes were wide and serious. "I will always want you to kiss me, Kate. Except maybe not when the other fellas are around. . . ."

She laughed and kissed him gently on the forehead, then she moved to turn down the light. "Are you sure you'll be all right, Ben, if I go for a quick sleigh ride with Sebastian?"

He laughed in the darkness of the room. "Of course, Kate. It's not like you're going to the North Pole or anywhere like that. . . . I'll be fine."

She smiled to herself and left the room, leaving the door slightly ajar. Then she went into her tiny room and dressed with care, though Sebastian would probably only see her cloak and bonnet. She patted her *kapp* into place and then went to put on her outer things and wait for Sebastian.

She soon heard the rich sound of many sleigh

bells ringing and flew to open the front door. The moon was out in full and perfectly illuminated the sleigh and driver, and she caught her breath in wonder.

The sleigh was an exact replica of the cutter sled that Sebastian had made for little Karen in the hospital: painted a rich, shiny burgundy and trimmed in coal black, its lines smooth and perfect. The new reins even stretched out to contain a prancing white gelding, whose white mane competed with the color of the snow.

"Sebastian . . . what . . . how?" she asked, unable to put a full thought together at the childlike wonder she felt gazing at the sleigh. He stepped down and extended a gloved hand to her.

"Tim . . . uh . . . a friend thought it might be a *gut* idea to make for you something special that we'll use on our wedding day and on nights like tonight." His voice was husky and romantic, and she let him lift her easily into the tight confines of the sleigh.

She ran her hand in delight over the velvet seat cover and scooted over to make room when Sebastian retook his place at the reins. The press of his lean hip and firm thigh against her was more than enough to send her senses spiraling upward, but then he spoke lightly to the white horse and they were off.

She'd never ridden in a sleigh so fine, she realized as they seemed to fairly fly over the dips and turns of the open fields.

"Do you remember the story I told Karen in the hospital?" he asked her tenderly and she turned to look at his handsome profile with love in her eyes.

"I do, indeed," she said.

"Tell me," he prompted.

She swallowed hard. "Once upon a time, two bears fell into love like it was a giant colored puddle, and they swam together happily for days and days. But then the winter came, a cold time between them, and the puddle froze over into long pulls of icy color and they couldn't swim together anymore."

She reached out to touch his arm, remembering her harshness to him the day she found out about his past.

"And then?" he questioned quietly.

Kate wet her lips. "And then, the Mr. Bear said, 'I will build you a sleigh to fly upon the ice, a sleigh fit for a princess bear so that we may be together when the cold comes.' And he did, a magical, special sleigh that cuddled them close together as they did, indeed, fly over the rose- and blue-colored ice, a sleigh ride with the promise of spring in its flight."

"Thank you," he whispered.

And she heard the love in his voice.

EPILOGUE

Daniel Zook carefully pulled aside the tarp that covered the baby sled. He picked it up with tears in his eyes, recalling how *gut Gott* had been to them in the past year and remembering the despair he'd felt two Christmases ago when they'd lost their little girl. But now that sister in heaven had a robust baby boy as a *bruder,* and it was a perfect time and day to take him for his first sleigh ride.

Dan quickly attached a pull rope into each hole in the sled, then left the woodshed to find Fran smiling and happy as she held their well-bundled baby, Kris, on the front porch.

"It's all ready." Daniel smiled and Fran looked at him with happy tears in her eyes.

"I'm so glad you kept it," she murmured. "It was a sign of a blessing, and many of our *kinner* will ride in his *gut* wood."

She passed the baby to Daniel, who put him securely in the little sleigh, then he turned and held out the rope to Sebastian, who stood nearby, with Ben on his shoulders, and Kate snuggled close under his arm.

"Sebastian, if you and your wife and Ben would do the honors. I think his first sleigh ride should be entrusted to your capable hands," Daniel said, smiling.

Sebastian nodded and moved forward, stretching out a gloved hand to take the sleigh rope while Baby Kris cooed excitedly.

They went slowly over the sun-kissed snow, the sleigh making a familiar whooshing sound complemented by Kris's happy gurgles.

Sebastian glanced down at Kate and squeezed Ben's hand where he balanced him on his shoulders. "Well, what do you think, *sohn*? And Frau *Christner*? Is it a fair enough day for someone's first sleigh ride on Ice Mountain?"

Kate laughed and Ben gave a tap to his hat, and Sebastian basked in their love as a united family.

A Mamm for Christmas

Amy Lillard

ACKNOWLEDGMENTS

Anyone who knows me knows how much my grandmother meant to me. I've dedicated one book to her, but wanted to honor her again. So I named the main character in this novella after her. Surprisingly enough—or maybe not—Bernice seems to have the same spunk as my grandmother did when she was alive. So thanks to my grandmother Bernice Davis, for lending your name and personality to Bernice Yoder.

I owe a debt of gratitude to my Lancaster friends for tirelessly helping me with the details concerning Amish schools, their teachers, and their Christmas pageants. Thank you to Becky, Nancy, Sadie, Rachel, and Sarah for answering my endless questions and for your continued efforts in making my books as accurate as they can be. I had the best team on my side; any mistakes are mine and mine alone.

Thanks to John and the team at Kensington for their continued patience and allowing me to be a part of this project. Each day I work with you is more fun than the one before!

And to my agent, Julie Gwinn. I know this is just

the beginning of many more fabulous projects to come.

Many thanks to my "Carl" for standing beside me and occasionally behind me to give me a nudge whenever I need it. I'm chagrined to say it is more often than I care to admit.

So many thanks go out to my family. You'll never know exactly how much you mean to me! Love you!

And to the readers. You are the reason I do what I do. Thanks for reading!

Amy

Now hear this, O foolish and senseless people, who have eyes but do not see; who have ears but do not hear.

—Jeremiah 5:21

CHAPTER 1

Snow was a'comin'. Jess Schmucker looked to the clouded sky, then across the pasture where his herd of dairy cows ambled along toward the barn. His girls would be home from school any minute, and together he and his oldest daughter, Constance, would get the animals all hooked up in their milking stalls and milked. But Constance was the only one of his three girls who was old enough to truly help in the barn. At eight she was not as much assistance as he needed, but for the time being she was all he had.

"*Dat!*" He turned as his youngest daughter raced toward him. She ran from the road as if he would disappear at any minute. They had talked about it time and again, but to Lilly Ruth the problem was simple. She had gone to her *grossmammi*'s house one morning last fall, and everything had been right in her world. She had returned that afternoon to find her mother dead and her father racked with grief.

He shook the thought away. Looking back to

the past never did nobody any good. All he could do was face the future and pray for the best. And that's what he was doing: the best he could.

"*Dat! Dat! Dat!*" Lilly Ruth flung herself at him, leaving him no other option than to swing her into his arms. Behind her clear-framed glasses, her eyes were worried and happy all in the same moment. "You're still here." It had been almost a year and her fear remained.

"Of course I am, *liebschdi.*" He planted a quick kiss to her forehead. He wanted to squeeze her tight and not let her go until the clouds left her eyes. But that would only make her clingier. Instead, he inhaled the scent of outdoors that wafted from her clothes and let her slide to the ground.

Constance and Hope had long since given up on their sister staying near. They trudged down the driveway, their lunch coolers swinging in their hands.

"Everyone inside," Jess instructed. "Let's get a snack before we start our chores." The girls didn't protest, but dragged their feet a little as they plodded to the house.

The girls removed their coats and changed into their chore clothes, then set about getting out paper plates for their quick snack. Constance poured disposable plastic cups full of milk for them all.

He tried not to think about the time long ago when they ate off the good plates and drank from glasses made from . . . well, glass. Of all the things that had changed, their use of throwaway dishes was at the bottom of the list of what he wished was different.

Constance and Hope shared a look as his middle daughter gave everyone three of the store-bought cookies, then sealed the bag shut. She placed it in the cabinet and came back to the table.

For some reason her serious face made the hair on his arms stand on end. Or was that the waft of cold air that had followed them in from outside? No matter. He bowed his head and his daughters did the same. A prayer before they ate, a quick snack, and it was back to the barn for the evening milking.

Jess idly chewed his cookie, the sweet treat tasting more like cardboard than he cared to acknowledge. He looked around the quiet table at each of his girls. Maybe it was just him. But what he wouldn't give for one of his *mamm*'s apple pies right about now.

"When's *mammi* coming back?" Hope asked, nibbling her cookie with what could only be described as reluctance.

With the holidays fast approaching and weddings to go to every single Tuesday and Thursday, Jess knew his *mamm* and his only sister were busy. His *brudders* had their own families and problems. It was time to face it; it was time to move on. Forward. And figure out what to do about store-bought cookies and his daughters. Or rather their everyday care.

"*Dat?*" Constance turned her blue eyes on him, eyes that were far too filled with pain for any eight-year-old's to be. "Is she ever coming back?"

Jess swallowed the lump in his throat. "Of course." Maybe sometime after the first of the year, once Christmas and the New Year had passed. Once wedding season had ended and they didn't have more of their own issues to take care of. Maybe after all that.

Despite his own doubts, his daughters seemed to accept the answer.

But now more than ever, he could see how hard his family was struggling without the care of a woman about the house. The girls needed someone to help them with their hair and breakfast. Someone to care for them and show them all the things a *mamm* shows her *dochders*.

But their *mudder* had only been gone a year, and the thought of marrying again . . . He shook his head.

"Come on," he said, motioning his daughters toward the pegs where their heavy coats hung. "Those cows aren't going to milk themselves."

Bernice Yoder pulled her buggy down the driveway that led toward the Schmucker house and told herself she was doing this for the girls. Constance, Hope, and Lilly Ruth needed her, and she had to stand up and do the right thing. But she had never in her eight years of teaching had to go to a family's house for something like this. She'd had to check on sick children and travel with the bishop to talk to the parents of some of the more spirited children. But never for neglect.

There, she let the word loose in her mind, but it was no comfort. She set the brake on her buggy and took a deep breath. It had to be done.

"Just go in there and take a look at the situation," she told herself. "If things are worse than you thought, just leave and get the bishop's wife." Ruth Mullet was always one to lend a hand. Or so Bernice had been told.

Mind made up, Bernice slid from her buggy and

headed for the porch. The wind whipped through her woolen coat as she made her way up the steps and knocked on the door. She would assess the situation. She had to. The girls deserved more than they were currently getting.

"Help you?"

Bernice whirled around at the sound of the deep male voice behind her. The man was tall, at least taller than anyone else she knew. And she was thankful that she was standing on the porch, three feet above him. Otherwise he would tower over her. Or maybe it was the frown pulling his brows together that made him seem so . . . menacing.

"Can I help you?" he asked again.

"Oh, I—" She cleared her throat, her mouth suddenly dry, her stomach twisting into knots. "I'm here to see Jess Schmucker."

He propped his hands on his hips. "That's me."

Of course it was. Just what she needed: to confront an angry man about the sad state of his daughters.

"Bernice!" Lilly Ruth came running out of the barn, her sisters trailing behind. Her coat flapped open in the wind, just one more thing Bernice needed to talk to the man about. Young girls shouldn't go around like that; she was liable to catch pneumonia.

Bernice bent down, preparing to be the recipient of one of Lilly Ruth's full-body hugs, when Jess snaked out one arm and caught his daughter as she passed.

"You know her?" he asked. As if she wasn't standing right in front of him.

Constance nodded. "She's our teacher."

He turned back to look at her, and Bernice couldn't help but nod as if that would add value to

Constance's statement. Maybe she should have come out here before now and introduced herself. She usually met all the parents before the school year started, but Jess Schmucker had sent his sister in his stead.

"Bernice Yoder." She stepped off the porch and reached out a hand to shake. She was right. He did seem to tower over her even though he wasn't *that* tall. But his frown sent her heart racing in her chest.

He looked at her hand long enough that she wasn't sure he was actually going to touch her. Finally his hand came up, but his eyes never left hers. She snatched her hand away as soon as politely possible. "What can I do for you, Bernice Yoder?"

"I would like to speak to you . . . if that's possible . . . alone." She pulled on her coat and tried to make her words ring with confidence, but sadly they fell way short of her goal.

"Girls, go on in the house."

They did as their father asked without question, though each one stopped and gave her a quick hug before scuttling inside.

"What's on your mind?" Jess asked as the first snowflake started to fall.

For a split second she almost abandoned her resolve, told him everything was fine and hurried over to her buggy. But it would do those sweet little girls no favors for her to chicken out now.

"It's the girls."

His frown turned into an all-out scowl. "*Jah?* Are they misbehaving?"

"Oh no."

"Having trouble with their studies? Lilly Ruth can be a bit headstrong."

Bernice smiled. "No, it's not that, either."

He waited, watching her as she gathered her thoughts. "*Jah?*" he said, his voice tinged with impatience. Not a good sign.

"It's their clothes." There, she said it. But the constriction in her chest remained.

"Their clothes?"

"They come to school a bit disheveled."

"Disheveled?" He repeated the word as if he'd never heard it before.

"Dirty." It was a stronger word than Bernice wanted, and it seemed to be harder than Jess could stand.

His face turned an unlikely shade of red, his freckles standing out stark against the vivid color. "Are you saying my children aren't clean?"

Bernice shook her head. She was ruining whatever chance she had of reaching him. "That's not what I mean. It's just that . . ."

"What?"

She took a steadying breath as the snowflakes continued to fall around them. "The other children are starting to notice." She dropped her voice in hopes that her softened tone would have a calming effect on him. "The girls . . . they are so sweet and smart. But when they come to school with stains on their clothes, their hair messy, and part of their breakfast on their faces . . ." She trailed off, but she didn't need to finish; Jess Schmucker knew exactly what she was talking about. She could see it in his eyes.

"Thank you, Bernice Yoder." His face was still

that frightening shade of crimson as he pushed past her and into the house. She turned as the door shut behind him, effectively sealing her off from him and his girls.

Bernice stared at the door for two long heartbeats. "I can help you if you'd like," she said quietly to no one, but she had a feeling Jess Schmucker didn't want her help. Not now anyway. Pulling her coat a little tighter around her, she dashed through the falling snow to her waiting horse and buggy. She had done her part. She had met with the girls' father. But, she thought as she clicked her horse into motion, her meeting with Jess had not gone according to plan. Not even close.

CHAPTER 2

Jess pulled the door shut behind him and was quite satisfied with himself when he didn't slam it closed with all his strength. Just who did she think she was, coming here and criticizing him and his efforts? He was doing the best he could. But he was both mother and father to his three girls. He had to run the dairy farm, see to the milk truck, get the girls dressed and ready for school, figure out what they were eating for lunch and dinner, and wash the clothes. And that was all before noon.

She had no right, he fumed. No right a'tall to come into his house and start pointing fingers over whose dress was stained and who had forgotten to wipe their mouth before they left the table. Well, he guessed she hadn't come into the house. Only onto the porch.

He looked around at the clothes that hung on the line stretched between the front door and the back porch. He hated having to duck under it to get anywhere in the house, but it was too cold to go hanging the garments outside. They would freeze solid before they would dry.

"*Dat?*" Hope stood in the entryway to the kitchen, a small frown on her smooth forehead. She was the image of her mother, light brown hair and pale gray eyes like the sky before the snow started. "What did Bernice want?"

He cleared his throat, unwilling to tell his middle daughter the truth. "She, uh, wanted to remind me about the Christmas program." *Lord, forgive me my lies.* But he would do everything in his control to keep them from knowing the truth.

Constance picked that moment to peek around her sister. Other than her blond hair, his oldest looked like her mother, as well. Two walking reminders of the past. "Really? You can come, right?"

Lilly Ruth bounced on her toes, excitement lighting her blue eyes. Of all of his girls she was the most like him in appearance. Red hair, freckles, blue eyes. "Please, please, please!"

"Of course." Jess let out a small cough. He would have to be at the program. Somehow, some way. He was struggling without his mother or his sister there to help. Yet tomorrow things would be different. He'd see to it. And the day after that and the day after that. He would get it all together. Surely that would put a stop to the pitying light he'd seen in the young teacher's green eyes.

"Constance!" Jess stood at the door to the house and hollered for his girls. "Hope! Lilly Ruth!" The milking had been done, breakfast had been eaten, and it was time for the girls to head to school.

After he'd gone to bed last night, he'd replayed the conversation between him and the teacher. He'd mulled over every word. Not that he actually said that many. He'd been too shocked. But he had realized one thing. He had to do something different. And he was starting today.

"Con—stance." His voice started out loud, then dropped to a normal tone as his daughters started down the stairs. He wasn't sure what they had been doing upstairs when they were supposed to be finishing up chores so they could go to school.

He needed to have them inside working on the dishes. The way they were piling up, it was going to take a week to get them all clean and put away. *Jah,* they had been using disposable plates and cups for nigh on a week, yet somehow the dishes seemed to pile up on their own. A cup here and there, a plastic container, a saucer, miscellaneous items that seemed to appear out of nowhere.

He said a small prayer of thanks that Bernice Yoder had stayed on the porch. The thought of her coming into the house and passing more judgments against him . . .

"Here." He stopped his girls one by one and gave their faces another swipe with a wet rag. He had done his best with their hair, but it still looked as if they had been caught in a strong wind. He used the rag to smooth down some of the worst of the flyaways, handed them their lunch coolers, then sent them on their way. He'd picked out the best of their dresses, ones without stains and tears. Thankfully, the snow had held off to a light dusting. Still they wore their warmest boots, coats, and knit scarves, ready for a blizzard if one decided to arrive that afternoon.

Let Bernice Yoder find fault with that, he thought as he watched his children traipse toward the road.

He gave the dishes one last look, then headed for the barn. The house needed his attention, but the north fence needed it more. Maybe this afternoon he'd have enough time to get started on the house, but until then . . . he grabbed the new fence post he'd gotten in town the day before and started across his pasture.

"Good morning." Bernice smiled to each of her students as they ambled into the one-room schoolhouse where she taught. Despite the fact the snow barely covered the ground, some of the more rambunctious *buwe* still scraped up enough to make snowballs to pelt each other as they raced toward the entrance.

"Johnny Lapp, get down from there," she called as the boy started to climb onto the outhouse to gather more snow. Heaven help them all when a big snow hit. She had a hard enough time keeping the boys busy when the weather was fine. But they would all get snow fever for sure when they got more than a dusting. And she had heard the talk at the mercantile. The elders had said this could be the snowiest winter on record.

Well, she would hoe that row when she came to it. For now, she waved the children inside and looked to see if she had forgotten any.

The playground was clear, but in the distance she could see three small figures heading for the school. They were a little late this morning, but of all her students, the Schmucker girls had to walk the farthest to attend. Sometimes Bernice wondered if it might not be closer for them to go to a different school, but since she had failed in her talk with their father, she thought it best that she have them remain in her school. At least that way she could keep an eye on them.

She was new to the area and hadn't met a good many people since she had been there. And she certainly hadn't heard what had happened to Jess Schmucker's wife. That was something she needed to find out. Perhaps the frowning Jess was still grieving for a love who had passed. Or maybe she had left him alone and bitter to care for their children while she enjoyed the pleasures the *Englisch* world had to offer.

Or perhaps she, Bernice Yoder, needed to quit reading those *Englisch* novels about Plain people.

But her buoyant mood fizzled as the Schmucker girls drew closer. Then it completely died as they came near enough for her to see every detail of their appearance. All three girls had mud caked to their boots, surely a result of yesterday's snow. But not the dark streaks on their hems and coats. Lilly Ruth's head scarf was even soiled with what could only be mud. Their faces were marked with smudges of peanut butter and jam, and their hair. Goodness! Their hair looked as if they had slept in the hayloft. And despite the fact that she didn't want to admit it even to herself, they smelled like they slept there, as well.

She cleared her throat and pushed her irritation with their father down deep inside and focused on what she could do now. Later she could examine why he had seen fit to send them to school in worse condition than ever before. And after she had gone to his house to help him.

He didn't want your help.

That wasn't exactly true. He'd slammed the door in her face before she could voice her offer of help, then she chickened out and scuttled on home. But her fears and reluctance weren't nearly as important as the three precious children who stood in front of her, with their big, innocent eyes and dirt-smudged, freckled cheeks.

"Girls, come in please and right over here." She led them as discreetly as possible to the hooks where everyone hung their coats and hats. On a top shelf, she kept a tub of wipes for when the children got dirty at recess. She helped Lilly Ruth get her coat off while the other two shed theirs and hung them on the hooks under their names. She would worry about the streaks of mud on the black wool once she got everyone seated and working on their lessons.

She hung up Lilly Ruth's little coat and turned toward the class. "Everyone, find your seat. I'll be there in just a minute. Until then, fifth graders, start reading. Remember we're on chapter ten of *Little House on the Prairie*. Eighth grade, help the first graders with their letters, and everyone else, get out your readers and pick up where you left off yesterday."

She didn't stop to see if they did as she said. The rustle behind her was testament enough. "Now," she murmured under her breath. She focused her attention on the three little girls.

"Is it bad?" Constance asked, eyes wide.

How could she tell the girl the truth? *Lord, forgive me this lie.* "Of course not."

"Oh," came Constance's reply.

Bernice took a couple of Wet Wipes from the tub. She hesitated, then snatched another one out just in case. "What happened?" she asked Lilly Ruth, who seemed to be the dirtiest of them all. Even her tiny fingers were coated in dried mud. "Did you fall on the way to school?"

"*Jah.*" She nodded her bright head, then she stopped and looked to her sisters. "I mean, I fell last night."

Bernice had hoped that her talk with Jess would bring about a few changes, but that optimism had been easily squashed. These *wunderbaar* children had been left to get dirty and not even cleaned up in time for bed. No wonder their clothes were on the ripe side and their hair tangled with rats' nests.

But mixed somewhere in between the smell of earth and barn was a hint of detergent. Perhaps there was more to the situation than she knew. Their clothes had been cleaned sometime or the scent wouldn't be there, but when and why did they look the way they did now were questions that remained. Not that she would ever get those answers. She couldn't keep going out to his house and badgering him until he got things right.

She had taken one look into those blue eyes of his, and her heart had skipped a beat. Unfortunately it had nothing to do with the scowl he wore. Not that it wasn't impressive, and she wondered if he scowled at everyone like that. Or was that look saved for teachers who cared a little too much? She would never know because she was not going out to the Schmucker farm again.

No, but there were other things she could do. She could wash the girls as much as possible when they got to school. She had two eighth-grade girls in the class. They could help as she redid their hair and wiped the smudges from their sweet faces.

And pray. She could pray for the girls and their father. Pray that the Lord provide them with everything they needed. God wouldn't forsake them. Of that much she was certain.

But as a new week began, the girls continued to arrive at school dirty, frowsy-headed, and increasingly smelly. What was a teacher to do but bring some lemon-scented body spray she'd picked up at the grocery store? Discreetly she sprayed the girls' coats when they were hanging by the door. She continued to wipe their faces and hands, spot-clean their dresses, and get angrier and angrier at Jess Schmucker.

She supposed some men were just like that, but he didn't seem to be unkempt when she'd been out there. He wasn't *clean,* but he worked on a dairy farm. Still, he wasn't overly dirty, either.

"You're not mad at our *dat,* are you?" Hope asked as Bernice wiped her hands clean. At the sound of her voice, Bernice realized that she might be wiping with a bit more force than necessary. But if she had thought the girls looked bad last week, this week they were downright scruffy. Dirt on their clothes, faces, and hands, dried food in all the same places. And yesterday come lunch, the girls only had one sandwich to split between the three of them. Luckily Bernice had made an extra sandwich in hopes that her cousin might stop by, but she didn't. No wonder since she was getting married in a couple of weeks, and Joy's absence allowed her to feed the poor Schmucker girls.

"Of course not. Why would I have reason to be mad at your father?"

Hope shrugged. "Because he doesn't wash our faces in the morning."

"Or our clothes," Lilly Ruth piped in.

Constance shushed them both. "It's okay, though." She sounded much older than her eight years, and Bernice had to bite her lip to fight the tears that sprang into her eyes. These poor, sweet girls deserved so much more than just her prayers, and it was becoming increasingly apparent that mere prayers were not all that was needed.

Action. She needed to take action. And quick.

"Don't be mad at our *dat*," Hope said, with a precious smile. "He's done the best he could since *Mamm* died."

Bernice pressed her lips together to keep her sigh of sympathy at bay. It wasn't the Amish way to grieve overlong. Life had to be lived, but how did a father tell his young children their mother would never tuck them in at night ever again? "I'm sure he has." She continued to clean the stains from their dresses, but this time with a gentler hand. Hope had a sticky spot that looked a bit like jelly, while Lilly Ruth had a stain that appeared to be ketchup. What kind of breakfast was he feeding them if they had jelly and ketchup?

They ate breakfast. That was the important part. And hopefully today they would have enough lunch to divide between them, but just in case, Bernice had packed an extra two ham sandwiches in her cooler. The Lord favored the prepared.

With one last swipe at their hair, Bernice sent the girls to their seats and her teaching day began.

CHAPTER 3

Bernice trailed her fingers over the bolts of fabric and tried to remember exactly what color she had chosen for the girls to wear in the Christmas program. It had been weeks since she had sent the bolt of fabric home with the first family, but the truth of the matter was that Jess Schmucker and his darling girls were a distraction like none other.

There was just a little over a week before the program. The mothers throughout the district were sewing matching dresses and shirts—one color for the girls and a different one for the boys—that the children would wear. But Constance, Hope, and Lilly Ruth didn't have a mother, just a father.

And just like that, the glowering, handsome face was once again at the front of her thoughts.

"I would have thought he'd remarry by now."

"I know. For the girls if nothing else." The woman *tsked*.

Bernice's ears perked. She hadn't meant to listen in on their conversation, but they were right behind her examining the large table of fabric while she studied the ones stacked on the wall. There was no way she wouldn't have been able to hear them unless she was stone-deaf. Yet just because they were discussing a man who needed to remarry for the sake of his girls didn't mean they were talking about Jess Schmucker.

"*Jah.* Those girls need a *mamm.*"

"Esther King said that his mother and sister had been over helping, but I hear these days that they have too much of their own to do. Frankly, I think they're trying to force him to see the truth."

"And what truth would that be, Abigail?"

"That a man shouldn't be in this world without a wife. The Bible even says so."

"I know what the Bible says." The other woman sighed. "So you think Jess will get married again."

So they were talking about him!

"I'm sure of it."

The women moved away before Bernice could find out how Jess's wife had died, but it was probably for the best. She shouldn't be listening in to other people's conversations, and she surely didn't need to be so interested in all things Jess Schmucker.

Bernice chose a dark purple that she was fairly certain had been the color for the dresses, then headed for the counter.

A tiny voice inside whispered that she might ought to ask Jess if he had someone to sew the special dresses for his girls, but she didn't want to risk it. She would make the dresses herself and keep them at the school until the day of the program. Jess Schmucker might not care how the district saw his children, but Bernice Yoder did.

*   *   *

He was dead tired, but Jess had no choice. He had a Christmas program to attend. It wasn't that he didn't want to go, but he was just worn out. The good news was he had managed to get all of the dishes washed. Now they had to be put away, though he had no idea where they all went. In the cabinets somewhere, of course. He had relied on his mother and his sister for too long, and he had no clue as to where Linda Grace had kept the dishes before she died.

As usual his wife crossed his thoughts at least once a day. He missed her like crazy, but time was a healer and now he could think about her without the stabbing pains of heartbreak.

He was moving on, living like those who are left behind are forced to do. But he couldn't say he was good at it. Right now he felt like a swimmer lost at sea. It was taking all of his energy just to stay afloat, and that was not living.

But he had a farm to see to and girls to raise.

"I'll do right by you," he whispered to his wife, hoping that she could hear him. "Just every now and then, give me some direction, okay?" He could use some bearing and a little more energy.

He pulled the buggy to a stop, and the girls scuttled down like the devil was on their heels. He knew they were excited to perform the program for all the fathers. But why did it have to be so late?

In past years the program was held in the middle of the day, when everyone could get away from their farm and chores. Since more and more Amish men and women were working outside their homes, and for English companies, the school had started doing the pageant twice—once during the afternoon for the *mamms* and visiting scholars from other schools, then again at night for the *dats* and the rest of the family.

Buggies were lined up next to the fence, their horses tied to the chain-link barrier that separated the school from the field next to it. Jess parked as far out as he could. He wanted to be near the road when everyone started to leave. He needed to get home and get to bed. Three o'clock came mighty early.

He hustled the girls into the building and wiped the grit from his eyes. An eighth-grade girl met them at the curtain and motioned them to come back and ready themselves for the program. Jess watched them go with a strange mixture of pride and exhaustion.

Jah, pride was a sin, but he had settled himself to times when resisting wasn't possible. And despite his tired soul, this was one of those times.

His girls disappeared behind the blanket hung at one end of the room, and he moved away to find a seat on one of the benches set up in the classroom. Husbands and wives sat together, along with their children who weren't in the program. Aunts and uncles, even cousins waited patiently for the program to begin.

Suddenly, Jess felt alone. More alone than he did when he arrived at church without his wife at his side, even more than he felt in his bed at night. Because his solo state was there for everyone to see. He could feel their pitying eyes on him, but he pretended to read his program handout and otherwise act like he had everything going his way.

Thankfully he only had a few minutes to wait before Bernice Yoder came around the side of the makeshift curtain and rang a bell to get the crowd's attention.

"Good evening, everyone." She smiled prettily at the room at large. Even though she never turned her gaze to him, Jess's heart skipped a beat as if she had pinned him with those gorgeous green eyes.

He shook those thoughts away. Beautiful or not, Bernice was a meddling busybody who had placed judgments on him and his family.

He stifled a small cough, realizing that while he'd been in his own thoughts, Busybody Bernice had finished her introductions and moved back behind the blanket.

As far as Christmas programs went, this one was not much different from any others. The children performed skits, recited poems, told Christmas jokes, and at the end, they all came out together and sang the English Christmas song "Jingle Bells." He laughed as the children shook bells and otherwise finished with big smiles. But it was in that moment that Jess realized the girls all wore the same color of purple. Even his girls.

Had they come home from school wearing the dresses? He couldn't remember. Did they have them on when they clambered into their buggy? Or maybe they changed when they arrived at the school. Why had he not noticed that before?

Because he had been so caught up in his own issues and problems that he hadn't thought of all the events leading up to the Christmas program. But he remembered in years past, Linda Grace sewing the dresses for Constance and then for Hope, as well. Dresses she made out of the material the teacher bought each year. But there hadn't been any material this year. So, who had made the dresses his daughters now wore? Surely his mother and sister would have said as much, so that left only one person—well, two if he counted Bess Lapp who sometimes took in extra sewing to help make ends meet—and that person was Bernice Yoder.

Jess pulled on his suspenders and tried to calm his temper. He was normally a levelheaded man, but something about the dark-haired teacher brought out the worst in him. Maybe he should leave a conversation with her until a better time. When he wasn't so tired. So cranky and angry.

He pushed up from the bench and nodded a farewell to those nearest him, then went to find his daughters. Instead he found Bernice Yoder. She should have been talking to the other parents, voicing her thanks and smiling at the compliments she received for her work. Yet, she looked like she was simply waiting for him.

"Jess Schmucker." She gave him a nod of greeting and another of those smiles. But this one trembled at the corners, and he had a feeling he wasn't going to like what was coming next. "Can I talk to you for a bit? Maybe tomorrow afternoon?"

He hardened his heart against the sweet tone of her voice. "I'm busy tomorrow afternoon." His words were gruff and coarse, but he had to stop this before it began. She had no right butting into his business, and he had better things to do than help her feed her own personal gossip mill.

"It's important," she pressed.

He braced his hands at his sides and fought the urge to reach out and touch her cheek. Her skin was fair and pale without a mark from the sun. Such an unusual case for an Amish woman. That had to be why he had the strangest urge to run the backs of his fingers down the side of her face. It was that reason and that reason only.

"*Nay.*" He shook his head to back up his words. Maybe then she would know he meant what he said and she would give up whatever mission she had set herself to.

If only he were so lucky.

She pressed her lips together, her green eyes flashing. "It's about the girls, Jess."

Of course it was. "Although I appreciate your concern, my girls and I are fine, just fine."

"I don't know how you can say that."

"I can say it because it's the truth."

Then they started talking over one another. "You have no right to tell me how to raise my children."

"Their cleanliness and care should be of the highest importance in the household, and I don't think that's happening."

"You don't think?" Jess raised his voice, then realized that all of the lingering guests were staring at them as intently as if they were the second round of the evening's entertainment. "Send my girls on out to the buggy when they are ready to leave." He spun on his heel and headed for the door. Stopping just short of completely storming out, he turned around. "*Danki* for making their dresses," he said without meeting her gaze, then he pushed his way into the cold night air.

Jess Schmucker was without a doubt the most stubborn and prideful man she had ever met.

* * *

Pride goeth before destruction, and an haughty spirit before a fall.

The verse from Proverbs popped into her head like it always did when Jess was near. And that was exactly what he was setting himself up for: a fall. Didn't he understand that she only wanted to help? His children needed him, and he was too blinded by his pride to see that he needed help.

She harrumphed as she watched him stride from the schoolhouse. She wasn't giving up. For the girls' sake something had to be done. Quickly. And whether he liked it or not.

CHAPTER 4

"Hold still, Lilly Ruth." Constance Schmucker pulled on her sister's arm, turning her around to face her. All the while, she smeared dirt on her sister's freckled cheeks. "Be still or you'll end up with this mud all over."

Lilly Ruth frowned in that way that looked so much like their *dat*, Constance wanted to take a step back and away. "What difference does it make?"

"*Jah*," Hope said, running her own dusty hands reluctantly down the front of her dark purple dress. It was the same one the teacher had made for them to wear for the Christmas program the day before. Constance knew that Hope had been extra careful not to soil the dress so she could wear it again today. And she was sure it was hard for her sister to purposefully dirty the pretty *frack*.

"You're going to need to use more than that if you want Bernice to notice."

Hope propped her hands on her hips in the way Constance had seen their *mamm* do on too many occasions to count. Was this how their father felt, faced with a reminder at every turn? No wonder he was struggling to get himself together. She wasn't sure exactly what that meant, but from the tone of voice she had heard her *grossdawdi* use when he said it, Constance was for certain it wasn't good.

In fact, every time she saw her grandparents, it seemed like someone was frowning. Most times it was her *dat*. He seemed to do nothing but glower at everyone these days. Glower. That was a *gut* word. She had heard her *aenti* Reba say that to her father the last time they all went over to visit. At the time, Constance wasn't sure what the word meant, but one look at her father's face cleared that right up.

"That's enough, *jah?*" Hope asked, looking to Constance for approval. She was always looking at Constance like that with hope and trust in her eyes. Both of them did. That was her duty as the oldest: take care of her sisters. But it was hard.

They had been looking up to her for the past year. Ever since *Mamm* died in that terrible buggy wreck. But this fall had been especially hard. Their grandmother and aunt had stopped coming by the house every day. That left the washing, cleaning, and cooking up to Constance, her sisters, and their overworked father.

That's when she came up with the plan to get a new *mamm* for Christmas. Well, the idea hadn't come to her right away, but after overhearing the conversation between their father and Bernice, she knew. She knew that Bernice Yoder was the mother for them. She was pretty and nice and she smelled good, like lilacs after a summer rainstorm. Constance had taken one whiff of their teacher and almost cried with the joy of an answered prayer.

She had prayed and prayed and God had sent her Bernice Yoder.

From there the plan fell into place as easy as slopping the hogs. If Bernice was worried about them showing up for school a little messy, then they would go to school *a lot* messy. She would have no choice but to come out to the house again and talk to their father. And this time, if God was on their side, their *dat* would notice how pretty she was and how good she smelled. He would stop frowning and that would be that. They would get married, and everyone would live happily ever after like the stories in the *Englisch* fairy tales.

"Constance?" Hope's voice brought her out of her thoughts.

"*Jah?*"

"Am I dirty enough?" Hope turned in a circle so Constance could see her from every angle.

"Mess up your hair a bit more and maybe put some of the jelly from your sandwich on your face and that should do it."

"I want some jelly on my face, too." Lilly Ruth bounced on her toes as she waited for her sister to smear her with today's lunch. Constance hated wasting food. Surely it was a sin, but a necessary one. And Bernice would expect them to come a sandwich or two short for the noon meal. Just one more way to show Bernice how much the Schmucker family needed her.

Constance looked at both of her sisters, gave her nod of approval, and proceeded to muss her own hair. Her father had worked so hard to roll the sides and pull it back into a lopsided bob at the back of her head. But this was necessary, and all of their efforts would soon be worth the deceit they had made.

"Let's go." Constance picked up her cooler and together the three of them headed toward the school. Her heart pounded in her chest. What if today was the day? The day that Bernice decided that another visit was necessary. Her mouth went dry at the thought. They were so close to getting a new *mamm.*

But Constance's footsteps faltered as she neared the schoolhouse.

"What's wrong?" Hope asked. She and Lilly Ruth stopped and waited for their sister to catch up.

"Look." She nodded toward the small porch at the front of their one-room schoolhouse.

"*Aenti* Reba!" Lilly Ruth made like to run and greet their sweet aunt, but Constance put out a hand to stop her.

"You can't go up there like that," she said, brushing at the mud she had so very recently used to streak her sister's dress.

"What's she doing here?" Hope asked.

"She's probably our substitute teacher for the day. Remember? Bernice said her cousin was getting married today, and she was going to the celebration."

Hope nodded.

Ach, how she wished she had a wet rag to wipe her sister's face. There was no hiding the jelly mess on her freckled cheeks.

Maybe they should just go back home. Or hide out somewhere in town until school was over.

But it was too late. Reba had already seen them.

"Come on, girls." She motioned them toward the school. "You're holding up the lessons."

Having no other choice, Constance, Hope, and Lilly Ruth trudged the rest of the way to school.

"What in the world happened to you three?" Their aunt plopped her hands on her hips and looked at each one of them in turn.

"We, uh . . . fell," Constance finally said.

"All three of you?"

Constance swallowed hard and nodded.

Lying wasn't *gut*. Wasn't good a'tall. But she would take the brunt of the reprimand. As the oldest, that was her responsibility. She would tell the lie to protect her sisters and then pray all night that the Lord forgave her this sin.

"Onto a peanut butter and jelly sandwich?" Reba wiped at the corner of Lilly Ruth's mouth.

"Maybe," the youngest Schmucker replied.

Hope bumped her with her shoulder to hush her up.

"Ow." Lilly Ruth rubbed her arm and glared at her sister.

"Take these and wipe your faces." Reba offered them the tub of Wet Wipes. "I'm not sure what to do about your hair." She shook her head as she looked at them each in turn.

Constance knew they looked a sight, but the show hadn't been for their aunt to see.

"Go on to your seats." Reba sighed.

Constance dragged her feet as she followed her sisters to their desks. All eyes were on them, and Constance had never felt so bad. Her plan had somehow gotten all twisted around. And there was nothing she could do about it now.

* * *

Jess came out of the barn, blinking in the sun to clear his vision. It might be overcast and gray outside, but it was still darker in the barn. But with such heavy clouds, he wouldn't be surprised if it started snowing again.

"There you are."

He started at the sound of his sister's voice. "Reba. What are you doing out here?" Dare he get his hopes up? Had she come back to help him get his house in order? Never again would he take her assistance for granted.

"Did I scare you?"

He shook his head, managing not to laugh at her crestfallen expression.

"Next time," she promised. She had been trying to scare him for so long that he had gotten accustomed to the ambush attacks from her. Maybe one day. When he was in a more charitable mood, he would pretend to be scared just to make her happy.

She swung down from the wagon, her violet dress swishing beneath the hem of her black woolen coat. The purple was a shock of a color and Jess wondered if their conservative bishop had seen it. Most church leaders didn't dabble so much in the everyday lives of their district. Bishop Daniel Mullet was not one of those.

"So, what brings you out here today, sister?" Jess managed to keep his hopes in check. Wouldn't do to let her know how desperate he was for her help.

Reba's normally impish smile fell. "Something happened at school today."

"The girls?" Jess whirled toward the house. They had come home just a few minutes before and headed inside straightaway. He was slowly catching up on things, but there were still a lot of chores to do.

"Are fine," she said. "But they came to school dirty."

Jess slammed his hands on his hips. Never in his life had he felt this close to violence. He knew he was being unreasonable but he was working extra hard—extra, *extra* hard—and he didn't need his sister coming over starting in like Bernice Yoder. "I've been wiping their faces before they leave the house, making sure their clothes are clean—" He let out a pent-up breath and tried to calm himself. He was overly tired, overly sensitive, and overly . . . everything.

Reba laid a gentle hand on his arm. "I know."

"Would you like to explain that?" He managed to tame his voice to a smooth tone without even the slightest hitch.

"I was at the school today as their substitute teacher."

Jess nodded. "Go on."

"Well, when they got to school they had mud on their coats and dresses, dirt and peanut butter on their faces, and their hair looked like they had been through a tornado."

"Did you say peanut butter?"

Reba nodded. "And jelly."

"You know I wouldn't let them leave the house like that."

"I thought so, but . . ."

"But what?"

Her blue eyes so like his sparkled with something akin to pity. "Losing Linda Grace cannot have been easy. I was concerned that maybe you had slipped a bit."

Slipped? He wasn't even going to respond to that. "I'm fine," he said. He had lost count of how many times he had said those very same words in the last week or so. But was he fine? Had he slipped? He thought he was on the track toward catching up and getting things back in order. But he couldn't work at this pace forever.

He needed to hire a hand to help him in the barn. Or a housekeeper to look after the girls. He needed a wife. The thought took his breath away. He wasn't ready for that. Not by far.

"I'm fine," he said again, but his voice had lost its earlier confidence. Or had it ever been there?

"So why did the girls come to school so disheveled?"

There was that word again. Bernice Yoder's heart-shaped face popped into his mind. When would he be free of her?

"I don't know," he finally said. "But I plan to. For sure and for certain."

Only Lilly Ruth came to dinner with a smile on her face.

Jess watched his daughters file into the dining area and take their places around the table. Constance and Hope looked as if the sky would fall any minute.

Jess didn't say anything as they settled in and bowed their heads. Silently they said their prayers and served their plates.

"Anything interesting happen at school today?"

Lilly Ruth gave him a huge smile that held great charm even though her two front teeth were missing. "*Aenti* was our teacher today."

"Is that so?" Jess took a roll off the paper plate in front of him and wished that he'd thought to put the butter on the table.

"*Jah.*" Lilly Ruth nodded enthusiastically. She bounced in her seat, and Jess knew she was swinging her legs under the table. That was his sweet Lilly Ruth, never still. "Bernice went to a wedding," she continued. "So Reba came."

"I see." Jess chewed his dry bread and waited for his daughter to continue.

"We didn't talk about much. Just peanut butter."

"Peanut butter?" He stopped and waited.

"And—ow!" She glared at her sister.

Constance shot Lilly Ruth her own look, and Jess hid his smile. His girls were spirited, and he wouldn't have it any other way. "*Dat* doesn't want to talk about peanut butter, Lilly."

"You didn't have to kick me." Lilly Ruth frowned.

"Constance, apologize to your sister."

"But I didn't kick her."

"Did, too."

"Constance."

"Sorry, Lilly Ruth," Constance said, but Jess noticed that his middle daughter had ducked her head, as well. Perhaps his firstborn was not the one responsible.

"Hope?"

"Sorry, Lilly Ruth."

"All right then. Anything else interesting happen?" He looked at each one of them in turn.

"No, *Dat,*" they said in unison.

His daughters were tight-lipped now, but if their downcast eyes were any indication, he'd have a confession before bedtime.

* * *

"*Dat?*"

Jess looked up from his Bible, pushing his reading glasses farther down his nose to better see his daughter.

Constance eased into the room as if it were filled with a den of poisonous snakes. "Can I talk to you?"

"Shouldn't you be getting ready for bed?" He wasn't going to make this easy on her.

She ran trembling hands down the front of her plain white nightdress and took a couple more cautious steps toward him. "I'm ready."

"What do you want to talk about?" Jess took off his glasses completely and used his finger to hold his place in the Bible. He gave his daughter his full attention.

"I've done something wrong, and I'm sorry."

"Oh?"

She nodded, inching closer still. She was near enough to touch, and Jess had to resist the urge to reach out and pull her into his lap. She needed to face what she had done. There would be time for forgiveness and love later.

"I—When Bernice—I mean—" She shifted from one foot to the other as he patiently waited. "Hope, Lilly Ruth, and me, we've been getting dirty on the way to school. On purpose."

Jess leaned back and pretended to think on the matter. "*Ach*, now, why would you go and do something like that?"

Constance shifted, studied the ground, then bravely lifted her gaze to his. "We—I thought that maybe if we were dirty enough, then Bernice would come back out here. And maybe if she did, you might notice how pretty she is. And sweet and kind."

He had noticed, all right.

"And maybe then . . . she would make a good *fraa,* no?"

"No. I mean, Constance, you cannot go around dirtying yourself in hopes of finding me a wife." Actually hearing her say the words was more painful than he could have imagined. Did his daughter think him that lonely? Or desperate? Or maybe it was that they needed a *mamm* far more than he needed a companion.

"I know, *Dat,* and I'm sorry."

"I'm not the only one you should apologize to." She nodded.

"And what of your sisters?"

"They had no hand in this. Only did what I told them to do."

"And you take all the blame."

"Yes, *Dat.*"

Jess sighed. He had raised a noble daughter to be sure, but his younger two were not without blame.

"Tomorrow you will go to school and apologize to your teacher."

"Yes, *Dat.*"

"All of you." He bit back another sigh. He was too tired and confused to think about this clearly tonight. Maybe after a good night's sleep it would all look clearer. "Go on up to bed now."

"That's all?" Constance's eyes held a gleam of hope.

"I'll decide what other penance you should serve tomorrow."

"Yes, *Dat.*" She turned and headed for the stairs,

her footfalls heavy. But before she climbed up to her room, she turned. "I truly am sorry."

So was he. "I know. Good night, daughter."

"Good night," she said, then made her way up to her room.

Jess watched her go, his heart sad, his breath heavy in his lungs. The lengths his children would go to in order to see a plan through. It was admirable and disturbing all at once. And he couldn't help thinking: She wasn't the only one who owed Bernice Yoder an apology.

CHAPTER 5

Jess walked up the steps leading to the school-house dreading what was to come. Two days ago he'd walked up these very steps never imagining that he would be returning so soon with his hat in his hands, so to speak.

Since the program, Bernice had placed a sheet of plastic over the door. It was decorated with a snowman and winter scene, across which she had written *All ye who enter, come with Christmas cheer and a joyful heart.* The message was surrounded by hand-drawn sprigs of green holly complete with bright red berries. The writing was neat and orderly, much like the woman herself, but seemed to have a flair that belied its tidy nature. Maybe there was more to the woman than he realized.

He snorted at his own thoughts. What was he, some sort of handwriting expert now? He needed to get a grip and soon. Maybe after this talk with Bernice, he would head over to the general store and see about putting an ad on the bulletin board. The sooner he got some help on the farm and with the house, the sooner these crazy thoughts would abandon him. And that couldn't happen soon enough.

Without another hesitation, he pushed his way into the schoolhouse.

Unlike his last visit, the desks were all in their proper place. Four neat rows ran the length of the room. Two large chalkboards covered most of the far wall and the one to the right. Various assignments were written there, waiting for the scholars to complete them. Paper candy canes hung from the ceiling on lengths of yarn. A chain of red and green construction paper looped around the perimeter of the room and added to the festive décor.

The children were reading and writing. The two eighth-grade girls were helping some of the younger children with their lessons, while Bernice worked with another group. None of them had heard him come in.

He cleared his throat and all eyes turned toward him.

"*Dat!*" Constance and Hope managed to keep their seats, but Lilly Ruth jumped up and flung her arms around him, dancing in place as she did.

Bernice straightened and nodded toward him. "Good morning, Jess. This is a surprise." Her eyes were guarded as she studied him, as wary as a deer in late November.

"I was hoping that I might have a word with you today."

She swallowed hard, but nodded. He could find no fault in her hesitancy. He hadn't actually been receptive the last two times they'd talked. Which were the only times they'd ever spoken. It wasn't like they had a good record.

"We have to sing first." A girl he thought was one of the Miller kids stood up next to her desk, gaining the teacher's attention. "We always sing for visitors."

He knew that was one of the school traditions, but one look at Bernice's face and he thought she might protest. Instead she gave a quick nod and the children all filed to the front of the classroom.

Jess eased down into a chair and smiled as the children sang. It had been so long since he had simply sat and enjoyed himself. Every night he read his Bible, but somehow that wasn't the same as letting the children's sweet voices wash over him. He really needed to get some help at the farm so he could relax just a little. That was the problem with dairy farming; there wasn't a slow season.

The last song ended and the children made their way back to their seats.

"Here." The same little girl who had announced that they had to sing to him thrust the visitors' notebook under his nose. Apparently she had appointed herself as keeper of classroom traditions. "You have to sign our log."

He took the book and the pen she offered, flipping through the plastic-covered pages. He would sign the book as quickly as possible so he could talk to Bernice, then get on back to his farm. But as the pages turned, one in particular caught his attention. He stopped, his gaze running over the brightly drawn picture. A house sat in the middle with smoke coming out of the chimney, a man in a blue shirt with a black hat stood to one side with three girls next to him. It didn't take a man with more schooling than he had to figure out it was his family. A brown-haired angel floated in the sky close to the smoke. Linda Grace.

He trailed his fingers over the image as tears stung his eyes. A person might not know if they were destined for heaven when they died, but he was as sure as the artist that his wife was with God.

He had seen the school's visitor log in the past. All the standard questions were there: name, age, parents' names, pet peeve, likes, and wishes. It was the last one that captured his attention. *A new* mamm *to help my* dat *and to love me and my sisters, Constance Schmucker.* His gaze settled on the pet peeve. *My* dat *works too much and doesn't have time to spend with me and my sisters.*

"Jess?"

He jerked his gaze from the book to the woman standing next to him. Was she the woman his daughters thought would be a suitable *mamm* for them?

He cleared his throat. "Can we talk outside?" He didn't need to add that he wanted privacy away from the many little ears that could overhear what he needed to say.

"Of course," she said. "Let me get my coat."

They walked out onto the small porch together. Instinctively he held her elbow as they made their way down the steps. That one touch made him miss being a husband, having a woman, a companion. The soft to his tough. The beautiful to his rough edges.

"I need to apologize to you," he said, reluctantly releasing her just this side of the playground.

"You get right to the point."

"It's cold out here." But in truth he didn't know what else to say. He wasn't about to explain his daughter's actions and plan to get herself a new *mamm*.

She nodded. "Accepted."

"You're making this too easy on me."

She smiled, then sniffed in the cold air. "I'm hoping that you will accept my apology, as well."

"What do you have to be sorry over?"

"Jumping to conclusions about your family."

He frowned.

"Your sister explained the situation to me. That your daughters thought to get us together." She smiled, a bit shyly. Or was that understanding? "And the girls apologized this morning."

"You're not mad?"

She shook her head. "It was a very nice compliment." She really was very pretty when she wasn't reprimanding him for one thing or another.

"You shouldn't have to worry about anything like this happening in the future."

"Oh?" she asked. "Why is that?"

"Because I'm going to find myself a wife."

Jess couldn't believe his good fortune. It wasn't the easiest thing he had ever done, going to Bernice Yoder and apologizing for his behavior. He wasn't sure how he felt about his sister telling off on his girls, but it was done now.

He tromped up the porch steps leading to his *eldra*'s house and let himself in. "*Mamm*," he called, watching for her to come out of the kitchen as usual. And she did. That was one of the most comforting things about his *mamm*, she could always be depended on to be the same time and again.

Mamm dried her hands on a towel, her smile stretching so wide it nearly ran off her face. "Jess. What a surprise! Come, sit, and have some pie."

He smiled and followed her into the kitchen. Before long he had a fresh cup of coffee and a slice of *snitz* pie in front of him.

"What's on your mind, son?"

He shrugged, then swallowed a bite of the delicious treat. "Why does there have to be anything on my mind?"

"You haven't been for a visit in months. Why would I not think you have something to talk about?"

He pushed his plate away. Suddenly the pie wasn't quite as tasty as it had been before.

"Well, there is one thing." Was he really going to do this? "I've decided to remarry."

His mother jerked away so fast Jess was tempted to ask her if her neck was hurt. "Remarried?"

"*Jah.*" He took a sip of his coffee for something to do, then gave an awkward nod. "It's time, I think."

"When's this wedding, and who are you planning on marrying?"

"I don't know."

"You don't know when the wedding will be, or you don't know who you are marrying?"

"Both, *jah.*"

She leaned back in her seat and crossed her arms, that *mamm* look on her face. "If you don't know who or when, how do you know it's going to happen?"

"Because it has to."

She raised one golden brow at him, but otherwise simply waited for him to continue.

"The girls need a mother. Linda Grace has been gone for a while now." He even said her name out loud without those stabbing pains in his chest. Yes, it was definitely time to move on. But the one person who kept popping into his thoughts was the one person who suited him least. "Bernice Yoder."

"You're going to marry Bernice Yoder?"

He shook his head. "No-no-no-no." Had he said her name aloud? He waved his hands around as if to erase the thought, but it was still there, lingering in the kitchen like the smell of baking bread and his mother's lemon furniture polish.

Marrying Bernice Yoder. The thought did not warrant such study, but it worked its way into his mind and wouldn't turn loose. But that was the last thing he needed, to marry a busybody who wanted to stick her nose in his business at every turn, challenge all of his methods and all the hard work he put into his family. *Jah,* she had accepted his apology, but how long would it be before she came to the house again?

Just because she was pretty and smelled nice . . . well, that didn't mean a thing. He was just overworked and tired of the smells that surrounded him. Seven days a week of smelling nothing but bovine was enough to make almost any other scent pleasing.

"Are you still with us?"

Jess snapped to attention and cleared the tangle of thoughts from his head. "*Jah.*"

"Would it be so bad?" she asked.

"Would what be so bad?" Reba asked as she swept

into the room. Whereas he took after their mother, his sister was the image of their father, sleek brown hair, soft gray eyes, and impish dimples that framed both sides of her mouth. She pointed to his abandoned plate and the half-eaten slice of pie. "Are you not going to eat that?"

He shook his head and pushed it toward her.

"So?" she asked around the first bite. "What would be bad?"

"Nothing," Jess muttered.

"Marrying Bernice Yoder."

Reba dropped the fork, her mouth hanging open. "You're marrying Bernice Yoder?"

"No!" The word exploded from him.

"Close your mouth, Reba."

He turned toward his mother. "See? This is exactly how rumors get started."

"Don't look at me. You're the one coming in here and talking about getting married," Reba said, finally recovering her bearings.

"She does have a point." As usual his mother took Reba's side. He guessed that was what happened when there was only one girl in a family of boys.

"I didn't say I was marrying Bernice Yoder. You did," he pro-tested.

"But you did say you were getting remarried," Reba said. "*Jah?*"

He nodded.

"So why not Bernice Yoder?" she continued.

"That's what I said," his mother added.

Jess pushed his chair back and rose to his feet.

"Where are you going?" Reba asked. She set the empty saucer on the table.

Away from here. "I've got milking to do."

His mother frowned. "You just got here."

"It's only two-thirty," Reba added.

"*Jah,*" he replied. What else could he say?

"Are you going to see Bernice?" his sister asked.

"No." He pulled on his coat and hat and reached for the door.

"It might not be a bad idea," his sister teased.

"Bye, *Mamm,*" he returned.

"Good-bye, son," she said.

He let himself out of the house, certain he could hear his sister's laughter trailing along behind him.

CHAPTER 6

Jess Schmucker had decided to remarry. The news burned through the district in record time. The thought filled Bernice with a strange combination of anxiety and sadness.

So what if Jess was one of the most handsome men she had ever seen? He spent too much time hollering and frowning. And if there was one thing she knew, all things happened at God's will. Unfortunately it hadn't been in His plans for her to have a husband and family of her own. But to think that Jess was out to pick a wife. . . . Oh, to have a man like him to set his sights on a girl like her. Well, it was nothing more than a dream, and one that would never be fulfilled. Best to clear those thoughts from her mind as quickly as possible.

Plus that was without considering the fact that she had accused him of neglecting his own children. Her face filled with heat whenever she thought of how she had come to his house to "help," only to discover his girls were crying out for attention.

"So will you go or what?"

Bernice turned her attention from her coffee to her cousin Sarah. Sarah King was the reason Bernice had moved from her home district to Paradise to teach school. Sarah's young husband had fallen ill after just months of marriage and died in the hospital from pneumonia. What better time to make a move to support her cousin and to take on the young scholars of the district?

Well, that and the fact that her own sister had married the man Bernice had thought God had made for her. But once Leah and Jacob had said their vows, Bernice knew that she had to get away. So here she had fled, to start a new life, become a new person, a better person, but not to fall in love. "I don't know." She stirred the creamy liquid in her cup. The last thing she wanted to do was go to one of those desperate meetings where everyone wasn't married and wishing they were. No, thank you.

She shook her head. "I mean, it's not like I'm a widow." *Just lonely.*

"I know, but no one's going to say anything. Not if you show up with me."

Bernice studied her fingernails and tried to think of a good reason to stay at home and an even better one to go.

"I hear it's going to be quite an event. Food, games, food."

Bernice jerked her gaze up to meet her cousin's. Sarah's eyes twinkled. "Like a party."

Sarah shrugged. "I suppose so, *jah.*"

Would Jess be there? Why would he? She had never heard tell of him going to these kinds of things before. Bernice had no reason to believe he'd start now. What difference would it make if he did? She wasn't getting married. Ever. And he was out to find himself a wife. Had he wanted her in that position, he would have surely said something the other day at the school. And he wouldn't be going to a singles meeting in his search for a bride.

"I think I'll pass," she finally answered.

"Whatever you think is best."

Best might not be the proper word to describe it, but it was certainly the most effective way to protect her heart. For given half the chance she could fall in love with Frowning Jess Schmucker.

Jess stared into the red liquid in his cup and wished he were someplace else. Oh, the punch wasn't that bad, but the atmosphere . . . He shuddered.

It hadn't taken a day for word to get around the district that he had decided to remarry. He should have never let his sister know of his plans. She could never keep a secret, and this was no exception. Now women he didn't even know lived in the district were showing up with pies and casseroles. *Ach*, women he didn't even know existed were doing the same. At the rate this was happening he'd have to choose a bride and fast.

He scanned the room, watching as the widows and widowers mingled, circling each other, laughing but not quite, wary, uncomfortable. It was worse than those awkward singings of his youth.

Why had he ever agreed to come here?

To find a *mamm* for his girls, that voice reminded him.

He allowed his gaze to wander around once again, this time taking note of who seemed to be part of a forming pair and which women were still trawling.

There was Constance Fitch. She was *gut* enough, he supposed, and her buttermilk pie was mighty tasty. But he couldn't imagine the confusion of having two Constances in the house. One would surely get a nickname, and the thought of his darling daughter named by his beloved wife taking on a new name so she could have a mother didn't set quite right in his craw.

Ruth Lapp caught his attention and gave a little flirty wave. He returned it in spite of himself and tried not to cringe. He supposed in the big scheme of things she was a candidate. She was easy on the eyes, and her chicken and noodles was good enough. It was her laugh. Somewhere between a donkey and one of those yippy Mexican hairless dogs. He shook his head. No matter how good her cooking was, he didn't think he could listen to that cackle for the rest of his life.

That left two women at the meeting who could potentially be a mother to his three girls: Mary Chupp and Carrie Byler. Mary was a nice woman. She had a caring personality and she could cook. But he hated the way she twisted her hair before she pulled it back. It was backward, rolling down instead of up before tucking underneath the edge of her *kapp*. Who did that? He might not be the best at fixing hair, but he knew better than to fold it under like that. And he didn't think he could spend the rest of his days with that upside-down roll without eventually cracking and redoing it himself.

Nay, that would never do.

Carrie Byler. He sighed. The young widow lived across from his *eldra* on the farm she once shared with her husband. Elmer Byler had died early in their marriage, if Jess remembered correctly, before the first year had even passed. He could remember little about their courtship since they were in a different youth group from him and Linda Grace, but if his memory served him, they had been crazy in love. Which would explain why Carrie still wore her widow's black though several years had passed since Elmer had died.

But he could not find fault in that. Maybe only that Carrie still held feelings for her deceased husband. Though he had to admit a special place in his heart would always belong to Linda Grace.

Carrie didn't have any children, so she might want a couple to add to the mix. That was to be expected, he supposed. And it was *allrecht* with him. If he wanted her to be a *mamm* to his young'uns he'd expect she'd want a few of her own. The thought made his heart pound in his chest. A couple more young'uns to round out the mix, maybe a son to help in the barn and carry on the Schmucker name. *Jah,* a son would be *gut.*

She caught his eye and sent him a small smile. He should go over there and talk to her, but he couldn't convince his feet to carry him across the room. Amish courtships were slow and easy. The young people these days weren't as secretive about their courting as their parents and grandparents had been, but second marriages were always hidden until the wedding approached. He wasn't sure why. Seemed to him that the second time around, couples had more to do and less time to sneak around. But he hadn't been allowed to set up those traditions.

He nodded at Carrie, then turned back to his half-empty cup of punch. If he was serious about this—and he was—he couldn't go over there and blow it now. He'd have to take his time, and for that he was thankful. No sense rushing headlong into things.

"So what do you think? See anyone who interests you?" Dan Troyer sidled up next to him and surveyed the room.

"That's not why I came," he said, immediately saying a quick prayer of forgiveness for the lie. How could he keep his courting a secret if he said anything to Dan? Maybe he shouldn't have said anything at all to anyone.

Bad mistake.

"*Jah.* Sure." Dan chuckled and Jess knew the man didn't believe him. But that was fine with Jess. He was sticking to his story, and that was all there was to say about it.

"Maybe you should ask her to go caroling with us next week."

Jess jerked his attention to his lifelong friend. He and Dan had known each other ever since he could remember. Funny how time and work, life and death could pull people apart. Dan's wife had died in a car wreck a few years back. Dan hadn't remarried, nor did he seem ready to, though if the rumors were true Sylvia Hostetler might have something different to say about that.

"Caroling?" Jess asked. "Like, singing?"

"Singing, *jah.*"

Jess shook his head. "I don't want to go singing."

"Sure you do." Dan smiled. "Get your *mamm* or Reba to watch the girls, and I'll make sure Carrie Byler is there. All you have to do is show up."

And sing, he thought. It sounded like a good plan. He could talk to her alone, but around the others. See what she thought about his plans to get married again. Not raise suspicions but still get to spend the evening with her.

It was the perfect plan. The perfect plan, indeed. So why did his heart skip a beat when he wondered how Bernice Yoder would feel if she knew?

"*Dat,* can we put up Christmas decorations?"

Jess looked up from his evening reading. Constance, Hope, and Lilly Ruth stood at the bottom of the stairs three across, as if standing shoulder to shoulder could keep him from denying them.

They should be in bed already, but at least they were dressed to go to sleep in their plain white nightdresses, their hair all brushed and shiny, teeth clean and faces washed. A far cry from where they had been a week or two ago.

He shook his head. "There's too much to do around here to mess with all of that." He was proud of his girls and the changes they had made, but adding more to their chores right now just wasn't a smart move. They had barely begun to see the light at the end as it were.

He did his best to make his words gentle, but tears welled in young Lilly Ruth's eyes. "We didn't have decorations last year, either."

Because they had been in mourning, only having lost Linda Grace a couple of months before.

"Please, *Dat.*" Hope danced in place, then pushed her glasses back up onto her nose.

"Please." Constance gave him that look, the one he had such a hard time saying no to. Well, the old Jess had. The new Jess had to stick to the plan. The house was clean and uncluttered for the first time in months.

He held his place in the Bible using one finger between the delicate pages. "I don't know. We still have so much to do."

Constance pulled herself to her full height, as if that would somehow convince him to change his mind. "The dishes are all washed. The floors swept. And the nice ladies keep bringing food. Everything is done. Why can't we put up Christmas?"

Everything was done for now, but it would start all over again tomorrow. Despite the satisfaction he felt at having caught up his work, it wasn't at the end. It would just keep on going and going and going. But he didn't want to disappoint his girls. They had been through so much already. The thought was exhausting. Maybe he should wait to decide until he wasn't so tired. "Can we talk about this tomorrow?"

"*Jah.*"

His girls seemed disappointed, but they came over one by one, kissed him good night, and trudged up the stairs. At least they weren't crying or hurt and that in itself was a good thing. True, they were all caught up in the daily chores and he vowed they would never get behind again. And yes, the eligible and interested ladies in the district had seen fit to feed them for the last several days, so cooking hadn't been necessary. How long that would hold out Jess wasn't sure. Maybe only until word got around that he had set his mind to Carrie Byler. As for decorating for the holiday, he couldn't find any reason in his heart or mind as to why not.

When the girls got home from school the following day, Jess was waiting for them.

Together they ate a quick snack of cheese and crackers followed by the monkey bread someone had left on the porch while he was out walking the fences. There was no note, just the bread, his favorite.

Thankfully they hadn't had any snow since that first set of flurries, but he knew it was only a matter of time. They needed it, though, if the farmers were going to have a successful season come the spring. But he couldn't help but be a little appreciative to the dry ground as he plodded up and down the fences. There would be plenty of snow and mud soon enough.

After the milking, the four of them went back to the house and stoked up the fire.

"Are you ready?" Jess asked his girls.

"For what, *dat?*"

"To put up the Christmas decorations."

Their faces lit up and Jess's heart melted. They needed this. Normalcy, every day, just being together as a family. Even as he struggled this past year to provide for them and be both mother and father, he realized now he had failed on both accounts. He could never be their mother, and he had been too wrapped up in his own problems to be a *gut vatter* to them, as well.

The girls danced around as he opened the boxes he had taken down from the attic that very afternoon.

With more delight than he ever remembered seeing on their faces, the girls unwrapped the decorations: fat white pillar candles, strands of dried cranberries, anise, and cinnamon sticks, and silky springs of holly with bright red berries. Then the most beautiful decoration of all: a faceless nativity set carved out of delicate wood.

"We need pine branches," Constance said. "*Mamm* always put out pine branches."

"They smelled so good," Hope agreed.

Jess's throat tightened. So this was what it would be like to start to live again. There was pain, but happiness. He loved that the girls fed their memories of their mother. That they wanted to honor past traditions and keep them going still.

"*Jah.*" He nodded. "Pine branches, it is. Everyone, get on your coats. Let's get out there before it gets dark."

"Tell me again why I'm here?" Bernice asked Sarah. They were standing in the parking lot at the market waiting to load into the wagon. Bernice pulled her coat a little tighter around her and shoved her hands in her pockets to keep them warm.

"Because you love to go caroling?"

She shook her head.

"You love the elderly? I mean, we are going to the nursing home."

"Not quite."

"Because you love being around widows and widowers."

Bernice shook her head. "See, that's just it. I don't like to sing, and I don't belong with a group of people who have all lost their spouses."

"But you do like old people."

Bernice shot Sarah a look, the one she usually reserved for Johnny Lapp on those days when he couldn't hold himself in check any longer. "Why am I really here?"

"Word around town is that Jess Schmucker is looking for a wife."

"*Jah.* He told me as much."

Sarah nudged her arm. "See?"

"See what?"

"He likes you."

Bernice's heart jumped a beat, then settled back into its normal rhythm. The scowl that Jess wore whenever she was around was a sure sign that he didn't like her. Then again, she didn't know if he scowled all the time or only when she was around. What difference did it make?

"There he is." Sarah elbowed her.

"Would you stop that?" She bumped Sarah's shoulder.

"He's looking over here."

He was. And there was the scowl. She hadn't noticed it before. That meant it was reserved for her.

"Go talk to him." Sarah nudged her forward,

and Bernice felt as if they had stepped back in time. They were fourteen again, and Bernice was trying to gain Jacob's attention when he only had eyes for her sister.

But Bernice didn't have time to decide before Jess Schmucker started their way.

CHAPTER 7

"Where are you going?"

Jess stopped and turned back to face Dan. Where had he been going? He hadn't even realized that he had started walking until Dan called him back.

They had arrived at the meeting site a little later than everyone else. Typical Reba, his sister had shown up fifteen minutes late to stay with the girls. Then he'd spent ten minutes arguing with her about whether or not Bernice Yoder would be there. Why would she? It wasn't like she was a widow. And he had no cause to believe that she would show up.

That had to explain why the minute he saw her he started in her direction without even telling his feet to carry him there.

"Jess?"

Jess frowned, shook his head, and turned his full attention back to Dan. "Nowhere," he said. It was almost the truth.

For some reason he wanted to go talk to Bernice, which was ridiculous. Why would he want to talk to a busybody know-it-all who thought she could tell him how to raise his children?

Except that wasn't really how it had happened. She had been concerned about his kids, worried that they needed help. And they did. But she had been the only one to see it and do something to help.

And what had he done? He had thrown it back in her face and all but tossed her off his property. He repaid her by frowning and scowling and telling her to leave. Not once had he thanked her for taking the time to come out to his house and care about his family. That was something he needed to correct—and soon.

"There's Sally." Dan pointed toward the front of the group of carolers. Sally Esh was waiting for the driver like the rest of them.

"I thought we were watching for Carrie."

Dan gave him a sly smile. "Sally was supposed to get Carrie to come."

But Carrie was nowhere to be seen.

"Let me see what happened." Dan brushed past him to meet up with Sally. The two talked for a few minutes before Dan returned at his side. "She's not coming."

Great. First he'd had to get a sitter, leave his children at home to come out to sing. Singing was not something he enjoyed. He just sang at church and only then when he had to.

"Maybe I can get her to—"

"No." Jess cut him off before he could finish. "I can handle this on my own," he said. And he would. Tomorrow he would head over to Carrie Byler's and talk to her about courting. Until then, he had senior citizens to sing to.

"I didn't expect to see you here tonight." Though he wondered if his sister knew something he didn't. It wasn't like Bernice Yoder was in the group of widows and widowers who went caroling each year.

"Sarah." She rolled her eyes. She didn't need to say any more. He had known her cousin almost as long as he could remember. The woman had always been a bit mischievous. Too much like Reba for him to want to be around either of them for long. "She said I needed to come and sing."

Thankfully they were inside now, going from room to room in the nursing home singing to the mobile and infirm alike. They had shed their coats and scarves in the lobby. Bernice wore a green dress that brought out the gold flecks in her eyes. Her dark hair gleamed under the artificial lights of the hallway where they stood.

Other carolers moved around them, but for a moment to Jess it seemed like they were all alone. He reached out a hand, for what he didn't know. He reached toward her for the sole purpose of brushing against that pale skin. Was it as soft as it looked? *Jah,* it was. Not only was she nice, pretty, and good-smelling, she was soft, too.

Amazing how once he stopped being angry with her and she stopped trying to boss him around that the two of them could connect.

Jess retreated and cleared his throat. Bernice lowered her gaze and gave a little cough.

"I should find Sarah," she muttered.

And he should find Dan, but he would rather spend time with Bernice Yoder than his longtime meddling friend. "Or we could go to the next room ourselves."

She smiled and something in Jess's chest tightened. "I'd like that."

Her voice was like an angel's, he thought as she stood beside him. His sounded more like caterwauling, but the Bible said a believer should sing, so he did. Plus there were enough of them that his off-key, off-pitch efforts weren't completely obvious. He hoped, anyway.

After an hour and more songs than he could count, they headed back to the market parking lot. A few of the members milled around, while most got in their buggies straightaway.

Jess looked around for a moment, then started for his own buggy. He wanted to say good-bye to Bernice, but somehow that seemed a little too intimate. Like a date. Which this wasn't.

"Jess!"

He turned as Bernice hurried across the parking lot toward him. The tails of her coat flapped behind her. "*Jah?*"

"It seems that, uh . . . Sarah may have forgotten that I rode here with her."

The gentleman in Jess rose quickly to the surface. "I can take you home."

"Are you sure? It's out of your way." Plus almost everyone had already gone home.

"Not really. We're practically neighbors." And they were. His back pasture butted up to the cornfield behind the little *dawdi haus* she shared with her cousin. He didn't have to pass her drive to get to his, but it wasn't so far out of the way.

"That would be *gut*." She smiled at him gratefully.

Not many carolers were still in the parking lot when he helped Bernice into his buggy, but those who were had their gazes trained on him and the young teacher.

Mentally he shrugged it off. Let them talk. That was all it would be, just talk. Then how surprised they would be when he and Carrie published their intent to marry. Served them right, the gossips.

He and Bernice rode side by side in a silence that was somehow both comfortable and a bit tense. He supposed they were comfortable around each other because there was no reason not to be. It wasn't like they were at the beginning of a budding relationship. But the strain came from knowing that he needed to thank her, an appreciation that was long overdue.

"Are you warm enough?" he asked.

She nodded, but shivered.

He reached behind his seat and pulled out a quilt. "Here. Use this."

Bernice unfolded the quilt and spread it across her lap, leaving plenty for him to do the same.

Jess winced. There was a big hole in one end, but thankfully it was his portion that was destroyed. A mouse or something must have gotten into the barn and chewed clean through the fabric.

Bernice either didn't see it or decided not to comment, but either way he was grateful. This was just one more reason why he needed to find a wife. Sad but true, he needed someone to look after him.

"*Danki*," he said. His voice was quiet and rusty in the cold air between them.

"What?"

"Thank you," he said again.

"I mean, for what?"

He cast a quick look in her direction. In the dim light from the moon and stars he could barely make out her features, but he couldn't read the expression in her eyes or fathom the small frown puckering her brow.

He shrugged. "For caring enough about my girls to come all the way out to the house and talk to me about it."

Her laugh filled the spaces between them. "Your girls." She shook her head. "They are something else, *jah*?"

"*Jah*." He returned her chuckle with one of his own.

"It was quite an honor to be chosen as a candidate as their new *mamm*."

"Thank you for that, too," he said. "For being so gracious about being deceived."

"They mean well. They love you very much, you know."

"I know." He was well and truly blessed. His girls were *gut maedel*. They were deserving of a *mamm* who would love them and care for them just like their own would. That was why he needed to find them a mother, and quickly.

He pulled his buggy into the drive. "Looks like a party." He nodded toward the row of buggies lining the drive.

"*Jah*. My aunt and uncle said they were having a few guests over tonight."

It looked to be more than a few, but Jess didn't say so. Christmas parties of that size tended to last long into the night with fellowship and games, lots of food, punch, and laughs.

Bernice lived in the *dawdi haus* back behind the main house. Talk was that she shared it with her widowed cousin Sarah King. The two were close to the same age, so he imagined it was a good arrangement. No doubt it gave her a measure of freedom but still kept her close to others. At least she wasn't coming home every day to an empty house and faraway neighbors. Surely that kept her safer than if she lived on her own.

He pulled his buggy to a stop, then went around to help Bernice down. The scent of oranges and something spicy wafted from her, bringing back memories of better times.

The moonlight washed her in a pale glow that made her appear otherworldly, like an angel, a dream, a mirage of sweet beauty and all things good.

Time seemed to stop; even the wind didn't stir as they stood there, facing each other. The urge to reach out and touch her, run his fingers down her cheek, was so strong he could almost taste it. He trembled with the longing. How easy it would be to lift his hand and test the softness of her skin once again.

She was as caught in the moment as he was. Breath held as they stood there face-to-face waiting for what was next. A caress? A kiss?

"Thank you for the ride home." Her softly spoken words broke the daze that surrounded them.

He blinked. "You're welcome."

It was better this way.

She nodded toward him, then turned and made her way to the house. He watched her climb the steps with relief and regret.

She was his daughters' teacher, young, never

been married. He supposed she was around the same age as him, but she held an innocence that belied that number.

He had been working too hard lately, that was all it was. And starting to think about getting married again. Those things worked together, against him, producing these crazy feelings he directed toward Bernice Yoder.

She turned back toward him at the door of the house, gave him one last look, then disappeared inside.

With a shake of his head, Jess swung back into the buggy and headed for home.

Bernice shut the door behind her and leaned back against it. She closed her eyes and stood there, trying to make sense of what just happened. Had Jess Schmucker almost kissed her? Magic had filled the night, like the English authors who wrote about love so often stated. Time suspended. And they were the only two people in the whole world.

Or maybe she had imagined the whole thing. What would Jess Schmucker want with an old maid like her?

"Bernice?"

"*Jah?*" She opened her eyes as her cousin came out of the kitchen.

"Did you have a good ti—Goodness! What happened to you?"

Bernice ran a hand over the scarf that covered her prayer *kapp*. "N-nothing."

"That must have been some nothing. *Kumm,* let me get you a cup of coffee and you can tell me all about it." In a flash she was across the room and before Bernice could protest, Sarah had dragged her into the kitchen.

"There's nothing to tell," Bernice said again as Sarah slid a steaming mug of coffee in front of her. She wrapped her hands around it, absorbing its warmth, though she was hot and cold at the same time. Maybe she was coming down with something.

Sarah scooted into the chair opposite her and braced her elbow on the table in front of her, chin in one hand. A most thoughtful pose. "Did Jess bring you home?"

"I knew it. You planned this, didn't you?"

"I don't know what you're talking about." But Sarah's sly smile belied her innocent words.

"Well, I'm certainly grateful that Jess was willing to bring me home. Otherwise, I might still be standing in the parking lot trying to figure out how to get here, since my darling cousin left me to fend for myself." She crossed her arms and glared at Sarah.

"And he's looking for a wife."

Bernice shook her head, though the thought of being Jess Schmucker's wife sent a tingle through her. So he was a bit grumpy and a little unkempt, he had a good heart. She just knew it. He had been through so much. And he had the most adorable girls that she had ever seen. "I'm not getting married," she said, reminding herself of the fact. She needed to keep her head about her and remember that when the night turned magical.

"What are you going to do if I get married again?" Sarah asked.

A fist gripped her heart. "Are you thinking about it?"

"Well, no, and if I was, I wouldn't tell you. But if I did, what would you do?"

Bernice shook her head, somehow sorting through her cousin's confusing words. "If you were to get married again, then I guess I would just live here."

"In the *dawdi haus*."

She nodded.

"All by yourself."

The thought of coming home every night to an empty house made her stomach pitch. If Sarah were to get remarried, then she would move out and Bernice would be out of an excuse to remain in Paradise.

"Maybe go back home." But she didn't like that idea any better. She shook her head. "Why are we talking about this?"

"I just think you should give it some thought."

"You *are* thinking about getting remarried! Who is it?"

Sarah smiled, but picked at the corner of the napkin on the table next to her coffee cup.

"Does *Onkle* know?"

"No, and you're not going to tell him."

"What's to tell?" Bernice asked. "You haven't said anything."

"You just make sure you keep it that way."

CHAPTER 8

"*Dat?*" Constance tried her best to make her voice sound like she wasn't nervous, but she was. Her sisters were depending on this. On *her*.

"*Jah?*" He forked up another bite of his dinner, completely unaware of the turmoil raging in her belly. At least he acted like he didn't know.

How could he?

"I—" The words just wouldn't come. "I—"

Her father turned his attention to her, then reached for the bread plate.

She tried again. "I . . ."

"Spit it out, child."

"I was standing in the line at the post office yesterday, just like you told me to do, and I heard some people talking. I didn't mean to listen, but I couldn't help it, and they said that you said that you were going to find us a new *mamm,* and well, we want to know if that's true." The words came out on one long rush of air, without pause or separation.

Her father stopped chewing, stopped buttering

the piece of bread, and looked at each one of them in turn. Her, then Hope, Lilly Ruth, then back to her again.

"You heard this?" He returned to his meal like nothing out of the ordinary had happened. Constance breathed a sigh of relief. If he was acting like it was no big deal, then surely he wouldn't punish her for listening in on others' conversations.

"*Jah*," she whispered.

"And if I tell you that it is true, what then?"

We want our teacher for a mother. That was what they had all agreed she would tell him, but the words were stuck in her throat. "I don't know," she mumbled with a shrug.

Thankfully he didn't fuss at her for not speaking up, but his next words were no more reassuring.

"I think it's time."

"Ow." Constance rubbed her leg and glared at Hope.

Her sister pressed her lips together and gave a sideways nod toward their father.

"Quit kicking me," Constance said where only Hope could hear.

"Constance." Lilly Ruth's tone was much like Hope's, but this was harder than Constance could have ever imagined.

Their *dat* was finally back to acting like normal. Was it worth the risk to upset him by suggesting that he marry Bernice Yoder? There had to be some other way.

"Just shush," she told them both in that same mumbly tone.

"Girls." Her father's voice was low and rumbled

like warning thunder. She knew that tone, and it was time to let it drop.

They finished their meal in silence, but Constance could feel her sister's stares as she pushed her food around. She just didn't feel like eating any more tonight.

Not since she had messed up the plan. Now how was she going to get her *dat* to notice their teacher? At this rate they would never get a new *mamm* for Christmas.

Sunday dawned, clear and bright, though the air held a strong reminder that Christmas was just a week away.

Jess bundled up his girls, loaded them into the buggy, and headed for his parents' house. It was their turn to host the service. He especially enjoyed when the services were held there. It was familiar, comfortable, and somehow soothing. He loved the old barn. Always had. Seemed like he'd spent more time in there as a child than he ever had in the house. He smiled a bit at the thought.

"Chris Lapp says we're going to have a white Christmas," Hope chatted as they rolled up the narrow lane that led to the house.

"Chris Lapp likes you," Constance teased.

"He does not. You take that back!"

"What's a white Christmas?" Lilly Ruth asked.

"I'm not going to take it back because it's the truth."

"Constance." Jess said no more than her name as he pulled to a stop in line with the rest of the buggies.

"Sorry, Hope."

"Huh," she replied.

He didn't look but he had a feeling that the sound was accompanied by her sticking out her tongue. "Hope."

"Forgiven," she said. Her tone carried a bit of a lingering huff, but he let it rest.

He really needed to talk to Carrie. The girls needed a *mamm,* a firm hand, a parent who wasn't so exhausted that the constant reprimanding of their antics wasn't enough to send them into fits. And that was almost where he was. He loved his girls, but they were acting out, proving to him more and more that his decision to get remarried was a sound one. They needed a mother. And even more, they needed a father who only had to worry about being a father to them.

"What's a white Christmas?" Lilly Ruth asked again.

Jess parked the buggy, then swung his youngest to the ground. "It's when it snows on Christmas Day and the ground is covered in white."

He watched the dreamy light dawn on her face, then he smiled a little to himself and helped Constance and Hope down to stand beside their sister.

"A white Christmas," Lilly Ruth murmured in awe. "I'm going to start praying for that right now."

Why, oh why, oh why did she have to sit behind Jess Schmucker during the preaching? Bernice stifled a sigh and tried to turn her attention back front. Or maybe the question was, why did she have to sit across from and three rows behind Jess and three rows behind Carrie Byler on the women's side?

Now she could see every time Carrie glanced toward Jess and every time Jess looked over at Carrie. Thankfully Bernice didn't have to witness any lengthy, loving stares. That would have been plain embarrassing. But there was definitely something going on there.

Sarah tapped her on the arm and nodded her head toward Jess. He looked sort of lonely sitting there all by himself. She supposed he wasn't completely by himself. His brothers sat on either side of him, his father, too, among the mix of Schmucker men. Jess's girls were sitting with their aunt and *grossmammi* two rows in front of Bernice and Sarah. They were old enough to know that their friends were sitting with their *mamms* and theirs had gone on to be with God.

Just then Jess turned his head to the left and glanced at the women's side. He might as well have had one of those fancy English flashing signs above him that said I WANT TO COURT CARRIE BYLER.

And any hope Bernice had of courting Jess shriveled up to nothing. She had prayed about it and asked God to give her a sign. So it wasn't fancy or English or flashing, but it was easy enough to read. Sometime in the near future Jess and Carrie would publish their intentions, and that would be that.

After the final prayer, the women got busy setting up the benches as tables and laying out food for everyone to eat. Thankfully, they could fit in the barn and in the house to keep out of the cold.

The women served the men, then got their own plates and found their places to eat.

Bernice was settling down with Sarah when Reba came bustling up.

"Bernice, can you do me a big favor?" The poor woman looked a bit harried and flushed.

"Of course." Bernice put her plate aside and stood, brushing the hay from her dress. "What do you need?"

Reba gave her a grateful smile, then handed her a plate with a single piece of cherry pie resting in the center. "Take this to Jess for me."

Bernice looked to the pie, then up to Reba's face. Was she serious? She looked serious enough. She reached out to take the pie plate. Reba let her. Maybe she was serious. It was too late to back out now.

"Go on," Sarah urged her from behind, sealing the suspicion that she had been set up into hard fact.

If she backed out now, these two would never leave her alone about it. No, it was best to meet this head-on, take the pie to Jess, wait on him to stare at her like she was off in the head, then come back and finish her meal.

She took the plate and headed off to where the men were sitting. It didn't take long to find Jess. He and his five brothers were a fine sight and hard to miss. All of them had hair the color of sunshine, red-gold and shiny. They were all big strong men, and Bernice supposed that their mother had to say a prayer every night to ask God's forgiveness over her pride in her family.

"Jess."

He looked up from his plate when she approached. In fact six sets of nearly identical blue eyes turned to survey her.

"I, uh . . . Reba said I should give this to you."
She kept her gaze glued to him, but that didn't
mean that she didn't see a couple of the brothers
nudging each other. Were they all in on this? And
why? Was this some sort of joke to them?

Jess took the plate she offered. "*Danki*," he said
as if it wasn't the strangest thing that had ever happened to him. Or maybe his sister sent him a piece
of pie via an unsuspecting woman after every
church service.

"You're welcome." She turned to leave, all too
aware of his gaze on her.

She had almost made it back to where she and
Sarah had been sitting, when Constance approached,
carefully carting a steaming cup of coffee.

"Bernice," she said, though she didn't take her
eyes off the coffee. She was trying so very hard not
to spill it. "Will you take this to my *dat* for me?"

Inwardly Bernice sighed, but not at all where
the young girl could hear her. She was too young
and sweet and innocent to be pulling the same
prank as her cousin and his sister. The *maedel* was
just trying to take her father something to drink.

"*Jah*, of course. Would you like to come with me?"

Constance flashed her that engaging smile that
Bernice had fallen in love with the first time she
had seen it. "Oh no, *Mammi* is waiting." She turned
on her heel and skipped away, leaving Bernice
holding the cup of coffee and staring after her.

"Here she comes again," Ben said.

Jess didn't need to look up to know that his oldest brother was talking about Bernice Yoder. And

why he knew was not something he was willing to think too much about.

"I think she likes you," Abner said. As the youngest, he was easily the most swayed by the thoughts of those around him, a dangerous habit as his *rumspringa* neared.

But Jess's heart gave a skipping pound as he thought of Bernice. Maybe he should get an appointment with a doctor. He'd never had a problem with his heart before, but these days it seemed to be constantly skipping beats, jumping in his chest, and sometimes it seemed to stop altogether.

She cleared her throat as she approached. As if he needed any reminder that she was near. "Constance asked me to bring this to you. Since it was so full and I didn't want her to burn herself, I naturally agreed." She held out the cup toward him.

"Naturally," he replied, taking the cup from her. It was a reasonable excuse. The cup was full and the coffee hot. Maybe Bernice wasn't coming over to him by any design of her own.

He had asked Reba to save him a piece of cherry pie. He'd seen Bess Ebersol bring them in, and everyone knew she made the best cherry pies in three counties.

Bernice gave him a quick nod, her prayer *kapp* strings dancing around her slim shoulders. Then she turned and made her way back through the milling churchgoers.

He watched her go without a backward glance. *Jah*, that was all it was. Nothing more than her being the friendly, kind person that she was.

After all, what would a beautiful young woman like Bernice Yoder want with an old widower such as himself?

* * *

"Did it work?" Hope poked Constance in the ribs.

"Ouch! Quit."

"Well, tell me what's going on."

"*Jah,*" Lilly Ruth said, planting what felt like a foot in the small of Constance's back.

"Quit pushing! I'm doing the best I can." In fact, it had taken all of her running skills to make it back to their hiding place before Bernice managed to get the cup of coffee over to their *dat.* But she had managed.

"Are they in love yet?"

"I told you, dummy. That's not how love works." Hope snorted.

"How do you know?" Lilly Ruth countered. "You're only seven. And quit calling me a dummy. *Mamm* would wash your mouth out with soap if she could hear you."

"Well, she can't." Hope sounded close to tears, but then again so did Lilly Ruth.

"Both of you hush up." Tears rose into her own eyes. "How can we get ourselves a *mamm* if we're fighting?"

"I'm sorry," Lilly Ruth cried.

"Me, too." Hope bumped her as her sisters hugged through their problems and tears.

"What's happening now?" Hope asked.

Constance shook her head. "She gave him the coffee and left."

"That's all?" Her sisters' disappointment was apparent.

"*Jah.*" But neither of them were more saddened than her.

"How are we supposed to make them fall in love?" Hope bemoaned.

Constance thought about it a moment, but the answer didn't come. They were just little girls. "We can pray about it," she suggested.

"Do you think God knows about love?" Lily Ruth asked.

"Of course He does," Hope started in, her earlier apology quickly forgotten. "God knows about everything."

"More than you, anyway." Lilly Ruth was right; Hope didn't know about love. She was only seven, but at almost nine, Constance didn't know much more.

But she knew one place where she might be able to find out. "Do you remember those books *Mamm* used to read?"

Lilly Ruth shook her head.

"*Jah,*" Hope said.

"They were about love, right?"

Her sister nodded.

"All we have to do is get one of those books. That'll tell us how to make him fall in love with Bernice." It was the perfect idea. Or at least the best idea she'd had so far.

"Here's the plan," Constance said, giving each of her sisters her best *mamm*-in-charge look. "When we get home, I've got to help *Dat* with the milking. You two get in the house as soon as you can. Get up to *Dat's* room and look in the old trunk at the end of their bed. I think the books are in there."

"Then what?" Hope asked.

"You take one."

Lilly Ruth gasped, but it was Hope who protested. "Won't *Dat* get angry?"

"Not if he doesn't know."

"I don't know . . ." Hope hedged.

"Do you want a *mamm* or not?"

"I want a *mamm*," Lilly Ruth said.

Hope nodded.

"Then get in there and get one of those books."

CHAPTER 9

"Can I have a word please?" Jess shifted and shook in his boots as he waited for Carrie Byler to acknowledge his request.

She turned and leveled clear blue eyes on him. They weren't hostile or unkind. So why was he so nervous? He wasn't this jittery when he talked to Bernice Yoder. Maybe he needed a rest.

"*Jah?*" Carrie prompted. She dressed in her usual black. He wasn't sure why that bothered him. It just did. She patted her hair in place and smoothed her hands down her apron as she waited for him to continue.

Jess cleared his throat. "I wanted to invite you to supper tomorrow night."

A knowing light dawned in her eyes. "That would be *gut, jah.*" She smiled and the tension left his shoulders. His nervousness remained, but at least he wasn't wound up like a wooden top.

"Should I bring something?"

"No." He shook his head. "Of course not. You just come and be my guest."

"Six o'clock?" she asked.

He nodded in return. "Six o'clock."

She moved away to stand by her cousin and her friends.

Jess paused for a moment, then spun on his heel and went in search of his sister.

He found her with their *mamm,* and thankfully for once, she wasn't glued to Bernice Yoder's side. "Reba, I need your help."

"*Jah?*"

"Carrie Byler is coming to dinner tomorrow night, and I need you to cook something for her."

Reba raised one brow, but didn't say a thing.

"I mean, I need you to help me cook something."

Reba looked to their mother, who only smiled. Their *mamm* had learned long ago with six boys in the house not to meddle in the affairs of the heart.

"Please, Reba."

His sister crossed her arms and gave him that look, the one that usually meant trouble for whoever received it. "One condition."

Of course. "What is it?"

"You have Bernice Yoder over for supper next."

He shook his head. He didn't want to give Bernice the wrong idea.

But she was his girls' teacher. Surely he could invite her over as a courtesy. After all, the parents were always doing one thing or another for their school instructors. Hadn't he just given nearly forty dollars to the gift fund to provide Bernice Yoder with a fine present for Christmas? "You'll cook then, too?" he asked.

Reba nodded.

"Deal."

But the smile on his sister's face made the hair on the back of his neck prickle. She was up to something. Just what was anybody's guess.

Jess slapped his gloves against his thigh and peered out of the barn. Where were the girls? It was past time to start the afternoon milking, and they needed to get everything done as quickly as possible before it was time to eat. School had let out long ago, but he hadn't seen hide nor hair of them.

He shook his head. In the new year he not only needed to marry himself a wife, but he needed to find a barn helper, as well. Maybe he could convince his brother Ben's oldest son to apprentice with him.

Behind him in the barn, the cows shifted and lowed. He couldn't wait much longer to milk. With a sigh he eased back into the barn and started the chore.

Half an hour later his girls finally showed up. They didn't offer an explanation, and he didn't ask. They had all been through so much the last few months, it didn't seem right to ride them too hard. They were only little girls, after all.

And they worked extra hard to complete the chores without having to be reminded.

His girls were growing up, no doubt about that.

"How was school?" he asked as they finally made their way to the house.

"*Gut, gut,*" Constance answered for them all.

"Just two more days and we're out," Hope added.

And three more days until Christmas. But before that . . .

"We're having a guest tonight, girls."

Out of the corner of his eye, he saw his children exchange looks. Not sure what it meant, he continued, "Carrie Byler is coming to eat." It might be a little unorthodox for him to involve his children this early on in the courting practice, but how much could they really know about what was going on? They would just think that a friend was coming to dinner.

"Carrie Byler from across the road at *Dawdi* and *Mammi*'s?" Constance asked.

"The very same."

"We've never had company before," Lilly Ruth mused.

"At least not since *Mamm* died." For the first time in a long while, he felt a stab of longing at the mention of Linda Grace's name. Or maybe it came from the fact that Hope mentioned it.

"Well, we are having company tonight," Jess said.

"Good thing the nice ladies left us some more food today." Constance pointed to the porch where a towel-lined basket sat to the side of the door.

That hadn't been there when he went to the barn, but he supposed with the noise the milking machines made, whoever left it could have arrived with bells on and he wouldn't have heard them.

Hope ran forward and scooped up the basket by its handle. She pulled back the towel. "It's that sticky bread again."

"Yum." Lilly Ruth ran to catch up with her sister.

Constance rolled her eyes and pressed her lips together. Jess had the feeling she was trying to act older but deep down she really wanted to rush to her sisters' side. Childhood was so short. He wanted hers to last a bit longer. All the more reason to have

Carrie over tonight. The sooner they made their plans and got married, the sooner his children could go back to being children. If only for a little bit longer.

"Is there a note?" Jess asked.

Hope and Lilly Ruth peered into the basket, each lifting the sides of the towel to check underneath.

"No, *Dat*. No note," Hope said.

"Nope," Lilly Ruth chimed in.

It was the third time that someone had left monkey bread on his porch when he was out and three times that they hadn't left a note. How was he supposed to know who to return the basket to? The rest of the food came in throwaway pans with a note so that the chef got the credit. But if he got one more casserole from one of the women in the spouses' group, he might have to start spreading rumors that he wasn't getting married again, if only to get some peace.

"Do you think *Mammi* made it?" Hope asked.

"I like *Mammi*'s monkey bread." Lilly Ruth rubbed her belly and licked her lips.

He did, too. In fact, it was his favorite, but why would his mother bake the bread, then leave it on the porch? Why didn't she come into the barn and talk with him for a bit? She would have, and that meant the bread wasn't from his *mamm*, but from someone else entirely. But who?

"Okay, everyone get upstairs and get washed up. Put on clean dresses, then come back down, and I'll redo your hair."

They frowned at him.

"Why?" Hope asked.

Constance gave her a sideways kick. The blow

seemed to be a warning and didn't appear to hurt
the girl, so he let it go without comment.

"Because he wants us to look nice tonight," Constance said. She smiled, though her teeth were
clenched so tight her jaw jumped.

"That's right." A knock sounded on the door.
"That's your aunt. Now go on, get ready."

They dragged their feet as they tromped up the
steps. It might seem like too much trouble right
now, but they would appreciate what the extra attention brought them: a new *mamm*. And just in
time for Christmas.

"I'm telling you. He's going to marry her." Constance made a face as she spoke. They were in the
upstairs bathroom washing the day's remains from
their faces. She twisted her mouth the other way
and wiped at the spot again. Was it chocolate or a
freckle?

"What about Bernice?" Lilly Ruth asked. "I
thought he was going to marry Bernice."

"I like Bernice," Hope said.

"We all like Bernice," Constance snapped. She
didn't mean to be rude, but they were running out
of time. He had invited Carrie Byler to dinner.
Constance suppressed a shudder. It wasn't nice to
talk about grown-ups, but something about Carrie
bothered Constance. First of all, she smelled funny,
like mint and mothballs. And she wore black all the
time. It was just sort of creepy. Constance knew that
when a loved one died, it was customary to wear
black for the first year, but she had never known
her *mammi*'s neighbor to wear anything else. And

then there was the constant fidgeting and smooth-
ing. Why was the woman continually pressing on her
hair and her dress? She was worse than one of those
English models Constance had seen on the television once in the Walmart. She might only be eight
years old, but she had never seen an Amish woman
so concerned with appearances.

But the worst thing of all about Carrie Byler?
She wasn't Bernice.

"What did the book say?" Hope asked again.

Not near enough, or maybe it was because they
didn't have time to read much of it before they
hurried out to the barn to help their father. Thankfully he didn't ask them why they were late. That
was the power of prayer in motion. Constance had
prayed and prayed that her father wouldn't be mad.
Not only was he not mad, he didn't even seem curious as to where they had been.

Lilly Ruth wiped her face with a wet towel, hitting only the high points as she washed.

"Well," Constance said, taking the washrag from
Lilly Ruth and performing the chore herself. "The
man thought the woman had eyes that sparkled
like diamonds and a laugh prettier than an angel's
song."

"What's diamonds?" Lilly Ruth asked, closing
her eyes against Constance's efforts.

"Jewels, silly," Hope replied.

Lilly Ruth, eyes still squeezed shut, turned her
face toward her sister. "I may be the youngest, but
that's no reason to call me silly."

Constance wrapped a firm hand around Lilly
Ruth's chin and turned her face back front. "Be
still."

"Ow! You're going to scrub my freckles off." She peered at her with one blue eye, the other still closed tight.

"Sorry."

"Bernice has sparkly eyes," Hope said.

It was true. Bernice seemed to shimmer and sparkle wherever she went. Or maybe it was just leftover glitter from that day's art project.

"Do you know what angels sound like?" Constance asked.

Her sisters shook their heads.

"Me, either." How were they supposed to know if Carrie Byler fit the description if they didn't know that?

"Did it say anything about the men?" Hope asked.

Constance shook her head. "I didn't get very far. Only that the man was handsome and strong."

"*Dat*'s handsome and strong." Lilly Ruth pulled away from Constance. "Everything else belongs on there," she groused, moving so that Constance couldn't reach her with the rag.

Constance shrugged. She supposed her sister's face was clean enough. It was hard to tell with all those freckles.

"*Jah*, that's *gut*, right? That *Dat*'s already handsome and strong." Hope ran a hand down her dress in a manner that reminded Constance all too much of Carrie Byler.

"*She* has to think so."

"And if she doesn't?" Lilly Ruth asked.

"I guess the deal's off," Constance said.

"How do you make someone ugly and weak?" Hope asked.

"I don't know," Constance mused. "But until we

figure that out, we'll have to make sure that *Dat* doesn't fall in love with her."

Doubt pulled at her heart. What were they going to do if Carrie Byler had eyes that sparkled like diamonds and a laugh like the song of angels?

"Would you like some more noodles, Carrie?"

Jess looked up from his plate to see Constance holding the bowl of chicken and noodles toward their guest. So far the dinner had gone as smoothly as he could have hoped. His girls had been on their best behavior. They had come downstairs clean and neat and remained so since the meal started. They had all remembered to use their napkins and their manners as they politely and quietly ate their meal.

"Oh, I don't think I can eat another bite." Carrie patted her trim waistline and gave Constance a smile. Why had he only now noticed that when she smiled the action didn't quite reach her cool blue eyes?

Or maybe he was being overly picky.

Think of the girls.

All of this was for his daughters.

"I can't imagine why," Constance started, her voice the example of innocence. "You've only had three helpings."

"Constance." Her name was out of his mouth before he could give a second thought to what she'd said. And the evening had been progressing so nicely.

"I'm sorry."

"It's all right." Carrie gave his daughter that cool smile once again. "Forgive me, but I do enjoy a home-cooked meal. And I get them so seldom these days."

She didn't cook?

Jess shook the thought away. He couldn't very well ask, now, could he? Maybe he just misunderstood. It would be hard to cook just for one person.

He shot Constance a look. "How about dessert?"

Lilly Ruth hopped to her feet. "We still have some of the monkey bread." She danced off toward the kitchen before he could agree one way or the other. But monkey bread, he supposed, was just as good a dessert as any other.

She returned a few minutes later, holding the container he had put the bread in that very afternoon. Not exactly the most impressive way to serve it.

"Not like that." Constance slid out of her chair and pulled on Hope's sleeve. "We'll help you warm it up, won't we, Hope?"

His middle child mutely nodded and followed her sisters into the kitchen, leaving Jess alone with Carrie.

"I can't believe you went to all this trouble for me." Carrie propped one chin in her hand and looked at him. This time, her eyes were soft, her mouth curved into a genuine smile.

"I had some help," he confessed. "My sister came over earlier."

"And she cooked this? Why didn't you say something before?"

He shrugged. "I had no idea you would think that I had cooked it."

Her smile lost a little of its warmth. "I see." She allowed her gaze to trail around the room and for once he saw it with another's eyes.

His jacket had fallen onto the back of the chair. Or had he entirely forgotten to hang it on its hook when he came in from outside? The mantel needed a good dusting. They had wiped it down the other day when they placed the nativity scene there, but it was covered once again. There were little bits of paper on the couch where Lilly Ruth had been cutting out snowflakes for them to have a white Christmas—just in case Chris Lapp was wrong, she had explained.

Carrie had walked in the house, saw all those snowflakes hanging from the ceiling, and said, "How quaint." At the time he'd thought it to be a compliment. Now he wasn't so sure.

"Is that what you want? A *fraa* to cook and clean for you?" Carrie made a face that wasn't the least bit favorable.

"I can't very well do it all myself." But he was doing the best he could.

"I see," she said again.

Jess wasn't able to respond. His girls came back into the room carrying the warmed monkey bread on a tray complete with steaming mugs of the coffee Reba had brewed earlier.

That seemed to please Carrie, and she smiled at them.

So why did he feel like she was smiling more because she was being served than at the sight of his daughters?

"Eat up," Constance said. "We have plenty."

"That's right." Lilly Ruth smiled and pushed her glasses back in place. "Someone keeps leaving it for us on the porch."

"You don't say." Carrie took the saucer Hope offered her and leaned back a little as Constance balanced the coffee mug and set it on the table in front of her.

Jess held his breath, unnaturally certain the hot liquid was about to go tumbling into Carrie's lap. He exhaled slowly as the danger passed. Surely his girls wouldn't do something like that. But he was getting the feeling that his daughters would rather almost anyone but Carrie be sitting in the chair she occupied. Especially Bernice Yoder.

There he was, thinking about her again, when he was supposed to be showing Carrie all the wonderful things she would gain when she joined his family.

Like what? Daughters who didn't seem keen on having her for a stepmother? A dirty house? Someone who expected his wife to cook and clean all day? Help out in the barn when he needed it? What exactly did he have to offer Carrie Byler? Certainly not love, though perhaps that would come with time. Even still, he wouldn't be the only Amish who ever settled for less than love.

His girls grabbed their own plates of sweet bread and scrambled back into their seats.

"This is delicious." Carrie shot him an approving smile as if somehow he was responsible for it showing up on his porch.

"Can you make monkey bread?" Hope asked the question, but he noticed that all three of his girls were intently watching Carrie.

She must have felt pinned to the spot. She stopped chewing the bite she had in her mouth and looked from one girl to the other. Then she resumed chewing and slowly wiped her mouth before answering. "I don't believe I've made it, no. But I'm not much of a baker. There are too many women who enjoy that sort of thing." She didn't finish that thought, just waved a hand in the air and took another bite. He didn't need her to complete the sentence. He could do that on his own. *For me to concern myself with that.*

If she didn't want to cook, clean, or bake, she surely wouldn't want to help out in the barn. So what did Carrie find fulfilling in life? That might be good to know before he asked for her to join her life with his.

They finished their dessert in silence. Jess bowed his head to begin their silent prayer, then the girls started to clean the table.

Carrie smiled as she watched them and confusion washed over Jess. Why did she get such pleasure from watching others work while she did nothing?

He shook the thought away. He was misunderstanding again. Surely that's what it was. Carrie was not lazy. She was a good Amish woman.

Who leased her fields to others for them to farm and took part of the profit in payment for her land.

How had he forgotten that? She also leased her pasture space and her barn. Come to think of it, he never saw a vegetable garden on her property, though he had seen her tending the flowers that grew around the house. Just because he hadn't seen a vegetable garden didn't mean there wasn't one.

"Would you like to stay and read the Bible with us?"

Carrie shook her head. "I should be getting back home. I like to have time alone before I go to bed."

Time alone? Jess wasn't even sure what that was. By the time he got the girls in bed, he had just enough time to spend with God before drifting off to sleep himself. Then he got up the next morning and did it all over again.

"I'll walk you out."

He helped her with her coat, ducked under one of the dangling snowflakes, then opened the front door. The night was cold and the sky looked heavy. Clouds covered the moon and stars. Only the light shining through the house windows shed any light onto the yard.

Maybe Chris Lapp was right and they would have a white Christmas this year.

"*Danki,* for supper."

"I'm glad you came." And he was, but not for the reasons that he would have originally thought. Still, he was grateful for the opportunity to get to know Carrie a little better. She was easy enough on the eyes, but there was something missing. He couldn't name just what.

She moved a little closer to him in the dim light of the porch. The hint was subtle but clear. She wanted him to kiss her.

He moved away and back, putting as much distance between them as he could. He wasn't ready for that, not at all. But even as the shadow of disappointment flashed across Carrie's face, another evening under the nighttime sky came to mind. But with a different girl he had wanted to kiss. More than anything he had wanted to pull her close and just feel her warmth next to his, absorb some of the beauty and grace that was Bernice Yoder. But the magic of that night had been broken and the chance slipped away like the smoke from his chimney.

"Good night, Carrie Byler," he said.

"Good night, Jess Schmucker." She moved toward her buggy and he watched her go, glad she was leaving even while he was filled with a longing for something he couldn't name.

CHAPTER 10

"You promised." Reba crossed her arms and glared at him. He was used to the look, having been subjected to it all the years they spent growing up.

"I'm tired, Reba." Jess dropped the bag of corn feed on the ground, missing her toes by mere inches. It was a trick Reba was used to and she didn't flinch, just kept up her argument as to why he had to spend tonight in Bernice Yoder's company.

"A deal's a deal, brother."

"*Jah,* but I didn't say I'd have dinner with her tonight." He plopped down another bag of feed, this one even closer to her feet.

"Too bad. She's coming anyway." She moved a little out of the way when he turned with the third bag. "When you're done here, go take a shower." She wrinkled her nose at him. "And shave." She pointed to his lip where the hairs were starting to grow back. "And put on clean clothes." Then she turned on her heel and headed out of the barn.

"Where are you going?"

Reba spun back around. "I'm going to cook dinner. Of course."

Of course.

Bernice pulled her buggy to a stop and set the brake before climbing to the ground. She reached behind the seat and pulled out the basket of gingerbread men she had stashed there. She had baked the cookies the night before, knowing that she wanted to bring them tonight. How much fun would it be to decorate the cookies with Jess and the girls? It was a Christmas tradition she had enjoyed since she was a child, and she had missed it terribly this year.

She hooked the basket handle on her arm and gave her horse a pat on the neck. "Give me just a second, girl, and I'll put you in the barn." It was too cold a night to leave the aging horse in the wind, even if she was only going to be here for an hour or two.

She was reaching for the fasteners when Constance and Hope came crashing out of the house. Their coats flapped in the wind as they raced toward her. They had scarves tied on their heads and covering their ears and grins on their faces as they skidded to a stop in front of her.

"You're here. You're here! You're here!"

"I'm here," she said, laughing as the girls flung their arms around her. As far as welcomes went, this one was fantastic. "Where's Lilly Ruth?"

"Inside with *Dat* and *Aenti* Reba."

"Reba's here?"

The girls nodded. "They said to tell you to go on inside and we'll take care of your horse."

"Thank you very much." Bernice gave them both a quick nod, then started toward the house. With each step her heart pounded harder and harder in her chest. She had been so very surprised when Jess had sent a note to school with his girls asking her to come to supper tonight. She had read and reread the missive until she knew each word by heart, each curve of his strong handwriting.

Don't read too much into this.

It was just a supper. Parents invited teachers to supper all the time. Some wanted to talk about their child in the schoolroom. Others wanted to show their appreciation. For Jess Schmucker it was more than likely a mixture of both. But that did not make this a date. Nothing more than supper, she told herself as she let herself into the house.

"Jess? Reba?"

"In here," her friend called.

The house smelled divine, like fresh baked bread and the forest when it snows. Pine boughs accented the mantel and the decorations that appeared to be spread throughout the front room. Paper snowflakes of varying sizes hung, suspended from the ceiling with lengths of yarn. A fire crackled in the fireplace, and in general the atmosphere was festive and cheery.

"Bernice!" Lilly Ruth came flying from the kitchen and ran headlong into Bernice, hugging her with all the might in her thin, little girl arms. "I'm so glad you're here!"

"So am I." Bernice returned Lilly Ruth's hug, surprised to discover that in spite of her nervousness, she was happy to be there. She was looking forward to supper and decorating cookies with the girls and in general spending time with the man and his daughters.

A lot of good it would do her. She needed to remember that he had called this to thank her for taking care of his children this school year and nothing more. Talk around town was that Carrie Byler had come to supper the night before. And Bernice was certain that the motivations behind that invite had more to do with an upcoming wedding.

"Come on." Lilly Ruth pulled on her hand, bringing her out of her stupor. "Come see what Reba made us to eat."

Bernice walked into the kitchen to bubbling pots and popping grease. "My goodness. All of this is for me?"

Jess whirled around, looking both surprised and chagrined. He had a towel slung over one shoulder, his cheeks reddened from the heat billowing around the room.

"Hi, Bernice. Almost ready," Reba called over one shoulder.

"Do you need some help?" Bernice set the basket of cookies on the sideboard.

"Oh no, I've almost got it." Reba started dishing up platters of this and that. A bowl of chicken and dumplings, fried okra, a basket of corn bread muffins. In only a matter of minutes, the table was covered with a feast.

Reba dusted her hands and pulled off her apron. "Well, that's that. Enjoy." And before Bernice could say another word, she swept out of the house and was gone.

Jess chuckled and shook his head.

Bernice followed suit. Sometimes being around Reba was like getting trapped in a whirlwind.

"You didn't have to go to all this trouble for me."

Jess smiled. "I didn't. Reba did."

"*Jah,* about that. You should have said something. We could have eaten at the *dawdi haus.* It would have been nice to cook for someone besides Sarah."

"But I invited you to dinner."

She shrugged. "No matter."

Jess studied her, a moment so intense she shifted in place to keep from running out the door.

"Is it ready?" There were footsteps across the wooden floors and Constance and Hope burst into the room. Their cheeks were pink from the cold, smiles stretching from ear to ear.

"Go take your coats off and wash your hands, then we'll eat." Bernice straightened and gave a little cough. "I mean, ask your father." For a moment there, she had forgotten this wasn't her little family. She was just the teacher. She didn't have the right to tell them to wash up, at least not outside the schoolroom.

He gave them a quick nod.

The girls filed out to wash their hands, and Bernice was left alone with Jess.

"I thought you handled that quite well," he said.

"I apologize. I didn't mean to overstep my boundaries."

He frowned. "I have no idea what you're talking about."

And the conversation ended as the girls came rushing back in. There was no way they had been gone long enough to wash their hands thoroughly, but neither Bernice nor Jess sent them back. Bernice was thankful. She needed the buffer the girls provided.

They sat down around the table, everyone bowing their heads to say a prayer before they ate. Bernice asked God to bless their food and to please take away the sense of yearning that filled her by just sitting at the table with Jess and his girls. Never before had she longed for a family of her own. Not even with Jacob. And never like this.

Jess lifted his head, and the others followed suit.

Bernice unfolded a napkin and placed it in her lap, hiding her smile when the girls mimicked her actions.

They passed around the bowls and platters of food, everyone serving themselves before passing it on to the next person. Conversation was lively, consisting mostly of the girls telling tales on each other and their classmates.

Bernice couldn't remember ever having a better time. Afterward, they cleaned off the table and did the dishes. Despite their protests, she helped the girls. She wasn't about to sit and not help clean up after one of the best meals she had ever eaten. Plus that meant they could begin decorating the cookies sooner rather than later.

The girls gasped and squealed as she brought out the cookies and the small tubs filled with colored icing and sprinkles.

"And you can use these for buttons," she said, pouring out candy-coated chocolates.

"Oh Bernice, you thought of everything!" What should have been a happy sentiment seemed to have Hope close to tears.

"Are you all right, *liebschdi?*"

Hope nodded, but wrapped her arms around Bernice's middle. The hot moisture of Hope's tears wet the fabric of her dress. Not knowing what else she could do, Bernice just held her, running a hand soothingly down her back as the girl cried.

"She misses our *mamm,*" Constance said in her not-quite-adult tone.

"Is that true?" she asked, her voice soft and low. Hope nodded.

"That's only natural, you know."

Hope tipped her face up to look at Bernice. Her heart melted at the sight of those tearstained cheeks. "It is?"

"Of course. Anytime you lose someone you love, you miss them. Even if they just move away."

"So it's okay that I cry?"

"Of course it is." Bernice smiled even as her eyes filled with tears.

Before she knew what happened, all three girls had wrapped their arms around her, surrounding her with all the love a young heart could hold.

They let go one by one. Hope squeezed her tight, then turned her loose and skipped back to her place at the table.

Bernice shook her head at the resiliency of youth. Was that all they needed to know? That it was okay to miss their mother? She would talk to Jess about it, but she had seen him with his girls. He wouldn't begrudge them their tears. Perhaps they didn't want to worry him or make him sadder.

"*Dat,* come get a cookie." Lilly Ruth licked the streak of blue icing from the side of her hand, succeeding in smearing it across her nose in the process.

Jess appeared in the doorway. "Are they ready to eat?"

"Come decorate one." Bernice waved him in.

For a moment she thought he might protest, then he sauntered in and grabbed a cookie.

Forty-five minutes later, the cookies were all decorated, the children were cleaned up, and Jess sat down with his Bible.

Bernice settled on the couch with Constance on one side, Hope on the other, and Lilly Ruth snuggled in her lap. The fire crackled as Jess read, his deep voice lulling her into another time and place. One in which this was her life and not just one happy evening out of so many lonely ones.

By the time he marked his place and stopped reading, Lilly Ruth's breathing had evened out to the steady rise and fall of deep sleep.

"Want me to take her?"

Bernice shook her head as Jess roused the other girls and led them up the stairs.

He directed her into the first room on the second floor. She settled Lilly Ruth on the single bed while Jess helped Constance and Hope into their bunk beds. Just seeing the sweet, shared room made her a little homesick. Or perhaps it was simple nostalgia for the simpler days of her youth, back before Leah and Jacob had betrayed her and life had been easy.

"Good night," Jess said, softly planting a kiss on each daughter's forehead.

"Bernice," Constance whispered, her sleep-weary voice beckoning. "Good night."

"Good night," she whispered in return. Unable to stop herself, she leaned in and gave each of them a small kiss.

"See you in the morning," Hope muttered.

Bernice's heart jumped. She wouldn't be there in the morning. She had been pretending all evening that this was her life, but it was time to return to reality.

She walked back down the stairs, so aware that Jess was right behind her.

At the bottom of the steps she took her coat from the peg by the door. "Thank you for inviting me to dinner. I had a really good time."

"Me, too." He grabbed his own coat from the peg next to where hers had been hanging and slipped his arms into the sleeves.

"Where are you going?"

"To help you get your horse."

It looked like her escape would be delayed a few minutes. But she nodded, wrapped a scarf around her head, and plunged into the cold, dark night.

Jess made short work of hitching up her horse.

Bernice was glad; it was past time to return to her real life.

"Thank you," he said as she placed her basket behind the seat.

"I should be thanking you."

Even in the dim light, she could see the quick flash of his smile. "I'm glad you came tonight."

"Me, too." She stood there for a moment, that yearning part of her needing to extend the night as long as possible. But the practical part knew it was past time to leave.

She turned to climb into the buggy, but stopped as he reached out one hand and touched the side of her face. His fingers were cool against her flushed cheeks. Then it was gone so quickly, she wondered if it had been there at all.

"Good night."

"Good night," he echoed, giving a little wave as she turned her buggy around and headed for home.

CHAPTER 11

Christmas Eve dawned with gray skies heavy with snow. If the heavens were any indication, Chris Lapp had called it, and they would have a white Christmas.

Jess was grateful to have his daughters home early after only a half a day at school. Tomorrow they would head to his parents' house for a family dinner, but today they were staying at the house, putting the finishing touches on the gifts the girls had started for their *mammi*. One day to enjoy family and not have to worry about anything else.

By the afternoon milking, the snow still hadn't started, and Jess wondered if the sky was deceiving them for a reason.

"Who's coming to supper tonight?" Hope asked as they headed back to the house.

"No one. It's just us tonight."

"Can we have Bernice over again?" Lilly Ruth asked.

"No, *liebschdi*. Bernice needs to be with her family."

But was she with her family? Or was she sharing a tiny supper with her cousin?

"If no one's coming to supper, then who's that?" Constance pointed toward the road where a buggy was turning down their drive.

"That's Carrie Byler."

The girls groaned.

"What's wrong?"

"Nothing," they mumbled in unison.

"Hello, there." Carrie waved from her seat in the buggy.

"Hello." Jess waved back.

"I just came to bring you a fruitcake." Carrie slid from the buggy and pulled a small box from behind the seat.

"A fruitcake," Jess repeated. "How . . . nice." And from the grocery store in town no less. The kind of cake that was baked in an English factory and wrapped by a machine before being sent out to sell.

"Let's go inside, and I'll cut us a slice."

He was really looking forward to an evening alone with his girls. He'd had company the last two nights, and he was ready for things to slow down a bit.

But it would be this way when he remarried. There would be a woman underfoot day and night. The thought of Carrie Byler in that position wore on his nerves more than he cared to admit. Scenes from last night's cookie-decorating party flashed in his head. Somehow time spent with Bernice was different, more relaxed, less . . . strained. Time with Bernice seemed to be less about Bernice and more about family.

Something niggled in the back of his mind. The hairs on his neck prickled as if to say he was missing something here. But he didn't have time to figure out what it was before he had to open the door and allow Carrie Byler to come inside.

"Constance," Carrie started, "be a good girl and cut us a slice of the fruitcake. We'll be waiting on the couch."

Constance frowned, but didn't say anything as she took the box from Carrie and carted it into the kitchen.

Carrie settled herself on the sofa and patted the seat next to her. "Come sit down, Jess."

He looked around. In a flash, his two youngest daughters disappeared. To where was anybody's guess, but he supposed they went upstairs to wash up before supper.

"Come on." Carrie patted the cushion again, and Jess was reminded of his mother's lapdog. She called the tiny beast much in the same manner, and the little dog came running every time.

He shook the thought away and settled down in the proffered space. "I don't think it's a *gut* idea to have cake before supper."

"Oh nonsense. It's Christmas Eve. Surely you can break a few rules on Christmas Eve."

He gave a small nod but knew inside that it wouldn't stop there. He wasn't sure how he knew; he just did. Carrie Byler had lived on her own for many years. She had been free to do what she pleased, when she pleased. Even if that meant having cake before supper every night of the week.

"*Danki*," she said with one of those smiles she seemed to save for the children, a little stiff, a little too polite.

"Will there be anything else?" Constance asked, sounding so much like the waiter at the last restaurant they had eaten at that Jess wasn't sure whether to laugh or frown.

"No, this is good for now. You can run along and play." She flicked a hand in the general direction of the stairs.

Constance forced a smile, then gave a small curtsy.

He would talk to her about her sass later, but thankfully Carrie didn't seem to notice.

"So, I guess you're wondering why I came over tonight."

Jess picked a nut out of his cake and idly chewed it. Maybe if he picked at it enough, he wouldn't actually have to eat the thing. "I figured you wanted to see us on Christmas Eve."

"*Jah*, well, word around town is that you want to get married again. That's true, *jah?*"

He nodded.

"And is it too forward to assume that since you invited me to supper, you have decided that I'm to be your new bride?"

He cleared his throat, unaccustomed to such frank talk. Wasn't he supposed to be the one to initiate this conversation? "I suppose, *jah*."

"Okay, good." She placed her saucer on the side table and her hands in her lap. "I think after the first of the year would be the best time to put your farm up for sale."

"Put my farm up for sale?" He was too stunned to say much else.

"Of course. I can support us both and the children with what I make leasing my farm. Why would you want to live out here and work yourself to death milking cows when you don't have to?"

The only part of the idea that held any merit was the fact that he would be living across the road from his parents. Or rather, his children would be across the road from their *dawdi* and *mammi*.

"I don't know, Carrie." The rest didn't bear thinking about. How could he sell his herd? Who would put up with Gigi's constant bellowing while she was being milked? Or Doug's stubborn attitude about going into the stall? The poor beast had to be rubbed behind the ears to get her to go in. Who would put up with a milk cow named Doug?

"Well, it's certainly something we need to think about if you're serious about this. You are serious about this?"

He had been. But he was growing more and more unsure, starting with the fruitcake and leading up to this moment here. Despite all his reservations, his girls needed a *mamm*. And that trumped everything. "*Jah*. I'm serious."

Carrie beamed at him. "I'm so glad. And there is one other thing. You don't want any more children, right?"

Bernice pulled to a stop behind the buggy and set the brake. Was Jess going somewhere? Most likely to his *eldras'* house for the holiday. She breathed a sigh of relief that she had arrived before he left. She had a few things for the family for their Christmas. It would be good to be able to talk to him for a little bit instead of just leaving it on the porch for him to find later.

She slid to the ground, then grabbed the wicker laundry basket from the seat next to her. So maybe there was more than a little something, but God had laid it on her heart to spread a little Christmas cheer.

Pfth. You are in love with that man and his children. Say what you want about God and Christmas cheer, but you know the truth. And we both know why you are going over there.

Sarah's words from earlier floated through her mind. *Jah,* okay. So maybe she was in love with him. Maybe she would trade everything she owned in the world to be a mother to those children. And maybe everything in the basket was just one more idea designed to show Jess love and hope-hope-hope that he might recognize it and return that love to her.

Surely she hadn't imagined the pull she felt between them. But she had never felt that way before. Did everyone in love feel the same? Could Jess feel it? Would he know it to be love?

Silly girl, she chided herself as she made her way to the porch. *One step at a time.* But there was this part inside her that wanted to fling her arms around him, despite the code of conduct she was expected to uphold, and confess her love for him. How else was a woman supposed to let a man know she loved him?

Perhaps with a basket full of Christmas cheer.

The first fat snowflakes started to fall as she reached the steps. She brushed them off her shoulders and made her way to the front door. She gave one small knock and let herself into the house.

The living room was warm and toasty. A fire crackled in the fireplace. Two cups of coffee and two half-eaten pieces of cake sat on saucers next to them.

Her smile froze as Jess jumped to his feet. He had been sitting next to Carrie Byler. On the couch. All cozy. No children around. The perfect atmosphere for a courting couple to get to know one another better. And if the flush on Jess's face was any indication, that was exactly what they had been doing.

"I—" she started, but the words were lost somewhere between her mouth and her brain. She tried again, doing her best to block the image of the two of them . . . together . . . from her mind. "I brought some things for the girls. I'll just leave them on the table and—" She rushed into the kitchen before Jess could even utter a thanks and was back at the front door in record time. She had to get out of there. Now. Had to get as far away from her crumbling dreams as she could.

Jess took a step toward her. "Bernice, I—"

"Merry Christmas, Jess." Her voice choked at the end, and her tears wouldn't be denied any longer. She whirled on her heel and rushed from the house.

Fat, wet snowflakes steadily fell. The ground was already covered with no sign of it letting up. They would have a white Christmas, but Jess was all she could think about as she climbed into her buggy. Jess and Carrie. She was too late. Jess Schmucker had fallen in love with another.

CHAPTER 12

"It's snowing," Jess idly commented. It was the clearest thought he had in his head. The rest were swirling around, elusive, as he tried to catch one and make sense of what had just happened.

Bernice had shown up with something for them for Christmas. Gift giving wasn't unheard of, but she seemed upset about something. Him and Carrie? Why would that bother her unless . . .

"My goodness, I would say it is. I must be going if I'm going to make it home safely in this weather."

Chris Lapp had been right. They were going to have a white Christmas this year.

Jess nodded. But he couldn't think of anything he should say as Carrie slipped into her coat and wrapped a scarf around her head.

He walked her onto the porch and watched as she dashed through the falling snow and climbed into her buggy.

Then he went back into the house and called the girls down for supper.

They were unusually quiet as they ate, not even the snow outside bringing about the excitement that he would normally expect on such a special day.

They cleaned up the kitchen, got ready for bed, and all gathered around his chair for the Bible reading.

He chose Luke and the story of the birth of Christ. It was a fitting reading for the night, but he wished that he had chosen something more challenging, less familiar. He had read the story so many times, none of it seemed real as he read. They were just words while there was something in his head that needed a name. Now, if only he could find it.

His girls went to bed and he stayed up long into the night, pondering, wondering, and trying to name something beyond his grasp.

He dozed off around two, only to wake up at four to start the morning milking. He didn't wake the girls. He needed the time alone, the work to pull him to the truth.

He bundled up and headed off into the snow. Inches had fallen during the night, and he was glad that his girls were snug in their beds. He would surely lose the girls to the snow as soon as they woke up. Lilly Ruth's prayers had been answered.

As he tromped out to the barn and gathered the cows into their milking stalls, it came to him. He couldn't marry Carrie Byler. How could he marry a woman who wanted to be the man of the family, provide for them all, and expect him not to work? What sort of message would that give his children? What sort of values would they learn from allowing another to toil on the land and for him to take the profits as a land owner? Not even an owner, for in his heart the farm would always belong to Carrie.

He finished up his milking and trudged back into the house.

The girls eased down the stairs, then finally raced to him as he came back in, doing his best to knock most of the snow from his clothes.

"*Dat! Dat! Dat!* Merry Christmas!"

"Merry Christmas!" He smiled at his girls, swinging them high into his arms as he did. Surely this was all a man needed. He set them on the floor and gazed around the house. It was clean, mostly. He had finally gotten the hang of doing the laundry. And the girls' hair had never looked better. Well, except for this morning. He was succeeding, against all odds, and learning to become both mother and father to his children. Maybe he had been a little too hasty in trying to find a wife.

"Can we open presents? Please, *Dat*." Hope grabbed his hand and bounced on her toes.

"*Jah*, please," Lilly Ruth joined in.

"Now, you know we're going over to *Mammi* and *Dawdi*'s this morning. We're supposed to take our presents over there and open them at their house."

Constance's eyes grew wide. "In the snow?"

"Of course."

"Can we open just one present?" Lilly Ruth asked.

"*Jah*, please," Hope added.

He scooped up his youngest, his heart light for

the first time in a long time. He could do this—
and without Carrie Byler. He knew he could. And
his family would be all the better for it. "Tell you
what. I have a basket in the kitchen from Bernice.
What if I let you open it this morning?" He had almost forgotten about it.

"The whole basket?" Hope's eyes grew wide.

"I'm sure there's something for everybody in
there."

Constance cheered and led the way. She hoisted
the large basket onto the table where they could all
see what it contained.

Right on top was a beautiful quilt made from a
selection of fabrics in a variety of colors and prints.
He thought he'd heard someone call a similar one
a crazy quilt, but he thought it was beautiful, unique,
and special, just like the woman who gifted it to him.
A note was pinned to it. *To replace the one in your
buggy. Stay warm. B.*

"A quilt?" Lilly Ruth wrinkled her nose.

Lilly Ruth might not be impressed with the gift,
but Jess was touched. He trailed his fingers over
the perfect stitches. She surely hadn't made the
quilt since the time they had ridden home together,
but yet she remembered and gave him something
unusual and beautiful.

"Here." Constance handed her youngest sister
a small package. "This one has your name on it."

Lilly Ruth took the package, her smile wide and
contagious. When Jess had said there would be
something in the basket for everyone, he had
thought of a gift to them all, not as individuals.

"Is there one for me?" Hope grew impatient
and danced in place as she waited for her sister.

"*Jah,* and one for me, too." She stuck her hand back into the basket, bringing out a disposable pan covered in foil. "This was in the bottom."

He took it from her as the girls tore into their packages. Inside were beautiful scarfs made from yarn as fine as spiderwebs. They were solid black in color and fit well into the *Ordnung,* but they had a shine to them, a sparkle that only showed when the light hit them just right.

"Do you think she made these for us?" Hope asked, wrapping the scarf around her head. She looked sweet and silly in the head covering and her pajamas.

"I think so," Constance answered. "What's that?" She pointed to the pan he still held.

He had almost forgotten he still had it. He was so wrapped up in watching the joy on his little girls' faces.

There was that feeling again. That feeling that he was missing something important.

"Well?" Hope prompted. "Are you going to open it?"

Jess pulled back one corner, strangely nervous. The pan was filled with monkey bread.

"Do you suppose Bernice has been leaving the sticky bread on our porch?"

His heart skipped a beat at the thought. There was no other answer. Except maybe her cousin had done it. He wouldn't put much past Sarah King, but he didn't want that to be the case. He wanted Bernice to be the baker who knew all his favorites.

And she was. Somehow he knew it. And just as he knew that he could make it without Carrie Byler, he also knew that he wanted a life with Bernice Yoder. A partnership of raising children, decorating cookies, and eating monkey bread.

"Girls, go get dressed."

"Are we going to *Mammi*'s and *Dawdi*'s now?" Lilly Ruth asked.

He shook his head. "Someplace better."

"In the snow?" Constance added.

"In the buggy?" Hope asked.

"I don't think so." Jess smiled. "I've got an idea. Now, go get dressed. And hurry."

The old sleigh was sort of a hand-me-down. His great-uncle and his grandfather had built it together so long ago that no one could quite remember when.

Jess pulled the cover off the sleigh and dusted his hands. It had been in the carriage house for so long now, he'd almost forgotten he had it. Why hadn't he taken it out more? Because he'd let life get in the way. The day-to-day chores and struggles. "I'm sorry, Linda Grace," he said under his breath. He should have given her more of his time. Not just at meals and evening devotionals, but always. And it was a mistake he wasn't about to repeat.

He slapped the side of the sleigh. The black painted wood could use a coat of varnish and perhaps another of wax, but it would get them where they were going.

"We're going to ride in that?" Lilly Ruth's eyes were as wide as saucers.

"*Jah.*" He smiled.

"Yay!" Constance cheered. "That'll be fun."

"Help me push it out so I can hitch up the horse." He didn't really need their help, but this was as much for them as it was for him and he wanted them to be a part of it all.

Together they pushed the sleigh out of the carriage house and into the crystal-white snow.

Constance ran to the barn and brought out Ginger, the mare Jess used to pull the buggy.

He hitched up the horse as the girls jogged in place to help stay warm.

"Everybody in," he called. They clambered aboard and Jess spread his new quilt across their legs.

"Where are we going?" Hope asked.

Jess just smiled. "We're going to get you a *mamm* for Christmas."

"What's that racket?" Sarah looked up from the pan of filling she was tossing together. They were due at her aunt and uncle's for Christmas dinner in a couple of hours. Bernice was thankful it was only a short walk to the house. With all the snow the night before, it would be a while before they got the roads plowed and they could get their buggies out.

After yesterday's debacle at Jess Schmucker's house, Bernice had cried and prayed herself to sleep. She had been a fool to think that Jess would be interested in someone like her. Especially since he had made his intentions very clear.

But she had awakened this morning with renewed spirits. It was the Lord's birthday. She couldn't be sad today. Tomorrow might be a dif-

ferent story, but for today she was going to celebrate and spend time with her family. She would
be grateful for all the things she did have and not
remorseful over the ones that she didn't.

"I don't know," Bernice answered. She had been
so caught up in her own thoughts that she had
barely noticed the sound in the first place.

"There it is again." Sarah rinsed her hands,
dried them on a towel, then peeked out the front
window. "Uh, Bernice?"

"*Jah?*"

"You're going to want to see this."

Bernice went over to stand by her cousin. Something in Sarah's tone sent her heart pounding.
"What is it?"

There in her front yard were Jess Schmucker
and his girls in a beautiful sleigh.

"Bernice!" he called.

She pushed past Sarah and whipped open the
front door. The blast of cold air nearly took her
breath away. She wrapped her sweater a little
tighter around her as she stepped out onto the
front stoop.

"Jess Schmucker, what are you doing?"

He stood up in the sleigh. "Bernice Yoder, I've
come to ask you to marry me."

The girls cheered and called to her from their
seat in the sleigh. They were wearing the scarves
she had made for them and the sight nearly
brought tears to her eyes.

Her heart gave a hard *thump.* "What?"

"Haven't you heard? I'm looking for a new
mother for my children."

She bit back her sigh. "And that's why you want to marry me?" For a moment she had been hopeful that he felt the same for her as she did for him.

He stepped out of the buggy and started toward her, trudging through the snow to her side. The girls stayed in the sleigh watching, their breath little puffs of smoke around their heads.

"No," he said as he came closer. He smelled like pine and outdoors and everything good in the world.

What was the question?

He reached out one gloved hand and touched the backs of his fingers to her cheek.

Bernice closed her eyes and savored the touch.

"I came here for me."

"You did?" She opened her eyes. He looked serious enough.

"*Jah.* See, somehow in all my plans I left out something really important."

Bernice swallowed hard, not daring to let her hopes rise any higher. "And what was that?"

"Love."

Hope thumped hard in her chest.

"I love you, Bernice Yoder. I think I have since the first time you came to the house and were all—" He waved a hand around, but didn't finish.

Heat filled her cheeks. "I was only trying to help."

"I know that. Now." He chuckled. "And I could use some of that help."

"*Jah?*" she asked.

He nodded. "For the rest of my life."

"I love you, Jess Schmucker."

He smiled and took a step back. "I love you, too. Now, grab your coat. We have a Christmas to celebrate."

Riding in a sleigh with Jess and his girls was about the best feeling in the world. The steady *clomp* of the horse's hooves, the wind stinging their cheeks. The love that surrounded them all.

They were wrapped up together in the quilt that she had made once upon a time. The air was cold on her face, but they were warm and happy.

"Are you really going to be our *mamm?*" Hope asked. "Really and truly?"

Bernice nodded. She could hardly believe it herself.

Jess chuckled, his smile showing just what he thought about the prospect.

"And you'll be at our house every day?" Constance, too, seemed unable to comprehend the joy.

"*Jah.*" She caught Jess's gaze. Every day as his wife, as the mother to his girls. It was the best Christmas she could have ever imagined. The best Christmas of her entire life.

"Can we make cookies, too?" Lilly Ruth asked.

"Don't be dumb, Lilly Ruth. We can't have Christmas cookies all year long."

"Constance." The girl's name on her father's lips was a gentle warning.

"But we can have them every year," Bernice said. Every Christmas with her new family.

"And a sleigh ride. Can we have a sleigh ride every Christmas?" Lilly Ruth pleaded.

"Of course," Jess said. "But only when it snows."

"A white Christmas every year," Lilly Ruth said in awe. "I'll start praying for it right now."

Constance started to contradict the words, but Jess silently shook his head.

Bernice smiled to herself. The chance of a white Christmas every year was slim, but Bernice knew that with God and love anything was possible.

An Unexpected Christmas Blessing

Molly Jebber

*To my wonderful loving husband, Ed,
and to my beautiful mother, Juanita "Sue" Morris.*

ACKNOWLEDGMENTS

Thank you to:

Dawn Dowdle, agent, and Editor-in-Chief John Scognamiglio, for believing in me. I couldn't ask for a better agent or editor-in-chief.

Misty Love, my daughter, and Mitchell Morris, my brother, Lee Granza, Debbie Bugezia, Elaine Saltsgaver, and the rest of my wonderful friends and family, for the unwavering encouragement, support, and love.

Patricia Campbell, mentor, author, and friend, and Diane Welker, author and friend, for her help and support.

CHAPTER 1

1910, Berlin, Ohio

Charity Lantz dug into her big pinewood sewing box for a piece of blue cloth to patch a hole in her boy's pants and eyed the faded torn gray shirt of her late husband, Aaron. The one she no longer had a need to mend. She lifted the soft material and held it to her nose, closed her eyes for a moment, and breathed deeply. His scent had faded away. She missed his laugh, touch, and advice.

She shook her head. His death had occurred a year ago yesterday. Time had passed quickly since that fateful day his heart failed him. She folded the shirt and tucked it back in her box. Someday she'd discard it, but not today. She darted her eyes to the toys on the floor. Josiah, five, and Beth, eight, should have a daed in their lives, but she couldn't imagine herself married to another man.

Maybe she should reconsider Abe Beachy's proposal for her kinner's sakes. He adhered to Amish law and would provide a gut living for them. Josiah and Beth liked him. Widowed and childless at thirty, why hadn't he remarried? She wrinkled her forehead and sighed. She couldn't picture herself wed to the soft-spoken, shy, and lanky Amish man. He walked as if he carried the weight of the world on his shoulders.

She bowed her head. "Dear Heavenly Father, am I being selfish wanting to fall in love again? Am I depriving Josiah and Beth of a daed? Please lead, guide, and direct me in the way You would have me go. Amen."

She crossed the room and glanced out the window at the fresh snow on the ground and ice-covered tree branches. Eyes wide, she grabbed her burnoose, threw it around her shoulders, and rushed outside to the new neighbor's haus. She waved the kinner over to her. "Josiah and Beth, you come home and stay in our yard. Don't bother our new neighbor. He's just moved in and doesn't need the two of you pestering him."

She smiled. "Hi, I'm Charity Lantz. I apologize for my curious kinner coming to talk to you on your first day here. They're not shy."

"Hi, I'm Luke Fisher. I hope it's all right, I've asked the kinner, and I hope you will call me Luke. You don't need to apologize. I'm enjoying their company."

She gasped as a gust of wind blew his hat across the snow. She caught it and handed it back to him. His full head of thick brown hair matched his deep brown eyes. She guessed his age around the same as hers, twenty-six.

Her cheeks warmed. "You're kind. You may call me Charity. Wilkom to Berlin."

Her neighbors, the Zellers, had told her they

sold their haus to Luke Fisher, an unmarried Amish man from Lancaster, Pennsylvania, before they moved to another Amish community in Ontario, Canada. Their brief description of him hadn't done the man justice. She'd expected a much older man. His deep brown gaze met hers, and the muscles of his arms fit tight against his coat sleeves. He was tall and more handsome than any other man in the community.

"Danki for rescuing my hat."

Beth skipped over to a black, medium-sized dog next to Luke. A blond curl peeked out from under her hat and hung in her eyes. She swiped it away. "Mamm, this is Star. Isn't he the prettiest dog you've ever seen? He won't bite. Pet him."

Charity smoothed her hand over the dog's head. She studied the star on his forehead, his wagging tail, and his long tongue hanging out of his mouth. "He has a clever name." She petted the animal. "Hello, Star. You're a gut-looking dog." She wiped a wet snowflake from her nose.

"He's well-behaved and loves people. You don't have to worry. He's harmless."

"I can tell."

They both laughed as Josiah and Beth peeled off their gloves and stretched out their fingers for Star to lick.

Josiah tugged at Luke's coat sleeve. "Will you take me for a ride on your sled sometime?"

Beth stared up at him with her big blue eyes. "Will you take me for a ride, too?"

"Kinner, mind your manners. Luke doesn't have time to take you anywhere. He has a wagon full of supplies to unload." Her cheeks heated. "I'm sorry for my kinner's impoliteness."

"Again, don't apologize. I'd be happy to take them for a ride on the sled tomorrow. Since the snow is solid and several inches deep, it'd be perfect timing."

Josiah bounced on his toes. "Can we, Mamm? Please?"

"If Luke's in agreement, then you may go." She smiled.

"Yippee!"

"Come knock on my door at noon tomorrow." He pointed to the full wagon. "I'll be ready for a break from unpacking by then. I'll pull you for a while, and then you can pull me."

Josiah giggled. "You might be too heavy for us."

Beth wrinkled her nose. "We both might be able to pull you."

He laughed. "I'm teasing."

"I'd better get home and start supper before they have a chance to embarrass me again. It's nice to meet you." Charity turned to head home.

Beth glanced over her shoulder. "Join us for supper, Luke."

Charity froze. Beth should've asked first. What should she do? Invite him? "You're wilkom to come for supper."

"Danki, what time?"

"Six, or we can make it earlier."

"No, six is fine. I'll be over. I appreciate it."

She escorted Beth and Josiah home. "I appreciate you being kind, but you should ask for permission before going to Luke's haus or inviting him to supper."

Josiah bowed his head and stuck out his bottom lip. "He said we could come over anytime. He likes us. Star does, too. Why wouldn't you want Luke to come here for supper?"

"I don't mind him coming for supper, but I need to make sure I have enough food on hand for a guest."

Beth grinned. "It's all right, Mamm. Don't worry. I'll scoop half my food onto his plate if you don't have enough."

No wonder her son and dochder bounced on their toes to have their new neighbor for a meal. She sighed. The Zellers had been talkative with her but only cordial to her kinner.

"Your offer is sweet. I'll find enough food to cook." She gently tapped her dochder's nose. "You and your bruder pick up your toys and arrange them on your bedroom shelves."

She retreated to the kitchen, unhooked a plain white apron, and tied it behind her back at the waist. She opened the maple wood cupboard door and selected small plates, bowls, and cups she and Aaron had purchased the day after they married. She frowned. She'd invited other women to share meals in her haus since then, but not another man.

The Zellers had had a gut impression of him when they sold him their haus. He seemed nice enough, and they did share the same Amish beliefs. She straightened her shoulders. No need to fret over whether she was doing the proper thing in having an unwed man for supper. If the kinner were going to spend time with Luke, she should find out all she could about the man.

After grasping a container of leftover stew out of the icebox, she dropped the mixture into the iron kettle hanging off a hook over the flames in the fireplace. This would free up enough room on the small stove to warm her bread and pan of canned apples. She rubbed her chin. Would this be enough food to satisfy his hunger? She hoped he wasn't expecting a hearty meal.

On the table, she arranged sliced homemade bread in a basket and placed a clean white cotton cloth on top to keep the slices warm. Firm and moist, it might be her best loaf yet. She studied the table, and then her stew. The vegetable and meat mixture boiled and bubbled hot. Steam rose off the top, and its aroma filled the air. She stirred the mixture. Thick, just the way she liked it. She placed butter in a small dish and then put it next to the cherry jam she had canned last summer. She grinned. He could fill up on bread, butter, and jam.

His cheeks pink and out of breath, Josiah ran into the room. "I want to sit by Luke."

"No, I want to sit by Luke." Beth rushed in behind him and pulled out a chair. She scooted it closer to hers. "He'll sit there and be closer to me."

"You can both sit next to Luke."

A rap on the door sounded, and the kinner ran and flung it open.

"You're on time. I've been watching the clock." Beth glanced past him. "Where's Star?"

Luke stomped the snow off his boots, stepped inside, and put his hat on the hook on the wall. He shrugged out of his black wool coat. "I left him at home."

Charity removed her apron, accepted his coat, and hung it on a worn wooden peg. "You could've brought Star. He's wilkom anytime."

Josiah tugged on Luke's pant leg. "Will you go get him? Please."

Beth stood. "Please!"

"Star has made quite an impression on the kinner. I like him, too."

Luke walked over to the table. "I appreciate you inviting him. I'll bring him next time." He paused. "Where shall I sit?"

Beth pointed to the chair on the end. "Sit by me."

Josiah wiggled in his seat. "And me."

Charity pumped water into a pitcher, filled glasses, and put them on the table. She poured the stew into a white china bowl, added a ladle for dipping, and sat. "Would you mind praying for our meal, Luke?"

"I'd be happy to."

Josiah and Beth reached for Luke's and Charity's hands. Charity's heart raced as she beheld the grins on her kinner's faces at having Luke at their table. She bowed her head.

Luke closed his eyes and did the same. "Dear Heavenly Father, danki for guiding me to Berlin safely. Danki for this food and for introducing me to this fine family. Please bless Charity for preparing this meal. All these things I ask and pray in Your name. Amen." He dipped the ladle in the stew and filled his bowl, then slathered jam on his bread and put it on the small plate beside his glass. "I haven't taken time to cook anything today. I'm hungry, and this looks delicious. I'm glad you invited me. Danki."

"You're wilkom. The Zellers told me you lived in Lancaster, Pennsylvania. Did you live there long?"

He held a spoonful of stew. "Jah, all my life. I

needed a change, and friends told me they had visited Berlin and liked the town. I visited a week ago and purchased Mr. and Mrs. Zellers' property. I sold my place to a neighbor who was looking for a haus and farmland for his dochder and her husband."

"Do you have family in Lancaster?"

"No, my mamm died giving birth to my schweschder. Neither of them survived. I had a bruder, but he left our community to live in the world. In my opinion, my daed died of a broken heart a year later. I don't have other siblings." He sipped his water. "Enough talk about me. Tell me about you."

She couldn't imagine having a sibling leave to live in the world and having to treat them as if they were dead, according to Amish law. His downcast eyes and frown at the mention of this told her it must not be easy for him.

Beth paused and held her spoonful of stew. "Mamm doesn't have a bruder or schweschder, either."

"No, but I had friends my age for neighbors, and we were close."

Luke lifted his eyebrows. "You're blessed to have your bruder. I would've liked to have had a sibling. I didn't have friends my age close to home. My daed taught me how to target-shoot and fix things. I enjoyed his company."

"We had a daed, but he's not here anymore." Josiah pointed to an empty oak chair in the sitting room. "Mamm found him in his favorite chair. He fell asleep and never woke up. I don't 'member much about him." He stared at Luke.

Beth set her glass on the table. "I do. I miss him.

He gave the best hugs and told the best stories. He made me laugh a lot." She stared at her bowl. "Mr. Zeller and Mr. Yoder put my daed in a box. Our friends came to our haus and brought lots of food. The bishop talked, and then we buried him in the ground. I cried." She gazed at Charity and squinted. "But he's in heaven, not in the wooden box. Right, Mamm?"

Charity put a hand to her heart. Beth's simple account of her husband's death proved accurate. She studied the pain in Beth's eyes. It broke her heart. "Yes, you're right. Your daed is happy, healthy, and in heaven." She put her hand on her dochder's and smiled.

"Your daed was blessed to have a kind family." Luke cleared his throat. "If you clean your plates, I'll take you for a sled ride after we help your mamm wash the dishes. The sled is on the porch outside."

Beth and Josiah's eyes sparkled, and they clapped their hands.

Beth finished her last bite. "Can we, Mamm, please?"

Josiah chewed and swallowed his last spoonful. "Please, Mamm?"

"Luke, you don't have to entertain them. You must have a hundred things to do. We expect nothing in return for supper."

"I want to take them." He winked. "It's no fun to go sledding alone."

Luke had changed the subject, probably to cheer her kinner. Her son and dochder behaved as if they'd known him all their lives. Maybe it was his calm demeanor and voice.

"You're very generous." Hands on hips, she addressed Josiah and Beth. "All right. You don't have to do the dishes. I'll take care of them." She kissed their foreheads. "Have a gut time."

They bundled up in their winter coats, hats, and boots. She held the door. Luke instructed them on how to hold on to the sled as they strode outside. They stood like little soldiers and didn't interrupt him.

She shut the door and peered out the window. They followed Luke's instructions to the letter. She giggled and held a hand to her mouth. Luke had more energy than her kinner. He ran, pulling Josiah on the sled first, then Beth. She loved their happy faces. They should sleep gut tonight.

Returning to the kitchen, she cleared the table, washed and dried the dishes, and then put milk on the small wood-burning stove to heat. She was enjoying his company as much as her kinner.

A while later, Luke and her kinner entered the haus breathless.

Josiah pulled off his gloves. "Mamm, sledding is fun!"

Beth preened. "Josiah fell off the sled three times, but I didn't fall off once."

Luke slumped in the chair. "Sledding is fun, but I'm worn out."

Charity studied the three of them, so full of cheer and life. Something this family needed. Too often she had let her loneliness rob her of joy, laughter, and lighthearted living. How many times had the kinner tiptoed around her sadness and retreated to their rooms to play and avoid her? Luke had taught her a lesson tonight. She and the kinner would play games and bake cookies more often.

Luke blew on his cold hands and held them over the fire. "Come join me, Beth and Josiah. My fingers are stiff and cold. Yours must be, too."

The kinner pushed their way over to Luke and stood on either side of him, stretching their little hands and wiggling their fingers next to his in front of the orange hue of the flames.

Charity added a dollop of cocoa powder to the hot milk and stirred and then poured the mixture into four mugs.

Beth held both hands out to her. "I'll hand Luke his."

"Be careful. I don't want you to burn yourself. Hold it like this."

Beth carefully wrapped her fingers around the cloth she used to hold her mug and held the other cloth underneath. She passed the mug to Luke. "Here you go."

"You didn't spill a drop. I'm impressed. Danki." He winked at Charity. "You have well-behaved and delightful kinner."

Beth and Josiah beamed at him.

Charity passed mugs to her kinner, then lifted hers and sat. "They can be a handful at times, but for the most part, they mind well."

Beth and Josiah set their mugs on the floor next to them and lifted their tic-tac-toe game out of the toy box. They arranged the pieces and began to play.

Luke blew the steam off his milk. "Who takes care of your farm during season?"

"Zeb and Peter Yoder do all the work, and we split the money fifty-fifty. I manage my garden and take care of my chickens, horses, and cow."

"If you need any help, I'd be happy to oblige.

I'll do anything for a gut meal. I'm not much of a cook."

She grinned. Having him at her table had been a wilkom change for her and the kinner's routine. "You're always wilkom to join us for meals. I'm sure my kinner would appreciate any time you can spare them." She wouldn't mind cooking for him again soon.

Luke crossed the yard and entered his haus. Charity's deep blue eyes matched the sky on a sunny, cloudless day and filled his mind. Her petite frame and dainty small hands added to her natural beauty. How would her golden-blond hair look falling down her back instead of wound in a bun? He tightened his jaw. He shouldn't ponder such thoughts. It wasn't proper, and he mustn't let his mind go there. No woman would find her way into his heart again. He wouldn't allow himself. Not after his fraa had left him. No man should suffer such pain. Marriage was out of the question for him.

He and Martha had been childhood friends and married at seventeen. Beautiful, she had melted his heart. He shook his head. She had been full of life, humorous, and stubborn. She had asked a lot of questions about modern conveniences and what the world had to offer, but he wouldn't have guessed she'd leave him and her Amish life behind. He fisted his hands. She'd betrayed him. He wanted nothing to do with her. He swiped a nervous hand through his hair. No use dwelling on the past and Martha. He had come to start a new life in Berlin.

Josiah and Beth's faces came to his mind. Her dochder's features mirrored Charity's. Josiah's curly red hair and freckles won his heart right away. The boy had an impish grin and a sparkle in his eyes. Innocent, they said whatever came to mind. His mouth hurt from smiling at their boldness to ask him to join them for supper and to take them on sled rides before requesting permission. Charity's blush and stricken face showed her embarrassment. He suspected not having a daed in their lives must be the reason they hungered for a man's attention.

Charity's life must be hard. She had to earn a living for her family. He sucked in his bottom lip. He'd keep his distance but help them as much as he could.

Her woodpile had dwindled. He'd replenish her stock. Her front door latch hung on a loose nail, the porch had an open space where a flat board had broken, and a cracked window needed replacing. He'd fix these things tomorrow.

He petted Star. "Our neighbors have fed me a gut meal our first day here. I'd say we're off to a gut start in Berlin, Ohio."

Friday morning, Luke arranged his maple wood furniture, unpacked, put away his clothes, and stowed his staples in the cupboards. He paused to brew coffee and sat to enjoy a cup. His living arrangements were cozy and in gut condition, and he liked his choice of a new home. He swung his head from side to side. His oak desk fit snugly in the corner, and his settee and favorite chair a few feet from the fireplace would be a warm place to read and rest.

He stood, shrugged on his coat, hat, and boots, tramped through the crunchy two feet of snow outside, and opened the barn door to feed the animals. How generous of the Zeller family to have left him hay and seed. This barn stood sturdier than the one he'd sold in Lancaster.

After he'd mucked the stalls, he strode to the workshop and arranged the building supplies he'd brought from Lancaster for carpentry repair jobs. He rubbed the knot out of his neck, sat on a stool for a minute, and crossed his arms against his chest. Would he find enough work to earn a worthwhile living here? Lancaster customers had kept him steadily busy. No matter. He'd saved enough money to sustain himself for the next six months. And he had enough land to expand his farm and garden if he needed to.

At three, he paused. Beth's and Josiah's giggles rang in his ears. He glanced out the barn doorway. They ran and threw snowballs at each other. He laughed as Josiah fell to the ground, waved his arms, and then stood to study his creation.

He grabbed his battered metal toolbox and trudged to greet them. "Did you enjoy school today?"

The kinner scampered over to him.

Beth pointed to her mouth. "Yes, but I lost my tooth. It's a little hard to chew on this side, but Mamm said I'll get a big maedel tooth soon."

"Jah, you will. In the meantime, be careful biting on hard candy. It may cause it to bleed."

"Eeeew. I wouldn't want to taste blood in my mouth. I'll be careful."

"Hello, Luke!" Josiah pulled his glove off, and Star licked his hand. He dug in his pocket and pulled out a small piece of butter cookie. He held it to Star's mouth.

Star licked it off his fingers and swallowed it.

Josiah put his glove back on. "His tongue tickles my hand."

"There are some foods Star shouldn't eat, so please ask me first. Bread and rolls are fine."

"All right. I wouldn't want Star to get a tummy-ache. He's my friend." He hugged the dog's neck.

"Star likes you, too." He patted the boy's shoulder. "Is your mamm busy? Will you tell her I'm here?"

Josiah gripped his hand. "Come on in. She won't care." He paused and pointed. "Be careful. Step over the hole in the porch." Before Luke could say a word, Josiah had dragged him to the door, pushed it open, and pulled him inside. "Mamm, Luke is here."

Beth skipped in behind them.

Luke stepped back. "I'm sorry. I didn't mean to barge in."

"It's all right. I'm sure the kinner didn't give you much choice. What can I do for you?"

He held up his toolbox. "I couldn't help but notice your door, window, and porch need fixing. Do you mind if I mend them?"

She blushed. "I don't have the money to pay you for your trouble, and I don't want to impose."

"It's no trouble." Had he insulted her by offering to fix things for her? He hadn't meant to.

She'd been kind and generous, offering him food and welcoming him into her haus. She trusted him.

He wouldn't want to do anything to change her mind. Maybe he should've given her more time to get to know him better. "Would you rather I come back at a more convenient time?"

"No, I appreciate it. Of course, I insist you stay for supper tonight if you like venison. Mr. Zook brought me some the other day, and I'm frying it in flour."

"Venison is my favorite." He removed his coat and hat and opened his toolbox.

Charity hugged Beth. "Come and help me prepare supper."

"Let's bake ginger cookies for dessert."

"I'll set out the bowl, big spoon, and ingredients. You can mix them."

Josiah sat on the floor opposite Luke. He peered into the box and lifted a hammer. "I wanna help."

"You hold the hammer and pass it to me when I ask."

His face beamed as he stood. "Tell me when you're ready."

Luke held a nail in the door latch and reached out his hand. "Ready."

Josiah pressed it in his hand and studied his every move.

Luke enjoyed having the young boy observing him. He'd assumed Martha would want a boppli, but after they got married, she shied away from him and said no. What would it have been like to have a son? Like this, he supposed. He bit his bottom lip. He wouldn't let his mind go there. No use. He wouldn't allow himself to consider marriage again. He would never have kinner. A price he'd have to pay for protecting his heart. He'd enjoy Beth and Josiah as much as he could. He repaired the latch and smiled at the boy. "I'll lift you. You check to make sure the latch works properly."

Josiah pushed it back and forth. "You fixed it. Now it won't fall off."

The young boy paused and then pointed. "We should fix the window. I get scared at night when the wind hollers through the crack."

Luke glanced over his shoulder. Charity stood watching them. He winked at her and returned his attention to her son.

He removed his tool belt, lifted out a few screwdrivers, and tied it in a big knot to Josiah's waist.

The child's face lit up like a bright star on a dark night.

"I need a hardworking helper. Do you want the job?"

"I can do anything you tell me to." He held up his arm, fisted his hand, and patted his small muscle. "I'm strong and smart."

"I've no doubt you are." He studied the crack in the glass. "I've got a new window in my workshop we need to put in place of this one. Would you like to join me?"

"Mamm, may I?" He tilted his head and stuck out his bottom lip. "Please?"

Charity met Luke's eyes. "Are you sure you want Josiah tagging along?"

"Of course. I need all the help I can get."

Josiah puffed out his chest. "Luke needs me."

"All right. Bundle up."

They crossed the snow-covered ground to his workshop. He opened the door.

Josiah's mouth fell open. "You have lots of tools in here." His small fingers touched the assortment of tools and different-sized wooden pegs. He rattled a box of nails and screws.

"Don't touch the saws. I don't want you to cut yourself."

"I won't. They look scary."

Luke raised his eyebrows and grinned. Josiah had obeyed him. He found the child a pleasure.

Lifting a small hammer, he handed it to Josiah. "You can put this in your tool belt."

"You mean I can keep the belt I'm wearing?"

"Jah. I have others. You'll need it if you're going to assist me."

"Danki, Luke." Josiah's smile spread wide as he shifted the belt on his slender hips.

Grasping the window, Luke gathered the supplies he needed and guided Josiah out the door. "Let's go put this window in. Then there'll be no more frightening noises."

Josiah grasped his hand until they reached the porch. Josiah lifted his hammer and held it. "I'm ready."

Luke grabbed a shovel and removed the snow, then replaced the broken board in the porch. He grinned as Josiah shivered. "You can go inside and get warm. I'll do this."

"No. Not until we're finished."

He wouldn't argue. The child's determination to stay by his side warmed his heart. He removed the old window and put in the new one. He asked Josiah to hold the nails and hand him the hammer now and then. He stepped back and eyed the repair. "We're done here."

Hands on hips, Josiah mimicked his actions. "Looks gut."

Luke stifled a chuckle. The boy was delightful.

He hadn't had this much fun in a long time. "Let's go inside." He followed Josiah.

The aroma of venison filled the air.

Beth carried a plate of warm, fragrant ginger cookies over to Luke. "I made dessert."

"Yummy. I may bite into one before I eat my supper." He grinned at her and reached for a cookie.

She pulled the plate away and waggled her finger. "No, you mustn't have a ginger cookie yet. You have to clean your plate first before you can eat dessert."

He withdrew his hand, stifled a laugh, and forced his mouth in a grim line. "All right, I'll wait."

Charity served them, then sat. "Beth, you should let Luke have a cookie."

Beth slid into her chair. "It's what you tell us, Mamm."

Luke waved a dismissive hand. "It's all right. She's right."

"She can be a little bossy at times."

"Don't be embarrassed. I understand they're going to say whatever is on their mind. I suspect some of your fondest memories will be funny and embarrassing words they've said while they're young."

"I'm glad you understand. Otherwise, I'll be apologizing every five minutes while you're here. Their words either make me laugh, embarrass me, frustrate me, anger me, or melt my heart. It doesn't matter how many times I ask them to mind their manners, they always say whatever comes to mind anyway. I've given up."

They both laughed.

She passed a bowl to him. "The Zellers said you mentioned your business is carpentry repairs for townsfolk and our community members. Will you farm and tend a garden?"

He accepted the bowl and spooned a heap of green beans onto his plate. "Jah. I can manage a small farm and garden and still have time for my business. I can control how much work I accept, and I enjoy it."

"I appreciate the repairs you've done for us." She sipped her water. "Danki for your patience. Josiah couldn't take his eyes off of you as you worked. I'm not smart about such things. It's kind of you to teach him how to use tools."

His heart caught in his throat. The gleam in her eyes while talking about her son's happiness touched him. Charity was vulnerable and open. Not haughty or stubborn. He yearned to protect and take care of her, but at the same time, he wanted to run from her. She had awakened something deep within him. He barely knew this woman, but something about her and her kinner had already pricked his heart. He'd better be careful and not get too close to this small family.

"Do your parents live in Berlin?"

"Daed died a few years ago. Mamm woke to find him dead next to her. Dr. Harris wasn't sure what was wrong with him. He'd had trouble breathing the last few months before he passed. Mamm lives next door."

No wonder Josiah and Beth gravitated to him. Like him, they had no daed or grossdaadi.

Beth wiped her lips with her napkin. "Grossmudder helps me with my spelling words. Today, I learned to spell the words kindness and peace." She spelled each word.

Luke held Charity's gaze and grinned, then

glanced at Beth. "You're a smart maedel. I'm impressed."

Josiah stood and adjusted his tool belt. "I'm a carpenter like Luke." He paused and peered at the empty pockets around his waist and then looked sheepishly at Luke. "Do you have any other tools I can have?"

Charity leaned in. "Josiah, it's not polite for you to ask Luke for things. Please apologize."

Luke patted the child's back. "I want him to ask me anything. I'm happy he's interested in learning about tools and doing repairs. I enjoy teaching him how to repair things. Josiah, I'll find some for you."

"He's thrilled to have you pay attention to him. Danki."

The kinner were cheerful and well-behaved, but they had a lot of energy. They'd kept Charity occupied much of the time he'd been there. What a patient and loving mamm she was to her boy and maedel. It must be exhausting, but she didn't complain. She was attractive and young—would she ever consider marriage again?

CHAPTER 2

Luke knocked on the bishop's door. He'd gone from one haus to another and repaired doors, floors, and furniture for members in the community the past week. Yawning, he stretched and rubbed his aching arms. He'd sleep gut tonight. Word of his skills had spread since he'd arrived. No longer would he fret there wouldn't be enough work for him to do in Berlin. He wrinkled his eyebrows. The bishop had requested he come fix his step and said he wanted to see him first. Maybe the bishop wasn't home after all. He rapped again.

Bishop Weaver opened the door. "Would you like to put your horse in the barn?"

"No. It won't take me long to repair your step."

"Come in and have a seat. I'd like to talk to you for a few minutes before you mend the broken step on the porch."

The bishop accepted Luke's coat and hat and hung them on a knotted maple coat tree. He gestured for Luke to sit on the blue cushioned settee.

A fire crackled in the fireplace. "Would you like coffee or hot milk?"

"No, danki, I'm fine."

Bishop Weaver opened a desk drawer and pulled out a piece of paper. "Bishop Yoder recommended that I and our membership accept you as part of our church. He wrote that you are an upstanding and fine Amish man who abides by our laws and has helped many in need in your Lancaster community. He considered your parents close friends."

"He is a gut friend, and jah, my parents thought a lot of him, too."

"He mentioned your fraa divorced you to wed an Englisch man you hired to help you. He explained you are innocent in this situation."

The bishop in Lancaster had told Luke he'd write a letter to Bishop Weaver passing along his recommendation and explanation of his divorce. Luke hadn't known when this conversation would take place.

He stiffened and pushed back in the settee. The familiar ache each time someone mentioned his former fraa coursed through him. "Jah, she did."

The bishop's sentence had summed it up. He had nothing more to say on the matter. He hoped his divorce wouldn't blemish his reputation.

"You are not at fault. We do not need to discuss the matter further, and I will not be telling anyone."

Luke blew out a sigh of relief, crossed his legs, and relaxed. "I appreciate your understanding and acceptance of me. Danki."

Bishop Weaver handed him three sheets of paper. "I've penciled out the rules we consider our Ordnung. It's what I do for each new member. Read it over. If you have any questions, come back tomorrow and I'll answer them. I suspect they are not much different from yours in Lancaster. Your bishop there and I are in agreement concerning our laws and rules."

Luke glanced over the small but precise print. "I will read them, but I doubt I will have any questions or issues with them."

"Gut, are you attending church tomorrow?"

"Jah, I am."

"After the service I'll ask the members to vote. How does this sit with you?"

This discussion had gone much better than he'd anticipated. "I appreciate your confidence in me. Please be assured I am a devout believer in God and in upholding our Amish laws."

"After reading this letter and talking to my friends here, I have no doubt." The bishop stood and stoked the fire. "I stopped by Charity Lantz's haus the other day to check on her. She told me you have been stockpiling her wood and repairing things for her. Josiah and Beth are happy you live next door and told me you took them sledding."

Luke's jaw clenched. Would the bishop reprimand him? "They've been kind to me."

"She is a hardworking widow, and I suspect it is difficult to make ends meet at times. Her late husband was a gut man. Aaron Lantz had a quick wit and a gut sense of humor. I enjoyed his company."

Why was he worried? He and Charity had done nothing wrong. The kinner were present anytime they were together. He bit his lip. The guilt came from his heart racing at the mention of her name. There was a spark there the first moment they met, but he'd pushed the attraction from his mind. He rubbed the stubble on his chin. Josiah and Beth had touched on the subject of their daed. He hadn't wanted to pry, but he wanted to learn more about Aaron. "What did he do for work?"

"He carved handles for knives, miniature toys, and different-sized building and hanging pegs. He sold them and earned a gut living. His friends helped him do chores, and he hired a man to farm his land and split the profits. Aaron said he was sick a lot as a child and had bouts of illness often as an adult. He was a gentle soul loved by his family and friends."

From what the bishop had told him, he would have liked Aaron. How sad his kinner wouldn't be able to ask him questions, learn from his talents, and enjoy his company. "I wish I'd had the chance to meet him."

"You do not have a fraa. Maybe you should consider Charity for a potential fraa. You and she are not getting any younger."

Luke cleared his throat and blinked a few times. The bishop was far from shy. He shuffled his feet and stared at the floor. "She's a gut woman, but I'm not interested in finding a fraa." He headed for the door. "I'd better get to work before we run out of daylight."

The bishop passed him his coat and hat. "Consider my suggestion. You would not want another man to snatch Charity away."

Halfway out the door, Luke pushed his arms through his coat sleeves and placed his hat on his head. He couldn't leave the bishop fast enough. The man meant well, but he had pushed the issue far enough. The hairs on his neck prickled as he considered the bishop's words. How would he react if another man showed interest in Charity? His head began to pound. He barely knew her, but he wouldn't like it one bit. No matter how hard he tried, he couldn't get her sweet voice and beautiful face out of his mind, as well as the faces of her kinner.

He flexed his gloved hands, strode to his wagon, and lifted out a new wood plank. The bishop's words rolled over in his mind. He shivered and pounded the nails into the new wood on the porch step, then bounced his feet on it. Sturdy, it would hold much better.

Footsteps crunched the snow behind him. He glanced over his shoulder and fought to hide the irritation welling inside. He had chores to finish at home, and Charity wasn't a subject he wanted to discuss any further with the bishop. "You didn't have to come outside. I'd have come in to bid you farewell."

The bishop's red cheeks dimpled. He pressed coins in Luke's gloved hand. "I needed fresh air and to stretch my legs. I've been inside too long." He studied Luke's work. "I've been watching you. You do fine work. I appreciate your coming out today."

Luke swallowed. A pang of remorse rushed through him. The man was gracious. He passed the coins back to the man. "I appreciate your willingness to pay me, but I'm happy to help you." He put a hand on the man's shoulder. "Several of your friends told me you have been spreading the word I'm a handyman. Danki."

The bishop shoved his hands in his pockets. "I like

to help young Amish men find work. It strengthens our community."

"Danki. You go inside and get warm."

"All right, but remember what I said."

Uh-oh, he'd better dash off quick before the bishop cornered him about Charity again. Luke waved and quickened his pace. He climbed in the wagon and headed home. Would the bishop mention his idea to her? He hoped not. He wouldn't want any awkwardness between them.

Charity sat in church next to Josiah and Beth on Sunday. She searched for Luke. He must have arrived early. He sat in the third bench on the other side across from her. The sight of him sent her heart in a spin. Like her late husband, Luke had ignited a fire in her. What was it about him? He had chopped and stockpiled wood for her, brought her food, and paid attention to Josiah and Beth, but those weren't the reasons she couldn't put him out of her mind. She liked his voice, neat appearance, and energetic way of living.

He'd joined them for supper almost every day for three weeks. On the days he hadn't joined them, she missed him. She wished he'd open up more about his life in Lancaster. Had he ever been married or even considered a *fraa?* Surely he wanted *kinner.* He'd gone out of his way to entertain Josiah and Beth.

Bishop Weaver lifted his Ausbund. "Please join me in lifting your hymnals and turning to page five."

She lifted the book and flipped the pages. She

shook her head a little and chastised herself. Her mind should be on the service and not on Luke, but his face popped into her mind when she least expected it.

The bishop led them in a song, then requested they kneel while he recited the Lord's Prayer. He raised his head and asked everyone to sit.

In his sermon he reminded them they should seek God's will for their lives and in each situation they encountered. She stared at her Bible. What would God have in store for her this year?

An hour and a half later, the bishop asked, "Luke Fisher, please join me at the front."

Luke joined the bishop, and the man prayed over him aloud. She found it hard to concentrate. A thrill coursed through her bones. This meant that Luke had grown roots in Berlin. She'd feared someone or something in his past would pull him back to Lancaster, until now.

The bishop's request to join him in prayer again jerked her out of her thoughts. The bishop asked Luke questions about his belief in God and his commitment to obeying God and the Amish law. Luke answered each question.

"Does anyone here object to Luke joining our membership?" The bishop waited. "Men, raise your hands to accept Luke into the fold."

"Luke, you've received a unanimous vote. Wilkom."

Luke stared right at her and smiled. Her cheeks warmed.

Josiah and Beth waved to him. He waved back and grinned.

After the bishop said a few more words and

prayed, he dismissed the members for the after-service meal.

Josiah and Beth tugged Luke's hand. "Come sit by us."

Charity approached him. "You're officially one of us now. Congratulations."

Men and women crowded around them to wilkom him. Charity noticed mamms introducing their dechder to him. She tightened her lips and stared at the pretty young women fawning over Luke. She had been silly. Why would he be interested in her when he could wed a younger woman who had no kinner? She gestured for her kinner to join her.

She glanced over her shoulder to Luke. "We'll go prepare for the meal."

She smoothed her black plain dress and righted her kapp. She stole glances at Luke, dressed in his black pants, suspenders, and a crisp white shirt as she uncovered her dishes. Relief washed over her. He'd joined a group of men. He had no problem making conversation. Setting the table, she turned her back to him. His laughter rang in her ears. She paused and recognized the pleasant sound right away. Her cheeks grew warm. His voice and laugh had become familiar. She couldn't pinpoint when it had happened, but she cared about him. She put a hand to her throat. It scared her a little but excited her more. He approached her.

"I fixed you a plate." She slid it over to him.

"Danki."

Josiah and Beth separated. Josiah patted the spot next to him. "Sit here, Luke."

She thought her heart would melt at his smile

as he sat between her kinner. He'd joined her and
the kinner, and not any of the other available
women who were staring at him. She smoothed
her cloth napkin on her lap and closed her eyes
for a moment. She must stop swooning over him.
He treated her like a schweschder. She raised her
spoon to her mouth but lowered it. She sat and listened to him chat with Josiah and Beth. He would
be perfect for a husband and daed for her kinner.
He was the first man she'd considered a potential
husband since the untimely death of her beloved
Aaron. He'd not broached the subject or even
hinted at it. She wouldn't want to pry.

She closed her eyes. "Dear Heavenly Father, did
You send Luke here for us? I don't know what Your
purpose is for bringing Luke into our lives, but
danki for him. Give me the right words to say to
Luke to make him comfortable to encourage him
to open up to me. I praise You and danki for Your
mercy, grace, and power. Amen."

A week later on Saturday, a loud scream pierced
the air outside. Josiah. Charity tossed the Amish
doll she'd been stitching on the chair and opened
the door.

Beth ushered her bruder inside the haus. Her
face paled. "Josiah's hurt real bad. I'm scared."

Charity rushed over to him. "What's wrong?" He
held his right hand with his left hand. Blood
flowed down his arm, dripped from his elbow, and
stained the floor red. Chills coursed through her.

His face drained of color, and tears stained his
cheeks. "It hurts. It hurts."

Charity knelt and held Josiah's arms. She willed

herself to stay strong. "Can you show me where you hurt yourself?"

Knock, knock. Beth answered the door. "Luke, Josiah hurt his finger." She opened the door.

"His scream startled me. What happened?" He hurried over to Charity and Josiah.

Charity's lips quivered. "I'm worried sick about him." She turned to Josiah. "Sweetheart, can you show me?" She heaved a big breath. She had to find the strength to handle whatever he was about to show her. This wasn't the time to faint.

Josiah removed one finger at a time. His last little finger hung to the side, and he cried and held it.

Gasping, her heart thudded against her chest. Dizzy, she grabbed the back of the settee and steadied herself. Her vision blurred, and she blinked to regain her composure. Her precious child's little finger had been cut off, except for a few threads of tissue still intact. She stood and grabbed a clean cloth and wrapped it around his hand. "How did this happen?"

Beth circled her arm around Josiah's shoulders. Tears wet her face. "We were in the barn jumping off haystacks, and then Josiah wanted to play hide-and-seek. I found him behind the trunk in the corner. He ran out of the barn and when he closed the door, he caught his finger in it."

Charity grimaced and gently held Josiah. The impact must've have been shocking and painful. She moaned. "Josiah, I'm so sorry this happened to you."

Luke opened the door. "Let's take him in my wagon to Dr. Harris. He'll know what to do."

Josiah's lips quivered. "It hurts, Luke." He rested his head on Luke's leg and sobbed.

Luke scooped him up in his arms and rubbed his back. "You poor child. Try to relax. I'll carry you." He faced Charity. "My horse is already hitched to the wagon."

Charity's mamm crossed the yard taking slow steps. "Who screamed? Is everything all right?"

Charity said, "Josiah hurt his finger. Luke's taking us to the doctor. You haven't been feeling well. You need to go back inside and rest. I'll let you know how Josiah is when we return."

"All right, sweetheart." Her mamm turned to go back inside her haus.

Charity followed Luke and climbed in the wagon. He passed Josiah to her, and she held him on her lap.

Beth sat close and tenderly stroked his cheek, whispering words of comfort.

Minutes later, Luke pulled the wagon in front of the doctor's office, jumped out and lifted Josiah from Charity's arms, and ran inside to Dr. Harris's office.

Beth followed on his heels.

Charity grabbed the reins and secured the horse to the hitching post. He'd left her to tend to the horse. She couldn't stand being away from her son at a time like this. She hurried to run inside. Dr. Harris already had his spectacles halfway on his nose, peering at Josiah's bloody hand.

"Ouch! It hurts." Josiah pulled back.

She swayed, caught a chair, and fell into it. She closed her eyes a moment and put her hand in her lap. The raw tissue, blood, and gaping wound flooded her mind. Fighting waves of nausea, she swallowed over and over.

Luke sat next to her. "Are you all right? Would you like some air? I'll stay next to Josiah and Beth."

"I'm embarrassed and ashamed. I should be comforting Josiah, but instead, I'm fighting to sit in this chair and not pass out. I've never been able to look upon blood or wounds and not get sick. You must think I'm terrible."

He had done the right thing by rushing Josiah inside and leaving her to secure the horse. She had a hard enough time keeping herself upright.

"No, you're a sympathetic and compassionate woman. You can't stand to watch your son in pain. I understand."

His concern and empathy touched her. The more she learned about this man, the more she liked him.

The doctor approached Charity. "I'll take your son to the exam room. My nurse will assist me. The room is not large enough for your whole family to join us. You will need to wait here."

She bit her tongue and drew Beth to her. The man was void of emotion. She watched Josiah's back until the door shut behind him. Her heart thudded against her chest. She should be in there next to Josiah. She stood but slumped into the chair again. She wouldn't want to anger the doctor. She had frequented the Englischer's office often to seek his help for Aaron more than once. He had treated the kinner for minor cuts before, but his bedside manner had been professional and nothing more.

Josiah might relax more if she were in the room. She fingered the corner of her scarf. His stiff personality aside, she considered the man a gut doctor. She trembled and circled her arm around her dochder. She whispered a prayer to God concerning Josiah, and Beth leaned against her.

Luke said, "Don't worry. I'll help you with whatever you need for Josiah's care. I can handle blood and wounds. My animals have suffered injuries, and I've cared for them."

What a relief. "Mamm usually helps me if Josiah or Beth hurts themselves. She understands my re-action to such things, but she's not been well lately. I wouldn't want to trouble her. I'll take you up on your offer. I really appreciate it. Danki."

Josiah's pitiful scream rang out.

She jerked, cringed, and tears dripped onto her cheeks. She stood but sat again.

Beth's tearstained face looked up at her. "I'm scared for Josiah."

"I am, too, but the doctor knows what's best for him."

Luke pulled a clean handkerchief out of his pocket and passed it to Beth. "I'm having a diffi-cult time listening to Josiah's painful cries. I can't imagine what it must be like for you. I wish I could say or do something to make this easier for you and your mamm."

Having him next to her and Beth eased the pain of the terrible accident a little. She drew strength from him. He had been such an unexpected bless-ing in her and the kinner's lives.

He removed his hat and raked a hand through his hair. "Sitting here is unnerving."

Minutes passed, and she stared at the exam room door and rubbed Beth's back.

"Enough is enough." He rapped on the examination room door. "Dr. Harris, please tell us something."

Beth gripped her mamm's arm and stared at Luke.

Charity sat on the edge of her seat.

The nurse opened the door. "Give us a few more minutes. The doctor's almost done stitching his wound, and then you can take him home."

She wiped tears streaming down her cheeks. How long was this going to take? Her heart ached for Josiah. Time passed slowly during a time like this. She glanced at Luke as he took a seat beside her, and his worried look and inability to sit still touched her. No doubt he loved Josiah.

She closed her eyes for a moment and breathed deeply. She bowed her head. "Dear Heavenly Father, please forgive me wherein I've failed You today. Please comfort Josiah and take away his pain. Give him strength to overcome this injury. All these things I ask and pray in Your name. Amen."

Luke whispered, "Amen."

The doctor opened the door and gestured them to enter. "He should be waking any minute. I put him to sleep for the time it took to amputate his finger and stitch the wound. It couldn't be saved."

The doctor's insensitive words sent a chill through her. Her knees buckled, and she fell against the wall. Her son had lost his little finger on the hand he favored most. "How will he write or use his hand?"

Dr. Harris crossed the room and opened a cabinet door. He removed medication and supplies, then returned to her. "Have him exercise his hand and fingers several times a day. He should practice picking up and holding small objects. These tasks will be easier once the bandage on the wound is removed. Encourage him and teach him to write with his other hand." He passed her packets of aspirin powder and supplies. "Have him keep the hand elevated and take one teaspoon of medication followed by a glass of water as needed for pain every four hours. Change the bandages each day. If the wound should become infected, come to my office immediately. Bring him back here in a week or so, and I'll remove the stitches."

The elderly man's cold eyes and harsh voice set her teeth on edge. Did he ever show emotion to his family? The man showed no compassion for her son. She just wanted to go home and get out of this place and away from this man.

Josiah blinked his half-open eyelids. "Mamm, I wanna go home."

The doctor helped him up. "Take it easy for the next few days. No jumping around."

Luke carried him to his wagon. "Josiah, I'm going to help your mamm take care of you. Don't worry about a thing. Star and I will visit you each day." He rubbed the child's back and pressed his cheek against Josiah's.

Charity and Beth followed alongside him and climbed in the wagon. She accepted Josiah from him and held him on her lap. "My sweet boy, you're so brave."

Beth patted her bruder's back. "When we get home, I'll tell you a story."

Josiah murmured and closed his eyes.

Charity avoided touching his bandaged hand, relieved he'd fallen asleep on their way home. How would Josiah handle this change in his life? Obedient, kind, and compassionate, her boy possessed a gut nature and took things in stride. She would do all she could to make this easier for him.

The sight of the bandage sent waves of nausea to her stomach. She couldn't expect Luke to come over each day. Mamm wasn't well. She wouldn't want to bother her. She'd have to muster the strength to examine the stitches and wound herself for Josiah's sake, in order to check for infection and change the bandages. She wrinkled her forehead. This would be one of the most difficult tasks she'd ever done.

Luke glanced at her. "When I said I'd help you with Josiah's care, I meant each day. I'll change his bandages and train him how to use his hand."

She put a hand to her heart. "Danki."

He'd stepped in and handled this situation as if he were a part of their family.

"You're kind. I'll cook supper for you in return." She liked having Luke's influence in Josiah's life. She relaxed a little. She and Josiah would benefit from Luke's help.

Luke dismounted, tied the horse to the hitching post, and scooped Josiah from her arms. He carried him inside and lowered him to his bed. He removed his coat and shoes and then pulled the covers up to Josiah's chin. He kissed him gently on the forehead.

Josiah moaned, but his eyes remained shut.

Charity put Josiah's coat on a peg in his room and put his shoes by a small chair in the corner. His hat must've blown off his head during the incident. She'd search for it later. As she gazed at him, curled in his bed, her heart ached and she kissed his forehead. Her son had suffered such a traumatic injury.

She studied him for a moment, then tiptoed out of the room behind Luke and Beth. "Danki, Luke. There aren't enough words to express how thankful I am for your thoughtfulness today."

"You find me anytime you or the kinner need anything. I'll be back tomorrow to visit Josiah. If he wakes in pain, please come and fetch me. This is traumatic for both you and him."

She studied his face and held his gaze. Her breath caught. He reached for her cheek but then withdrew his hand.

Beth had gone to the kitchen, but she returned. "Are you leaving so soon?"

Her heart sank. Would he have touched her cheek if Beth hadn't come in? She hoped so.

Luke dropped his hand to his side. "I'll be back tomorrow. Your mamm's letting me change Josiah's dressing."

"I'm glad you're coming to tend to Josiah. Mamm gags if we cut ourselves. She can't look at blood. I don't like for Mamm to get sick if I have to show her a cut. Grossmudder has to take care of us when we get hurt, but she's not feeling gut right now."

Charity's cheeks warmed. "I wish I could conquer my bad reaction to such sights."

Luke stooped to Beth's level. "Not everyone can handle the sight of blood and wounds. They have big hearts and don't like to see people in pain or suffering. She loves you, and it hurts her when you or Josiah experience pain. You and I need to help her take care of Josiah, all right?"

Beth clasped her mamm's hand. "I'm sorry. I didn't mean to hurt your feelings."

"I accept your apology."

She dropped her mamm's hand and faced Luke. "What can I do to help Josiah?"

"You can be my nurse."

"Maybe I'll be a nurse when I grow up."

Charity patted her dochder's shoulder and pointed to Josiah's room. "Take a peek at Josiah. If he's sleeping, don't disturb him. If not, maybe you can tell him your favorite Bible story about Moses and the burning bush."

"Gut idea." Beth scampered down the short hallway.

It had been a long day, but Charity wasn't ready for Luke to leave. She had a glimmer of hope after the moment they'd shared. "Would you like some hot coffee or tea?"

He shuffled his feet. "No. I must go home to do chores and feed my animals. I'll come by tomorrow. I'll go to your mamm's next door, too, introduce myself, and tell her Josiah is home."

"Danki. I appreciate all you're doing for us."

"I'm sorry you've had such a terrible day. Try to get some rest."

She eyed his back as he left. She wouldn't ask inappropriate questions, but she wanted to find out more about him. She'd asked him about Lancaster, but he refused to open up about his past. Maybe her mamm would have some suggestions.

Aaron had always been an open book. She talked to him about everything. He had been a loving husband, but he had been frail and unable to do many of the chores or tasks around the haus. She had grown weary at times, handling most of the work. Luke had already come to her rescue and eased her daily workload. She liked having a strong, able-bodied man to help her. A gut-looking man like him must've had plenty of available women interested in him in Lancaster. Why hadn't he married?

Tuesday afternoon, footsteps trampled the snow outside. Charity peered out the window.

Beth and Josiah joined her. "Is Luke here?"

"Grossmudder's next to him. He's escorting her. She must've been walking over and met him coming to our porch. Mamm must be healed from her cough and sneezing."

Beth and Josiah clapped.

Josiah took slow steps to the door and opened it. "Hello, Luke and Grossmudder." He hugged them.

Beth reached for their coats and hats. "Grossmudder, I see you've met Luke. He's our friend."

"He stopped and introduced himself the day Josiah got hurt. He was kind enough to let me know the doctor had bandaged his wound and sent him home." She smiled and passed Beth her coat.

Charity greeted them.

Beth clasped Luke's hand and led him to the floor, where she had a game for them to play. Josiah sat close on his other side.

Charity kissed her mamm's cheek. "I'm glad you're here. Your color has returned and you're moving around better. Your voice sounds clearer, too. Are you feeling all right?"

"I am." She whispered, "The kinner and Luke get along well."

"Yes, they love him." She recounted how Josiah

had hurt himself and how Luke came to their rescue. "He comes over each day and changes Josiah's dressing and teaches him how to use his hand."

"How's Josiah handling the loss of his finger?"

"It's been three days since his accident. He's adjusting, and he does have soreness now and then. He takes less medication each day. Luke created some games to teach him how to use his hand. He's the most patient man I've ever encountered. Josiah will do anything Luke tells him to do."

Luke glanced over his shoulder. "I'm going to change the dressing now, if you'd like to go to the kitchen."

Her mamm raised her eyebrows and leaned in close. "I take it you've told him about your reaction to injuries? It's thoughtful of him to consider you."

"Luke's been a blessing. Would you like to join me?" Charity padded to the kitchen.

Her mamm followed and sat at the table. "I caught Luke stealing glances at you while we were talking. I'm certain he's smitten with you and the kinner. Are you interested in him?"

Charity pulled leftover ham from the icebox and corn bread from the bread box. "He's a smart and hardworking, God-fearing Amish man who has all the qualities I want in a husband and daed for Josiah and Beth, but he confuses me. One minute I find him gazing at me, and the next, he finds excuses to run from me. I don't understand him."

"What has he told you about his life in Lancaster?

"Not much."

Her mamm had been a great support for her

and the kinner. Anytime she needed someone to mind the kinner, her mamm came to her rescue. She could talk over any subject, and Mamm listened and offered gut advice. She admired and respected the wisdom, caring attitude, and strength she showed after her daed's death. She shivered. The idea of her mamm leaving this earth one day frightened her.

Charity put her cooking pans on the already warm stove. "I'm sorry you haven't been able to get out of the haus for the last few weeks due to your health. I'll fill you in on what little I do know." She recounted the story of Luke's acceptance in the church. "Friends and neighbors in our community have asked him to do repairs. I've not heard anyone say anything bad about him."

"Why hasn't he married?"

Charity spilled beans on the floor and stooped to clean them up. "He's said nothing about why he's not married. Any suggestions on how I can encourage him to open up? I sense he's hiding something, but what?"

Her mamm stood, raised a pitcher, and poured water into a glass. "Ask appropriate questions, be attentive and listen to his answers, but don't pry into his personal life. Pray and ask God for guidance. God will work this out for you if it's meant for you and Luke to grow close."

"He plays games, puts together puzzles, and patiently answers the kinner's questions. He listens to what they have to say, no matter how long they prattle on to tell their stories."

"He sounds a lot like your daed."

Charity missed her daed. They'd had a close daed and dochder relationship. Her daed and Luke were so much alike. Both were physically strong, Amish law–abiding men who were loving and kind. Her husband had been a kind soul, but frail and weak, not able to play or interact with the kinner like Luke could.

Her daed had loved her mamm, and it showed by the way he gazed at her, helped her, and talked to her about everything. She'd had a marriage like theirs once, and she wanted to experience it again one day. "Josiah and Beth obey and respect Luke like they did their daed. I would like to have a husband and daed in our lives again someday."

"Maybe Luke will be the one God has planned for you." She gently tapped Charity's nose. "Like I've told you several times throughout your life, be patient."

She groaned. "Patience isn't my best quality. I'm not getting any younger." She eyed Luke coming in the room and paused.

Luke sat at the table. "Josiah's injury has no sign of infection. It's healing as it should."

Her mamm crossed the room, lifted plates and utensils, and began to set the table. "Luke, it's nice of you to help my dochder and the kinner. I appreciate it."

"I'm happy to do it. Charity repays me with her gut cooking, and I get to play my favorite games with the kinner. I've never outgrown playing tiddledy-winks or tic-tac-toe."

They laughed.

Charity eyed Luke sitting and chatting to her mamm. He fit into her family like her favorite warm, cozy, and comfortable quilt. Did he dread going home to an empty haus?

CHAPTER 3

A week and a half later, Luke finished cutting wood and hung his ax in the barn. He snapped his fingers. He had an idea and strode to Charity's haus. He rapped on the door.

Beth answered and waved him in. "Are you gonna have time to piece together a puzzle?"

"I'll make time." He approached Josiah. "How's the hand?"

"It doesn't hurt."

Charity adjusted her apron. "Would you like some hot tea?"

"No. I came to take Josiah to Dr. Harris to have his stitches removed. He had said to bring Josiah in about this time."

"I had planned to take him tomorrow, but today would be fine." She untied her apron. "I should go, too."

"You're wilkom to go, but it's not necessary. We'll be back in no time. Josiah, would it be all right if I took you to Dr. Harris to have your stitches removed?"

"Yes. Mamm better stay here. It might make her sick if she goes."

Beth grabbed her coat. "I wanna go."

Josiah clasped Luke's hand. "No, this is a boy's trip. Right, Luke?"

Charity put her hands on Beth's shoulders. "You can make bread pudding. I'll lay out the ingredients for you."

"I like making bread pudding. All right, I'll stay here."

Luke swiped his forehead. "You saved me from an awkward moment. Danki."

They chuckled.

Luke and Josiah bid Charity and Beth farewell, went outside, and climbed in the wagon. He chuckled as Josiah prattled on about his day at school. Pulling in front of Dr. Harris's office, Josiah stopped talking. "Are you all right?" Luke asked.

Josiah's lips quivered. "I'm scared."

"Let's pray." He bowed his head. "Dear Heavenly Father, please protect Josiah as Dr. Harris removes his stitches. Comfort and strengthen him during this time. Amen.

"Are you ready?"

Josiah threw back his shoulders. "Ready."

He loved the child as if he were his own son. Josiah had compassion and strength like his mamm. They walked inside. Dr. Harris sat at his desk.

"We're here to get Josiah's stitches removed."

Dr. Harris stood and pushed his spectacles up his nose. "Very well, come with me." He waved them toward the exam room.

Luke followed. He was determined to stay next to Josiah this time.

Dr. Harris glanced over his shoulder and stared at him for a moment.

Luke darted his eyes away from Dr. Harris and helped Josiah onto the table. He kept his hand on his shoulder. "I'm right here."

Dr. Harris washed his hands and began to remove the stitches.

Josiah closed his eyes from time to time but didn't make a sound. The boy was a brave little soul.

The doctor applied saline solution. "Your wound has healed well. You no longer need a bandage. Keep it clean. You may go." He walked out of the room.

Luke helped Josiah off the table. He couldn't understand why Dr. Harris had chosen this profession if he wasn't happy talking to people. He was glad they wouldn't have to visit him again anytime soon. "Did it hurt?"

"Not too much. God took care of me."

He guided him out the door. "Jah, He always does."

"Luke, danki for taking me. Your sitting next to me helped, too."

"I wouldn't have it any other way." He pointed to jars sitting on the counter in the window. "Let's buy some candy to take home. You deserve it for being such a gut boy."

Josiah beamed.

They went inside the general store, and Josiah picked out his favorite red and orange hard candy. He picked Beth's favorite color, green, and the store owner put the pieces in a bag and passed it to him.

Josiah held it up. "Can you put this in your pocket? I'm afraid I'll drop it."

Luke stuffed the bag in his pocket, and they

crossed the dirt-covered road and got in their wagon to ride home.

Luke halted the horse in front of Charity's haus. "You go inside. I'll take care of the wagon."

"I want to help."

He grinned. The boy never turned down time to spend with him. His heart warmed. They secured the horse in his barn and strolled inside Charity's haus. She stood in her flour-stained apron in the kitchen. Her kapp had shifted, and strands of blond hair hung loose. The word beautiful popped into his mind.

Josiah held up his hand. "Dr. Harris pulled out my stitches."

Charity hugged him. "Did it hurt?"

"No." He lifted his chin and shoulders. "Luke called me brave."

"He held up his hand, watched the doctor, and didn't make a sound. I doubt I would've been as courageous as Josiah."

Beth rushed over to her bruder. "There's no more blood." Beth stretched out her hand and held it up next to Josiah's. "I can't imagine not having my finger."

Charity hugged her dochder. "None of us ever consider that something like this will happen to us, but Josiah has taught us we can overcome anything with God's help. Right, Josiah?"

The child nodded and grinned. "I prayed and asked God to take the pain away, and God did. Luke, you prayed I'd be able to use my hand in no time, and I can."

Luke met Charity's bright blue eyes. Jah, he loved her. No matter how hard he tried, he couldn't stop his heart from racing at the sight of her. He had warned himself not to let it happen, but his heart wouldn't listen. Coming to her haus each day, he'd gotten accustomed to their routine. Could he put his fears aside and trust a woman again? Not yet. The familiar ache he'd suffered when Martha left him came rushing back.

Josiah scampered to the table. "I'm hungry."

"Danki for taking him. You made this much easier for Josiah and me."

"I enjoyed taking him. I like helping you."

Beth and Josiah closed their eyes and bowed their heads. Neither said a word.

Luke chuckled. He accepted the hot, steaming chicken and dumpling bowl and quilted pads from her and centered it on the table. "We have two hungry kinner on our hands." His "*we*" hung in his mind. He hadn't given it a thought, but "*we*" did have a nice ring to it.

They sat and she served them.

Josiah recounted his visit to Dr. Harris. "Luke bought me candy for after supper. It's in his coat pocket."

Beth stared at her lap.

"Don't worry, Beth. We bought you and your mamm a bag of hard candy, too, but you must ask your mamm's permission before you eat any of it."

Beth softened. "Danki, Luke."

The kinner cleaned their plates.

Josiah asked, "May we be excused and get a piece of candy?"

"Yes, you may." Charity waited until the kinner left and then pushed her plate aside. "You don't talk much about your past in Lancaster, Luke. Is there a reason?"

She'd finally asked him the dreaded question.

He still wasn't ready to talk about it. How embarrassing and humiliating.

His jaw clenched. Anger flashed through him as the memory popped in his mind. "The passing of my parents and some other incidents prompted me to move and start fresh here."

A loud knock on the door interrupted them. Charity rose. "I'm not expecting anyone." She opened the door and her eyes widened. "Mrs. Troyer, what brings you here? Please come in."

The Amish teacher stepped inside. "I should come back later. I don't want to interrupt your supper, and you have company."

Josiah and Beth rushed in. "Who's here?" They frowned and stared at the floor.

Josiah stood stiffly. "Hello, Mrs. Troyer."

Beth whispered, "Hello, Mrs. Troyer."

Luke glanced at the kinner. Why the long faces?

Closing the door behind the woman, Charity said, "Mrs. Troyer, please have a seat." She pulled an empty chair to the table for the teacher. "May I get you something? Let me take your burnoose."

Mrs. Troyer sat.

Charity gestured to Josiah and Beth. "Come and sit."

The kinner took slow steps to their chairs next to each other.

"Mrs. Troyer, have you met Luke Fisher? He's our neighbor."

The teacher pinched her lips. "I've not been formally introduced, but I've seen you at church." She addressed Charity. "I really should come back later. What I have to say should be told to you in private."

Charity waved a dismissive hand. "Anything you

have to say, you can tell me in front of Luke. He's a family friend."

The stout, gray-haired Amish woman had a pinched face and a stern tone. She frowned and her demeanor appeared serious. What could Charity's sweet kinner have possibly done to bring this somber woman here today?

Luke stood. "Mrs. Troyer, Charity, I can leave if you wish."

"No, please stay." Charity glanced at Luke, puzzled.

He shrugged his shoulders slightly and sat. He hoped whatever news this teacher had to say wouldn't be upsetting to Charity. He furrowed his brow.

"What I have to say won't take long."

Charity faced the woman. "Have the kinner done something to upset you?"

The woman darted her eyes at Beth.

Beth winced and shifted in her seat.

"During playtime outside today at school, Matthew Oyer said unkind words to Josiah about his hand and shoved him to the ground. Josiah asked him to stop. I headed in their direction to reprimand Matthew, when Beth pushed him. I understand her intention to defend Josiah, but she shouldn't have put her hands on Matthew. She should've let me handle the situation."

Luke's eyes widened, and he held his breath for a moment. This woman couldn't be talking about the same sweet and kind Beth Lantz who was sitting at this table. He couldn't imagine her pushing anyone. She had a direct manner at times, but never had she exhibited this type of behavior before.

Charity gasped and put her hand over Josiah's. "Are you all right? Why didn't you tell me about this?"

He lifted his shirt. "I have a bruise, but I'm fine." His lip trembled. "I didn't want Beth to get in trouble. Please don't punish her. She helped me, and Matthew scared me."

Charity patted his arm. "I understand. I'm sorry this happened to you." She eyed Beth. "You should never have put your hands on Matthew to settle this. Apologize to Mrs. Troyer."

"I'm sorry, Mrs. Troyer." Beth stared at her lap.

Charity turned to the teacher. "Is Matthew all right?"

"Jah, he's fine."

Luke narrowed his eyes. "Have you talked to Matthew's parents?"

"Jah, I visited them before I came here. They asked me to tell you how sorry they are for Matthew's rude actions. They are punishing him, and so am I. He will be responsible for cleaning the school, stocking the fireplace wood, and writing Bible verses during playtime for two months."

Luke cleared his throat. He'd be upset if Beth received the same punishment. Her actions were to defend her bruder, not to torment or start a scuffle. "What is Beth's punishment?"

"She's to write Bible verses at playtime for two weeks."

Charity bit her lip. "Your punishment is fair, Mrs. Troyer. I'll speak to Beth concerning this. Danki for bringing it to my attention."

Mrs. Troyer stood. "I wasn't sure Beth would tell you about the incident and thought I should make you aware of what happened."

Beth's lips trembled. "I would've told her tonight at bedtime."

Charity met Beth's eyes. "I do believe her. She isn't deceitful or secretive."

Luke wanted to hug Beth. She shouldn't have put her hands on Matthew, but she loved her bruder and hadn't wanted anyone to hurt him. Mrs. Troyer's stern eyes and voice set his teeth on edge.

Mrs. Troyer frowned. "Nonetheless, I always visit the parents of a student involved in such matters."

Luke clasped his hands. Mrs. Troyer must be one of those people who insisted on having the last word. He doubted she had a humble bone in her body, given her demeanor.

Charity opened the door. "I'd appreciate your keeping an eye on Matthew. He's older and bigger than Josiah. I don't condone Beth's behavior, but she was protecting Josiah. I wouldn't want this to happen again."

Luke shifted his weight in the chair and glanced out the window. He couldn't have said it better himself.

"I understand, and rest assured, I will monitor him closely." She turned on her heels.

"Gut day to all of you."

"Gut day, Mrs. Troyer." Charity shut the door behind her.

"Josiah, stay far away from this boy. He sounds like trouble."

"I will, Mamm."

"Why don't you go to your room and practice writing your alphabet, while I talk to Beth for a few minutes."

Her son clasped Beth's hand resting on the

table for a moment before he slid out of his chair. He dragged his feet to his room.

Luke smiled. What an endearing picture. The kinner loved each other. Mrs. Troyer, what a somber woman. The kinner had to endure her cold personality each day. He'd had young and kind teachers in school. There wasn't a sign of anything kind about this teacher. Maybe he should speak to the bishop about Mrs. Troyer. He glanced at Charity. No, he wouldn't interfere. She might not like it.

He sat and sipped his water.

Charity pointed her finger at Beth. "You will not be allowed to go outside and play for a week. You will go to your room right after school, do your homework, have supper, and go to bed."

Beth's tears stained her face. "I'm sorry, Mamm. I told Matthew to stop, but he went to push Josiah again. I had to do something."

She reached across the table and put her hand on Beth's. "I understand you wanted to protect your bruder, but putting your hands on Matthew shouldn't have entered your mind. You could've used your voice or waited for the teacher. She would've handled the situation." She shook her head. "Please go to your room and do your homework."

Beth glanced over her shoulder at Luke.

He bit his lip and glanced out the window.

Chin to her chest, she padded to her room.

Charity slumped in a chair. "Beth pushing Matthew is terrible."

Luke reached for her hand, then withdrew it quickly. He had reacted and not thought first. He suspected his heart had taken over. "I'm surprised at Beth's behavior, but it doesn't sound like the teacher would've crossed the yard in time before Matthew delivered his second shove."

Charity stood and crossed her arms. "Are you condoning what Beth did?"

"No, but I don't agree her pushing the boy is *terrible,* given the circumstances."

Charity tightened her lips and crossed her arms. "I disagree. There is no room for compromise on this issue."

"You're overreacting."

She stiffened. "I'm disappointed we don't agree. You and I have both been raised not to impose physical harm to anyone for any reason. Beth must understand she can't do this again." She nervously touched her kapp and glanced toward the hallway. "I should check on the kinner."

Her abruptness caught him off guard. "Charity, I didn't mean to offend you. Let's sit and discuss this. I don't want to leave under these circumstances."

She stared at her feet. "I'm sorry, Luke. I'm tired, and it has been a long day. May we discuss this another time?"

He nodded, lifted his coat and hat from the wooden peg, and left. He would allow her time to digest what had happened before talking about this again. He'd said the wrong words. She'd misunderstood him. What Beth had done deserved punishment and she shouldn't ever repeat her action, but he understood it. He'd apologize tomorrow and listen to what Charity had to say.

Charity pressed a hand to her forehead. Her head throbbed and her teeth hurt from gritting them so hard. He had been Amish all his life, so how could Luke defend Beth's putting her hands on the boy in such a way? *Overreacting? How dare he?* He hadn't understood at all, and she wasn't *overreacting*. She filled and warmed a large basin of water on the stove and then carried it to Beth's room.

The child's lips quivered.

Charity's face softened. At least Beth showed remorse. "Please get ready for your bath."

Beth trudged to the washroom and stood silent.

Charity returned from the kitchen and poured warm water from the wash boiler into the cool water already in the tub. She touched it. "The temperature is all right. You can step in."

Beth undressed, put one foot in at a time, and inched her body into the water. "Danki, Mamm."

"You're a gut schweschder to Josiah. I'm glad you care about him, but do you understand why you mustn't let this happen again?"

Beth's shoulders slumped and her lips trembled. "Yes. I'm sorry."

Her dochder had a strong will, determination, and wasn't afraid of much. She hoped Beth had listened and learned her lesson. Charity left the room and checked on Josiah. Snuggled under the covers, he slept. She left him in his clothes and covered him. He'd been through a tough time suffering the loss of his finger, and now this. Her kinner were close and couldn't stand it when she punished one or the other of them. She hoped they'd remain close as they aged.

After Beth bathed and put on her bedclothes, Charity listened to Beth's prayer. "Dear Heavenly Father, forgive me for pushing Matthew, but please help him not to push Josiah again. Make his parents real mad at him and punish him gut. I love You. Amen."

Charity opened her mouth but then shut it. She wanted Beth to say whatever was on her mind to God anytime she wished. She was certain Beth had learned her lesson.

Later, she lit the kerosene lamp and opened her bag. After pulling out a half-finished scarf, she wound yarn around her needles and began to knit. Luke was too tolerant where her kinner were concerned. She'd put distance between them for a while. Maybe time apart would be gut for her, too. She couldn't figure him out.

Her frustration mounted, not knowing where he stood concerning his emotions for her. Pushing the needle through the blue yarn, she paused. Maybe she'd taken her irritation and embarrassment concerning the situation out on him. No doubt he loved her kinner and wanted the best for them. Nonetheless, she couldn't allow Luke to diminish what Beth had done in any way. Even angry, she couldn't stop her heart from skipping a beat at the picture of Luke's handsome face in her mind.

Luke carried a cooked chicken and a pint of peach jam he'd bought from a peddler in town to Charity. Maybe his gifts would show her he cared and wanted to make amends. "How are the kinner?" he asked.

Charity gave him a faint smile as she held the door half-open. "They're fine. Beth's in her room and not allowed to play, and Josiah is playing with his wooden train." She eyed the food in his hands. "It's best if you and my kinner don't spend time together for a while. Beth needs to take her punishment seriously, and I don't want you to insinuate in any way that her behavior was justified."

Luke lifted his eyebrows. "I wouldn't do anything to interfere or go against you. I apologize for speaking out of turn. I should've listened to you and kept my opinion to myself."

She met his eyes. "I accept your apology, but please help me impose this punishment on Beth by not allowing her to visit with you for a week or so. I would really appreciate it."

"I understand." He passed her the chicken and jam.

"Danki, Luke." She bowed her head and closed the door.

A whole week before he could darken their doorstep again. He wouldn't want this disagreement to harm what they had between them. He'd wait, then approach her again.

During the week, Luke repaired furniture and doors and painted inside walls for his friends and neighbors. He was sick of eating ham sandwiches. The loneliness was even worse. Had Beth and Josiah asked about him? What had Charity told them about why he hadn't visited them? He closed his eyes. He could picture their angelic faces and melodious voices. Their giggles and stories about school delighted him, as did Charity's full lips and wide smile and the sparkle in her eyes. He frowned. The loss of them from his life this week had been difficult. He readied for bed. Tomorrow was Sunday, and they'd be at church. Would she allow him to talk to the kinner?

He woke to the Sunday morning sun peering in the window. Maybe it would melt the snow and ice. Hot coffee sounded gut. Climbing out of bed, he paused to stretch. He couldn't wait to go to church. Charity, Josiah, and Beth would be there. Would Charity speak to him? Had she missed him? He hoped so.

He dressed, readied his horse, and rode to the church barn. He passed the reins to the young stable hand and stepped inside. He searched for the Lantz family. They were seated on a bench several rows back from the front. He took slow steps to sit behind them. His throat dry, he coughed.

The Lantz kinner turned around and grinned widely.

Beth waved. "Hello, Luke."

Josiah shifted in his seat. "We've missed you. Mamm said you couldn't come over because Beth was bad and it was part of her punishment. She said a week. It's been a week. Will you sit with us at the meal today?"

Charity smiled.

He nodded and grinned. Maybe everything would return to normal.

After the service, he made small talk with Charity and the kinner while they enjoyed their meals. It was as if they'd not had a disagreement. He bid them farewell and looked over his shoulder at Charity one more time. His eyes narrowed. Mr. Young was asking her a question. He strained to hear Mr. Young's exact words. Haus? Had he asked Charity to his haus? The chatter around them drowned out most of their conversation. He couldn't understand when Mr. Young had invited her to visit him.

She was nodding. Oh no, what was she agreeing to? The man was a widower. This couldn't be gut.

He went home, fixed another cold ham sandwich, and read the first few pages of the book of John in the King James Bible, then fed his animals. His body ached and he couldn't keep his eyes open. Cold one minute and hot the next, he pulled back the covers and climbed in bed. He'd shut his eyes for a few moments before changing into his bedclothes. A little while later, he shivered and pulled his knees up to his chest. Tossing and turning, he couldn't get in a comfortable position. Legs and arms aching, he rubbed them.

Star licked his face, and he pushed him away.

Whining, Star jumped off the bed and paced.

Luke gritted his teeth at the sound of the dog's nails tapping on the wooden floor. "Settle down, boy." He shivered. Hot one minute and cold the next, he piled quilts and blankets on himself. Sweat beaded on his face and soaked his bedclothes.

CHAPTER 4

Sunday evening Charity sat in her favorite over-sized oak chair and sipped hot cocoa. Luke had brought her food and apologized. The man had gone out of his way to help her, and she had taken her anger out on him. It hadn't been fair to punish him as well as Beth, although she was disappointed he hadn't agreed on the seriousness of Beth's transgression.

On the other hand, her kinner loved and missed him. She had missed him more than she thought she should. Was God testing her? She bowed her head. "Dear Heavenly Father, please forgive my anger and frustration this week. I'm confused. Guide me in what You would have me do where Luke and Mr. Young are concerned. Should I wait on Luke? Is he a friend or something more You have planned for me? Give me the right words to apologize to Luke. Danki for Your love, grace, and mercy. Amen."

She would rather spend Thanksgiving with him than with the Young family. He shouldn't be alone on Thanksgiving. Maybe she should invite him to her haus. No. She had accepted Mr. Young's invitation for her family to join his for Thanksgiving. He had been a widower for a year. His wife had had a deep cough and weakness for a year before she died. Ten years older than Charity, he was a decent man, bald with pale skin and freckles. He was thin and tall. She liked his kind demeanor, and he went out of his way to talk to Josiah and Beth after church meals.

Luke had gazed at her a few times during their suppers as if he wanted to say something endearing, but then he shied away. She frowned. Maybe she'd misunderstood his expression and it was wishful thinking on her part. She couldn't wait forever. She owed it to herself and her kinner to find out if Mr. Young could be a potential husband.

She cocked her head and listened. *Scratch, scratch.* She crossed the room and opened the door. "Star, what are you doing here?"

Josiah and Beth joined her. "Where's Luke?" The kinner rushed outside into the cold.

"Kinner, please come inside. You'll get sick without your coats on."

Beth's teeth chattered as she rubbed her arms. "Star came here alone." She petted the dog's head. "What's wrong, Star?"

Star padded in but went back out before Charity could shut the door. He barked and paced on the porch.

Beth glanced at Charity. "He wants us to follow him."

Charity stared at her bright dochder. The child was right. Beth never ceased to amaze her. She paid attention to detail and hardly missed a thing. "Get your coats on. We'll return him to Luke."

Josiah clapped his hands. "Gut. We'll finally get to visit Luke. I've missed him. When can we visit him again?"

She kissed his forehead. "I'm sorry I've kept you from Luke. It was wrong of me. I'll talk to him about it soon." She grabbed a lantern and herded them outside. They hurried to match Star's pace.

Josiah hugged her arm. "Danki, Mamm."

Beth nodded. "Yes, danki, Mamm."

She swallowed. The kinner would be lost without Luke if she chose Mr. Young. She knocked and the door swayed open. Luke had left it unlatched. She went inside. "Luke, may we come in? Are you all right?"

A moan came from a far room.

Josiah and Beth followed her with worried faces.

The haus was eerily quiet and dark. She lit the kerosene lamp closest to the door on a small table in the entryway. She squinted and noticed dirty dishes and a half-empty glass of water on the kitchen table. That wasn't like him. He'd always put his tools away and cleaned up his mess after doing repairs at her haus. Her breath caught. Something was wrong. She found another lamp and turned it up. She gestured toward Josiah and Beth. "No, you two stay in the sitting room." She ran her hand along Star's soft black fur. "Play with Star. I'll be right back."

She crept down the hallway and found Luke in his bed. She stepped gingerly to his bedside but kept her distance. His face appeared flushed, and his body trembled. Moving a little closer, she touched his forehead and quickly withdrew her hand. Warm and clammy. He had a fever.

He opened his eyes and his lips quivered. "Charity, what are you doing here?"

"Star scratched at my door. He must've sensed something was wrong. You need a doctor. I'll ask Mamm to mind the kinner and fetch him. First, I'll get you a drink of water." Not waiting for his response, she returned to Josiah and Beth. She explained to the kinner about Luke's condition and why she'd need to drop them off at her mamm's. "Leave your coats on. I'll be back in a minute. I'm going to the kitchen to get Luke some water. He's sick."

They frowned and nodded.

She hurried to the kitchen and pumped water into a pitcher and poured him a glass. With one hand to her churning stomach, she returned to his room. He shivered and winced. She grew lightheaded.

"Can you sit up?"

He struggled to raise his head.

She held the glass to his lips. Her heart ached for him. He barely had the strength to sip the water, his body quaking. "I'll be back. You rest."

His voice was weak. "No. I don't want you to go out in the snow and cold. I'll just sleep and be better in the morning." He reached out and took her arm. His hand shook against her skin. "I'm glad we've moved past our disagreement. I missed you." His eyes closed and his body trembled.

She put a hand to her heart. She shouldn't have shunned him. "I'm sorry for being rude to you, Luke. I took my frustration out on you, and you didn't deserve it." She put a hand to her chest. "Please rest. I'll be right back." She retrieved the kinner and trudged through the snow to their haus. She retrieved her horse and wagon, then she and the kinner headed to her mamm's. She was glad it was a short distance. The wind blew cold.

Beth knocked on the door. "Grossmudder, Luke's sick."

Josiah hung his hat on a hook. "Star came and told us."

"How did Star tell you?"

Charity hugged her mamm and recounted how Star had led them to Luke. "I'm worried about Luke. He's a vibrant man, and the raging fever has him weak and shivering. I'll rest easier if Dr. Harris examines him. Maybe he'll have medication to help lower Luke's temperature. Do you mind watching the kinner?"

"Of course not. You be careful."

Charity bid the kinner farewell, climbed in the wagon, and guided her horse to town. Her heart ached for Luke; he had looked miserable. Throwing a blanket, then a saddle over her horse and fastening it, she paused. What if this was more serious than just a fever? She adjusted the bridle, then pushed the thought from her mind.

Dreading bothering the harsh doctor, she hoped he'd agree to come back to Luke's. Arriving at his haus, she rapped on his door.

He appeared and frowned. "What brings you here?"

"Luke Fisher is ill." Charity recounted Luke's symptoms. "Will you please come to his haus?"

Dr. Harris grabbed his coat and medical bag. "I'll tell my fraa where I'm going and meet you there."

Returning home, she put the horse in her barn, then waited for Dr. Harris on Luke's porch. She rubbed her arms. *It's so cold.* A few minutes later, Dr. Harris arrived. She accepted his animal's reins.

"You go on in. I'll stow your horse out of the winter air and then I'll come inside." She hurried to secure his horse, then went inside and added logs to the dwindling fire. Flames burning bright, she removed her gloves and held her hands close to the fire. *Warm at last.*

She put a hand to her forehead. She hoped his illness wasn't serious. She'd done all she could for now. She went to Luke's kitchen and washed and dried the dishes. She stretched the damp dish towel on the counter to dry.

Dr. Harris entered. He lifted his chin and stared down his nose at her. "His fever is high, but he doesn't have a cough or nausea. I've given him two spoonfuls of medication to lower the fever and to help him rest. I put the bottle on his bedside table and told him to take two teaspoons every four hours until his fever is gone. I don't suspect anything serious. When his temperature breaks, he'll feel much better. If not, please fetch me."

"I will. Danki." She followed him outside, escorted him to the barn to get his horse, and waited until he left before she went back to check on Luke. The doctor's cool demeanor hadn't changed since the last time she'd encountered him. No matter. She was grateful he'd come to Luke's to check on him.

She went inside, got a glass of water, tiptoed to Luke's bedroom, and stood a few feet away from him. "Are you doing all right? Is there anything I can get you?" She set the glass next to his medication.

"Danki for getting the doctor. I'll be all right. I just need sleep, and I'll take the medicine."

"You're wilkom. Get some rest."

"Danki again, Charity. Your being here is the best medicine." He managed a weak smile.

Her cheeks warmed. "It pains me to find you ill. I hope you're better soon. I'll check on you tomorrow."

He pulled the covers tight. She turned down his lamp and left. Heading for her mamm's haus, she fretted about Luke. Pale and in obvious discomfort, it was difficult to watch him suffer. She put a hand to her heart. She would fix things between them after he healed.

She knocked, then walked inside her mamm's haus. "Hello."

Mamm met her. "How's Luke?"

Josiah and Beth hugged her.

Beth wiped cookie crumbs from her mouth. "Is he all right?"

"His fever is high. I'm hoping the medication Dr. Harris gave him helps lower it. Dr. Harris left the medication on his bedside table. He's to take two teaspoons every four hours, but I'm not sure he'll be in gut enough condition to take it. He really shouldn't be alone, but it would be improper for me to stay at his haus at night."

"Why don't you take me over to Luke's? At my age, no one is going to question me watching over him until morning. I can give him the medicine."

Her mamm had stepped in and eased her mind more times than she could count during her lifetime. She was doing it again. She had a generous heart, and nothing flustered her. She should've been a nurse. Beth resembled her mamm in this regard. "I'd rest easier if you'd tend to him. I'll be glad to take you." She gestured to Josiah and Beth. "Get your coats, hats, and gloves. We need to get Grossmudder to Luke's and you to bed."

Beth peered up at her. "I want to help Luke."

"It's thoughtful of you, but no, he needs his rest. Grossmudder is going to take care of him."

Josiah let out a deep sigh. "Feed Luke your chicken broth and bread like you do me when I'm sick. That'll make him better."

Her mamm chuckled. "Gut advice, little one."

"Can you walk to Luke's?"

"Jah, the exercise will do me gut."

Charity and the kinner escorted her mamm to Luke's. She yearned to check on Luke herself, but her kinner needed to get to bed. The time had gotten late. "Will you be all right, Mamm?"

"Jah, child. Go home and get some rest."

Charity and the kinner left and arrived home. "Change into your nightclothes, and I'll tuck you in." She hurried to stow her horse and wagon in the barn.

The kinner sat on the floor in Josiah's room.

She knelt beside them.

Josiah yawned. "I'll go first." He bowed his head and folded his hands. "Dear Heavenly Father, please forgive me for my sins. Please make Luke better so he can take me sledding and we can fix things together. I love You. Amen."

Beth then bowed her head. "Dear Heavenly Father, please forgive me of my sins. Please heal

Luke and take away Mamm's sadness. Please tell her to let Luke come back. He makes her laugh and us, too. We miss him. I love You. Amen."

She had been blessed with loving kinner. She kissed their foreheads and tucked Josiah in his bed, then held Beth's hand to her room and tucked her in.

Her precious kinner would be asleep in no time. Her heart lay heavy. This past week had been the longest and loneliest week she'd experienced in a long time. Maybe she should wait a little longer before giving up on Luke. She groaned and rubbed her temples. She should've put Mr. Young off a bit. She might have gotten herself into a mess.

Luke woke early. He dressed and followed the aroma of baked bread to the kitchen.

Mrs. Vogel grinned. "You have your color back. How are you?"

"I'm weak but on the mend. I'm starving."

She straightened her apron. "I have hot tea on the stove and warmed chicken broth. If your stomach accepts the broth all right, then you can have something more substantial."

Luke was fond of Mrs. Vogel. She had her gray hair wound in a bun under her kapp, and wire spectacles rested on her nose. The frail little woman moved slowly and winced in pain now and then, but she was always full of cheer. Charity's mamm took slow steps and care in lowering herself to a chair.

"Danki for taking care of me and for breakfast. I'll take you home after we're finished."

"You've done so much for my family, I'm happy

to do it. You take it easy today. It's not far. I can walk home. I'll stop by Charity's and tell her you're doing much better."

Her concern touched him. "I insist on taking you home." He spread a cloth napkin on his lap. "I'll feed the animals, but I won't venture out. I have no repairs scheduled today. Once my strength returns, I'll be as gut as new." He sipped the tea she passed to him. "You raised a kind dochder. She's a wonderful mamm and a hard worker."

Mrs. Vogel buttered a slice of bread. "Charity's a strong and determined woman, but money's been tight since Aaron's passing. The wood, food, and supplies you've brought her have helped tremendously." She sipped her steaming hot coffee. "Are you happy here in Berlin?"

Luke sipped his broth. The salt rolled over his tongue. "Jah. I've grown roots here. I plan to stay for a long time."

"Your news will make Charity and her kinner happy."

"They are the main reason I'm happy living here."

She grinned. "I'm glad to hear it." Mrs. Vogel sipped her coffee and conversed with him about gardening while she tidied the kitchen. "I should head home and tend to my animals."

"I'll hook my horse to the wagon."

He shivered in the bitter cold and headed to the barn. He rubbed his thighs. His legs hadn't regained their strength yet. He hitched his horse to the wagon and pulled it outside.

Mrs. Vogel joined him, and he helped her climb in. He took her the short distance to her home, bid her farewell, and shut the door for her. On his way home, he had an idea. He guided his horse over to Charity's. A thrill jolted through him. He tied his horse to the hitching post, stepped onto her porch, and rapped on the door.

She opened it, a puzzled expression on her face. "Luke, you shouldn't be out in this weather any more than you have to be. You need to give your body a chance to heal."

"I won't come in. I realize the kinner are in school." He spread his mouth in a wide grin and ran one gloved hand over the other. "Will you, your mamm, and the kinner join me for Thanksgiving? I'll get a turkey from the peddler, and I'll cook dinner."

She frowned and whispered, "I'm sorry. Mr. Young has asked us to join him, and I accepted."

He removed his hat and raked a hand through his hair. His concern about Mr. Young talking to her after church had been right. "Mr. Young, the widower who has six kinner?"

"Yes, and my mamm is joining us."

"*No, no, no*" hung on his tongue. The idea of her with another man rendered him speechless. The way he felt on the day Martha left him. He needed a minute alone. Turning on his heels, he hurried to step off the porch and move toward his haus. He groaned. It was his fault for shying away from her questions and not sharing his feelings.

"Luke, please come back later. We do need to talk."

He shook his head and waved over his shoulder. He needed time to digest what she'd told him. He flexed his gloved hands. Another man might snatch her away from him. The bishop had warned him that another man might show interest in Charity. He should've listened.

On Thanksgiving, Luke cooked eggs, bacon, and grits for dinner. The haus stood quiet, except for Star's panting and tail slapping the wood floor. He pictured Charity, her mamm, Josiah, and Beth in his haus. He shut his eyes. He could almost hear their voices ringing out over the snap of game pieces on a tic-tac-toe board as they teased each other and laughed. What if Mr. Young won her heart?

He trudged through the wet snow to the barn and checked on the animals, then headed back to his haus. Eyes wide, heat rose to his face. There stood Martha. "Why are you here?" He wouldn't invite her in. He owed her nothing. They were no longer even married. She'd played him for a fool. He had hoped never to lay eyes on her again.

Cheeks tearstained, her dark hair hung in ringlets around her face. A long red wool coat fit snugly to her small waist and thick hips. The matching hat and velvet ribbon tied at her chin outlined her sweetheart face. Elegant, but none of it was appropriate as far as he was concerned. They were a harsh reminder of her desire for the world.

"Aren't you going to invite me inside?"

"How did you find me?"

"I went to our old haus in Lancaster. The couple who bought our place told me you had given them your address here." She hugged herself. "Let's go inside. It's cold. I need to speak to you. It's important."

He heaved a big sigh. She'd ripped his heart in two the day she destroyed his trust and left with the Englischer. "I've nothing to say to you, Martha."

She fell against him, hugged him tight, and pressed her lips against his. "Please, Luke, please."

His eyes widened. He shrugged her off and stepped back. He wiped his mouth with the back of his hand. "Keep your distance, Martha." She was married to another man. What was she thinking putting her arms around him? During their marriage, he couldn't wait to have her in his arms each day, but not anymore. Hands on hips, he glared at her. "Where is your husband?"

"I've left him. He gambles and is a drunk. I found him last night in the arms of another woman. I can't stand him."

Married or not, he had no interest in her personal life. He felt nothing for her.

She clutched his arms. "I made a horrible mistake leaving you. Please forgive me. I love you. Please take me back." Her lips were inches from his. "We had a gut life. I'm sorry. I'll never leave you again. We can sell this place and buy a haus in Massillon. You'll love living in the world. The food, clothes, dancing, modern conveniences, and music are wonderful. Let me show you. We can experience it together."

He clenched his teeth and stepped back from her again. Who was this stranger he'd once loved? She hadn't known him at all, or she wouldn't even suggest such a thing. More than anything, he wanted her to get on her horse and never return. He crossed his arms against his chest. "You've turned your back on God, Amish traditions, and me. You have no place in my life anymore."

She looked at him with pleading eyes. "You can't turn me away. I have no money. Where will I go?"

He heaved a big sigh. He wouldn't leave her stranded. He dug in his pocket and pressed some coins and paper money in her gloved palm. "Take this and don't come back."

She stepped over to him, threw her head back, and beat his chest with her fists. "You make me sick."

He moved away from her. "Please go."

She swished her coat skirt. Her mouth spread in an evil grin. "You can have your boring Amish life. I'll have no part of it. I'd rather have your money anyway." She spit in his face and mounted her horse.

He wiped her spittle from his cheek and shook his head. The world had changed her. She was self-indulgent and rude. He'd found her beautiful before they married. She'd had a gut sense of humor, but she could be as stubborn as a mule. They'd argued more than any couple should, but he'd given in to her most times to keep the peace. The gut times outweighed the bad for a time, but he'd sensed she always wanted more than he could give her. He wouldn't want any harm to come to her, but if she returned again, he'd refuse to have one word with her.

A barn door shut next door. Startled, he turned his head and caught sight of Charity hurrying across the yard to her front door. He cringed. Had she seen Martha? He hoped not. He should've told her he had been divorced and why. He'd tell her everything about his past soon. Pulling his coat tighter, he lowered his head and went inside.

He'd allowed Martha's indiscretion to affect his

future. Otherwise, he'd have been the one sitting next to Charity and her family today. He closed his eyes for a moment. Martha had ignited an angry fire in his stomach. Stiff, he rolled his shoulders, then bowed his head. "Dear Heavenly Father, please forgive me for getting angry and having bad thoughts toward Martha. Please prevent her from returning here. Give me the right words to say to Charity tomorrow. I love her. I'm asking You to intervene and prepare her heart to hear and accept what I have to say about my past life and to answer jah to my marriage proposal. Please, Heavenly Father. Amen."

The day dawned gray the next morning. His strength had returned. *What a relief.* Rested, he cooked a hearty breakfast. Ham sizzled in the skillet, and the smoky aroma filled the air. He inhaled, then exhaled. After he finished his meal, he tidied the kitchen and strolled over to the barn.

Should he approach Charity today and tell her everything? He glanced over to her porch. A man stood at her front door. He twisted his lips. Mr. Young. What was he doing at her haus? His heart sank. This couldn't be gut. She had all the traits a man would want in a fraa. No doubt Mr. Young appreciated them. He suspected the man was in a hurry to wed her, since he needed a mamm for his six kinner. Her door opened and the man went inside.

Luke must do something before he was too late. He tramped through the snow and knocked on her door.

Charity gasped when she opened the door. "This

isn't a gut time for you to visit, Luke. Mr. Young is here. Please come back later. We do need to talk."

Mr. Young might propose at any minute. Luke wasn't leaving. "Please put on your coat and step outside. I have something important to say to you, Charity."

"Luke, Mr. Young is in my sitting room. He might hear us. Not now."

Cheeks flushed, she stared at her feet. He'd caught her off guard, and his timing wasn't the best. No matter, she must listen to him. "Please, Charity, I must speak to you right now."

"Please understand, it would be rude to leave Mr. Young for long."

Josiah and Beth ran over to Charity and Luke, shrugging into their coats. "Can we go over to Luke's?"

She glanced at him.

"I'll take them for a sled ride. Don't make any decisions until you talk to me. Please." He glanced at the kinner and then at her. He clasped the kinner's hands and stepped off the porch.

"Danki." She retreated inside.

The kinner piled up snow to make a little hill for the sled to go over as he and the kinner played outside. Mr. Young left the haus minutes later. What had the man said to the woman Luke loved? He shivered. No matter. He still had a chance. She wasn't married to Mr. Young yet.

Beth tugged on his coat sleeve. "You should've been with us at Mr. Young's for Thanksgiving. His kinner threw food at each other at the table and made a mess. They got up out of their chairs and ran around during the meal. They were funny."

"What did you do?"

Josiah cupped his mouth. "We laughed but we minded our manners. Mamm would punish us if we behaved that way."

Beth's eyes widened. "Mr. Young talks a lot with his mouth full. Mamm scolds us when we speak with our mouths full, but she didn't say anything to him." She paused. "He has lots of rooms in his haus. He showed Josiah and me two of them and said they might be ours if Mamm agrees to marry him one day soon. I told him Josiah and I already have you picked out for our daed."

"What did Mr. Young say to that?"

"He frowned and looked at me funny, then said we'd better join Mamm in the kitchen."

Josiah bobbed his head up and down. "Luke, will you marry us?"

"I'm working on it. This isn't just my decision. Your mamm has to agree."

Beth swayed from side to side. "She likes you better. I can tell."

"I hope you're right." He checked his time-piece. "You should go home. We've been out here for a while." He kissed their foreheads and watched them until they were inside, then went over to his haus. He couldn't let this man have his family. Life would be empty if Charity and her kinner weren't a part of it. He'd tell her about his former fraa and then propose. He'd invite her, the kinner, and Mrs. Vogel for Christmas dinner. He'd enjoy buy-ing presents and watching their faces as they opened them on Christmas Day, and hopefully, they'd set a wedding date.

He grinned. Charity must've been appalled at the Youngs' behavior. She'd taught her kinner gut manners. Her haus was neat and orderly. The kinner wore clean clothes and wouldn't think of throwing food. The time he and Charity had spent together had to mean something to her. She barely knew Mr. Young. Had the widower told her what the kinner had said to him? Had Mr. Young questioned her about him?

CHAPTER 5

Charity sat in her favorite oak rocker and knitted a wool scarf to sell. The kinner were asleep, and the haus was quiet aside from flames snapping in the fireplace. Cozy and warm, she was glad she'd gone to check her animals an hour after she came home from the Youngs', or she would've missed the woman hugging Luke in front of his place. She'd peeked around the corner of the barn and strained to understand their words, but the wind muffled their voices. She'd watched them a minute or two, then run back inside. She'd tossed and turned last night, unable to erase the Englischwoman from her mind. Who was she?

She hoped Luke hadn't caught sight of her gawking before she scampered into the haus. Had he been waiting for this woman to return to him? It didn't make sense, since the woman was an Englischer.

Dinner at the Youngs' had been a disaster, the worst she had ever experienced. She chided herself for being ungrateful and critical. The man had hired Mr. and Mrs. Pine to cook the meal and join them for dinner at the long oak table decorated with candles. He'd been generous and insisted they take food home. It would last for a week. His prayer for the meal had been heartfelt, and he'd been attentive to Josiah and Beth. His proposal that they marry for convenience hadn't come as a surprise. He needed a fraa to raise his six kinner. He had a big home, had plenty of money, and was a gut Amish man, but he wasn't Luke.

The next day, she strolled over to Mamm's. While the kinner were in school, she could have Mamm to herself. Voicing her concerns about Luke and Mr. Young might ease her mind a bit. She went inside. "Are you busy?"

Mamm crossed the room and hugged her. "Don't be silly. I'm never too busy for you, child. Come, sit. You're wearing a frown. What's troubling you?" She sat back down in her oak rocker.

"Mr. Young asked me to marry him."

Mamm gasped. "You didn't say a word on the way home after we left his haus. I wondered what was wrong. I thought you were just tired. Are you considering accepting his proposal?"

"I'm hesitant, but yes."

"You and Luke have spent a lot of time together. He loves your kinner, and he can't do enough for you. I've caught you gazing at him. Am I wrong? Do you love Luke?"

"Yes, but he hasn't said a word to me indicating he feels the same. I damaged our friendship by not allowing him to say his piece when we disagreed about Beth's transgression. I want to make amends, but I haven't yet."

Mamm leaned over and pulled two quilts off a quilt rack. She passed one to Charity and covered her own legs with the other. "Why have you waited?"

She clutched the quilt. "I have more news." She recounted the story of the woman she had caught sight of visiting Luke.

She loved him, but no matter. He obviously had another woman in his life. She heaved a sigh. She couldn't wait for him. Her kinner needed a daed, not just a kind neighbor. "He meant something to this woman or she wouldn't have been so comfortable throwing herself at him. I'm curious to learn more, but I doubt Luke will say anything. He's so tight-lipped."

"From what you've told me, I'd guess this woman has no place in his life any longer, or she'd have been a part of his life all along."

"What's your advice?"

Mamm leaned forward. "As far as Luke's concerned, you should mend your friendship. Don't marry Mr. Young. I've no doubt you could whip his haushold into shape and discipline those kinner of his, but it wouldn't be easy."

Charity groaned and rubbed her eyes. "If I say no to Daniel Young, I might not have any other offers."

"Be patient. Don't do anything rash. Pray and ask God to guide you. Seek His will, and everything in your life will fall into place."

"I love Luke, and you. I'm blessed God chose you to raise me."

Her mamm pressed a hand to her chest. "My

heart aches when you're burdened. Your happiness is important to me."

She hung her quilt back on the rack, hugged her mamm's neck, and bid her farewell. She stepped outside and met Josiah and Beth coming home from school. "How was your day?"

Beth held up a paper and rolled her eyes. "I have more spelling words to learn."

"My day was gut." Josiah pointed. "Mr. Young is on our porch. I wonder if he has candy."

"I wonder why he is here." She clasped Josiah's hand. "Don't ask about candy. It wouldn't be polite. Let's go say hello." She forced a smile to her face, held her kinner's hands, and approached him. "What brings you here, Mr. Young?"

" 'Mr. Young' is too formal, especially after our chat. Please call me Daniel." He gently tapped the noses of the kinner. "You can call me Daniel, too." He lifted his basket. "I brought you jams, a roast, and potatoes." He pulled a small bag from under the cover and dangled it. "And here's hard candy for the kinner."

Beth and Josiah bounced on their toes and accepted it. "Danki, Mr. Young."

Charity opened the door. "Kinner, please take one piece each and then place the bag on the counter. You can have another piece after supper." She returned her attention to Daniel. "Would you like to come in?" She hoped he wouldn't. It rattled her nerves to have him here at this moment. Especially after she and Mamm had just discussed Luke and he was fresh on her mind. She had half a notion to tell Daniel she couldn't marry him, but she shut her mouth. Her kinner's excitement stopped her.

"I won't stay long, but I would like to ask you a question."

She gestured him to a chair. She mustn't be rude. "Would you like something to eat or drink? I've got sweet rolls, and I could warm up some milk."

Mr. Young shook his head. "No, I don't want to trouble you. Please sit."

She folded her hands to keep from fidgeting. Mr. Young prattled on and on about how much he had enjoyed their company on Thanksgiving. She'd hardly said two words.

"I couldn't sleep last night. I tossed and turned. I told you I'd give you until Christmas to give me an answer, but I'm too impatient. Let's get married before the holiday. I'll buy presents for your kinner, and we'll enjoy a gut meal and have our first family Christmas."

She swallowed around the knot in her throat. This man had determination. Again, he hardly paused for air while pleading his case.

"I'm sorry, Daniel. I need more time. This is a big decision. I'll need until Christmas, as we agreed."

"I'm sorry. I'm rushing you." He frowned and stared at his feet. "Take all the time you need."

Sadness was in his voice. It couldn't be easy taking care of six kinner. He was a kind and gentle soul, but she wouldn't marry him out of pity. The marriage must be beneficial to both of them. She bowed her head and went to the door. "Danki for your gifts. It was kind of you. I'll honor your request and deliver my decision in person before Christmas. I hope you enjoy the rest of your day." She hoped he got the message not to visit and suggest this again.

"I'll be praying for gut news."

He mounted his horse and traveled down the dirt road. He had been kind and generous to her and her kinner. She liked him as a person, but no spark of excitement was there at the sight of him. She groaned and rubbed her temples. Headaches happened every time she found herself burdened. With her chin to her chest, Luke popped into mind. The Englischwoman had hugged him. She must be the reason he had shied away from her. Her heart sank. She never had a chance.

She had to do something to get her mind off of Daniel and Luke. She went inside and pushed her arms through her coat sleeves, exchanged her shoes for boots, and headed out to the barn. She grabbed her shovel and mucked the stalls. Maybe work would clear her head. Footsteps padded behind her. She glanced over her shoulder and her breath caught. "Luke, what brings you here?"

"Is this a gut time to talk?"

She set her shovel aside. "Yes. Would you like to come inside? I have bread pudding. Does a warm cup of milk sound gut, too?"

"No, danki. I need to tell you something."

She shifted her weight from one foot to the other. "I have something to tell you, too."

He opened his mouth but then shut it, circled his arms around her waist, and kissed her full on the lips. "I love you, Josiah, and Beth. I'm sorry I've waited so long to tell you."

Tears pooled in her eyes. "Why have you waited?"

"I was afraid."

"I caught sight of you and a woman outside your haus. Who is she?"

"Her name is Martha. She's my former fraa."

Charity, eyes wide, gasped and covered her mouth. She stepped back. "You were married?"

"Jah, for four years."

"What happened?"

"A year ago I hired an Englischer to farm my land so I could do carpentry work for extra money. Six months ago she divorced me and married him. She wanted to experience living in the outside world."

"Is your divorce the real reason you moved to Berlin?"

"Jah. My friends visited and tried to cheer me up. They offered their sympathies over and over again. Their pity wouldn't allow me to move on. Her leaving was the talk of the town. I was broken, confused, and angry. I vowed never to trust another woman again, and then I met you. You, Josiah, and Beth changed my mind, opened my heart, and showed me love." He caressed her cheek. "I love you, Charity."

No wonder the man had been afraid to open his heart to another woman. "I've waited a long time to hear you say those words. I love you, too."

"Will you marry me?"

She bounced on her toes. "Yes! Yes! Yes!"

He twirled her around and kissed her again.

"I'm so sorry she hurt you. I won't leave you. You can trust me." She gasped and covered her mouth. "Oh no! I have to tell Mr. Young I can't marry him. I'm supposed to let him know before Christmas."

Luke's eyes narrowed. "You told Mr. Young you'd consider marrying him? Were you going to say anything to me about his proposal?"

She searched his face. "Please don't be angry.

Yes, Mr. Young's proposal was the news I had to tell you." If Luke had waited another few weeks to ask her to wed him, he might've been too late. "I don't have any attachment to Daniel Young, but he'd have been a gut daed for Josiah and Beth. I doubt I would've gone through with it, though. Most importantly, I was hoping to hear from you what you've told me tonight."

He caressed her cheek. "I couldn't stand the thought of losing you and the kinner."

"I'm thankful we've finally had this conversation. I'll visit Mr. Young tomorrow and tell him I decline his offer." She grinned. "The kinner will be thrilled. They treat you like a daed already. How could I say no?"

"Let's tell the kinner and your mamm our news on Christmas Day, and we'll pick a date together. We'll keep it a secret until then."

"Yes, I like your idea. Our announcement will be a wonderful Christmas present for them. I'll have Christmas at my haus and fix a big dinner."

"If you don't mind, I'd like to have Christmas at my haus. I have some surprises for all of you."

She grinned. "It sounds like a wonderful idea."

The next morning, Charity waved to the kinner as they left for school. She saddled her horse and rode to Daniel Young's haus and found him in the barn.

He lifted a saddle from his horse and lowered it to a sawhorse. He secured his animal in the stall and approached her. He beamed. "Charity, I hope you have come to tell me gut news."

Her knees threatened to buckle. She was confident in her decision but dreaded disappointing him. She winced and swallowed. "You've been kind and generous. I appreciate the food, gifts, and Thanksgiving dinner. You are a gut man, but I must decline your proposal."

Frowning, his eyes widened. "Why?"

"Another man has asked me to marry him, and I've agreed to wed him." She wanted him to learn this information from her. After Christmas, word would spread. She clasped her trembling hands and waited.

"Is this man Luke Fisher, your neighbor? He must've visited you after I left yesterday or you would have said something."

She folded her gloved hands and willed them to stop quaking. Mr. Young's distraught face pricked her heart. "I must keep the man's name a secret until I've told my kinner." She paused and stared at her feet.

"It's all right. My friends have observed Luke Fisher stockpiling your wood and pulling your kinner around on a sled. When I showed your kinner the rooms they'd have in my haus, they told me they'd already picked a new daed. I suspected they meant Luke Fisher."

Charity stifled her gasp. Josiah and Beth hadn't spoken a word to her about their comment to Daniel. Their declaration to him had been inappropriate, but it wasn't a surprise. "The man is Luke, but please don't share my news. We want to tell the kinner and Mamm on Christmas Day." She met his eyes. "Again, I'm sorry to disappoint you. I'm certain you'll find a suitable fraa within our community."

He shook his head. "I won't say a word." He

rubbed his forehead. "I wish you the best. You're a kind, sweet, and strong woman. Luke is a blessed man to have you say jah to his proposal."

"Give my best wishes to your kinner, and danki for being a gentleman about this."

"I care about you, and your happiness is important to me."

Her eyes pooled with tears, and she bid him farewell. The man's forlorn face sent a pang of guilt through her chest. He was sweet, and she disliked having to add to his pain and disappointment. "Dear Heavenly Father, please comfort Daniel Young. Bring him peace and introduce him to his new fraa. Help her to love him and his kinner. Bless him and give him the strength he needs to raise his kinner in the meantime. Amen."

She wiped her eyes. She hadn't liked adding to his sadness. She traveled home, guided her horse to the barn, removed the saddle, and fed him. She sighed. She could now put the unpleasant task of delivering her news to Daniel behind her and look forward to a future with Luke. What would marriage to Luke be like? Would they live in his haus or hers? There were so many things for them to discuss.

Entering her haus, she paused. Memories spun. Aaron reading his Holy Bible in his favorite chair, the kinner sitting on his lap, and their quiet evenings together as a couple after Josiah and Beth had gone to sleep. Aaron would always hold a special place in her heart, but she was ready to move on.

She pumped water into two tubs, added soap to one, and washed, then rinsed clothes. She strung a thick string across the room in front of the fire and hung them to dry. She grinned. It would be hard to wait until Christmas to tell her and Luke's news. Should she tell Mamm beforehand? No, she wouldn't want to ruin the surprise.

The next day, Luke joined them for supper. She reached for the potatoes.

Luke raked a hand through his hair. "How did Mr. Young take your news?"

She inhaled, then exhaled. "Josiah, Beth, if you're finished, you can be excused. I'll wash the dishes tonight."

Josiah and Beth went in the other room and called for Star.

She slumped in the chair. "He was sad and upset but gracious and kind. My heart sank for him. He is a gut man and has suffered so much heartache this past year. I didn't want to add to it, but I had no choice. I told him you proposed to me and asked him to keep our secret. He said he would."

"Would you like it if I talked to him?"

She lifted her eyebrows. "Yes, I would. I don't want to run into him at our church services and have things be awkward between us. I would like the kinner to play together as usual. If he needs anything, I would want him to ask us for help."

"I agree. I'll take care of it."

"Danki, Luke. I would really appreciate it."

"Anything for you."

CHAPTER 6

Luke grabbed his coat and put it on, walking out the door. Charity had a compassionate heart. Her wrinkled brow told him she was worried about Daniel. He wanted to eliminate any distress she had over rejecting the man's proposal.

He paused as he readied his horse and rode to Daniel Young's haus. How he handled this was important. Charity respected him. He tied his horse to the hitching post out front and rapped hard on the door.

Mr. Young swung it open. "Luke, I'm surprised to find you here. Please come in."

He removed his hat and stepped inside. "I won't stay long."

The kinner rushed to him. His heart flip-flopped. Their clothes were stained and wrinkled.

Sweet faces stared at him. "Will you play with us?"

He tousled the little maedel's curly black hair and grinned at the five other little ones surrounding her. "I'm sorry. I don't have time. I must have a word with your daed and be on my way."

Daniel hugged her. "Go play, and when Mr. Fisher leaves, I'll read you a story."

The kinner waved and scampered off.

"Let me take your coat."

"I'll keep my coat on. I should head home soon."

Daniel gestured to an oversized oak chair. "Please sit. Would you like hot coffee? I made a pot earlier."

Luke waved a dismissive hand. "No, danki. You have beautiful kinner."

Daniel sat across from him and nodded his head. "Before their mamm got sick, she cooked, cleaned, and tended to me and the kinner. I loved her very much. I miss her." He paused. "Charity was the first woman I considered for a fraa. She's a strong but kind woman. You're blessed to have her say yes to your proposal."

"She's an exceptional woman. I'm thankful she's agreed to marry me, but I don't delight in your disappointment. We don't want any awkwardness between us. Josiah and Beth enjoy your kinner, and we'd like them to still play together."

Daniel glanced at the kinner playing a game on the floor. "I appreciate your concern, and your visit erases any awkwardness. Danki."

"Gut. Please don't hesitate to ask for our help for whatever you may need." He stood and stretched out his arm.

Daniel shook his hand. "Charity will be blessed to have you for a husband. You're a kind man to have come here today. I've gained a new friend."

Luke bid him and the kinner farewell and guided his horse to Charity's haus. What would it be like to find himself in Daniel's position? He shivered.

He couldn't imagine losing Charity. Daniel Young had a rough road ahead of him. Luke secured his horse and went inside. The kinner sat on the floor in the sitting room playing tiddledywinks, and Star rested between them. "Who's winning?"

Josiah raised his hand. "Me!"

Beth said, "The game's not over yet."

Charity waved him over. "Luke, come in the kitchen."

Luke reached for her hand. "Please sit."

She leaned forward, her eyes full of worry. "How is he?"

"Everything's all right."

"What a relief." She blew out a breath.

"He appreciated the visit. I'm certain he'll speak to us at church services and community dinners with ease. He and I had a nice chat. I admire and respect him. He's doing the best he can under difficult circumstances."

"It was thoughtful of you to visit him for me."

"Now we can put this to rest and plan our own future."

Charity crossed off the day on her calendar. Three and a half weeks had passed since Luke had proposed. One more day, and she could tell her family their news. She poured hot tea in a mug, then bit into a biscuit. Soon they would all live together, and she'd no longer have to bid him farewell each evening. She looked forward to referring to him as her husband. What had his fraa done for him when they were married? What were his expectations?

Later after supper, Luke visited and read Josiah

and Beth their favorite story about Jonah and the big fish, tucked them in bed, and then joined her in the sitting room. "It's getting late. I'd better go."

She patted the spot on the settee next to her. "Sit here for a minute."

He sat. "Is anything wrong? Your furrowed eyebrows and frown say jah."

Charity fingered the corner of her apron. "I have unanswered questions."

"You can ask me anything."

"Where will we live after we're married? What are your expectations of me?"

"My haus is larger. Wouldn't you want to live there? I have extra rooms for Josiah and Beth." He frowned. "Would you be sad to leave your haus?"

"I'm a little sad but ready to start life anew." She darted her eyes from the fireplace to her favorite chair. "Would we sell my haus? My furniture?" She swallowed. She wasn't sure she could watch someone take over her haus right away. She liked Luke's furniture. They wouldn't need two of everything. He had beds and dressers for the kinner.

"Jah, it wouldn't do any gut to have the haus sit empty. I'm certain we could sell your furniture, too. There are always young couples getting married who'd need it. The haus would be a burden for you to keep clean. We'll save the money we earn from the sale and agree on how to spend it."

"The money doesn't bother me." Of course he was right. She hadn't thought of the extra work it would entail. Again, he was thinking of her. Their life would change when she became his fraa. She relaxed. "I agree. It would be silly to keep it all, but do you mind if I bring my favorite chair with me?"

"Charity, you can bring whatever you like."

She leaned forward. "What are your expectations of me?"

"You'll choose what you want to do. My goal is to make you and the kinner happy and secure."

"Do you want more kinner?" She'd wanted more kinner, but she hadn't gotten pregnant again. She hadn't yet put a number to the idea.

"Jah, I would like to have more kinner. Two more bopplin?"

"I agree." He couldn't have said anything more perfect. "Two would be gut. Danki for putting my mind at ease. Please understand, I trust you, but living in your haus and as your wife will be different from what we're used to." She stared at her hands. "I don't want to disappoint you."

He lifted her chin and met her eyes. "You have nothing to worry about."

He stood and she followed him to the door. "You get a gut night's sleep. We have a big day tomorrow, and I've got surprises for you." He leaned in and kissed her.

A thrill of excitement went from her head to her toes. She was ready more than ever to marry him. It would be their first Christmas together. She watched him leave. What kind of surprises would he have in store for her?

The next afternoon, she walked to Mamm's. She sat mending socks. "I've got news."

"Is it gut news?"

"Yes. I told Daniel Young I'm not going to marry him."

Mamm's eyes twinkled. She rocked back and forth in her rocker. "I'm delighted. You've made the right choice. Now I can't wait to see what God has in store for you and Luke."

Charity covered her grin. She wanted to blurt
out their secret, but she could wait one more day.
Mamm might consider it her best present and an
unexpected Christmas blessing.

Luke rose at four on Christmas morning, prepared the turkey, and put it in the wood oven.
Shrugging on his coat and hat, he crossed the yard
to the barn to put his final touches on his present
for the entire family.

Star followed him outside.

He'd thought he'd have trouble hiding it from
the kinner, but the cover on his surprise hadn't
been disturbed. He grinned. If Josiah or Beth had
peeked, they wouldn't have been able to keep it a
secret this long.

After he put his tools away, he went back inside
and studied the hearth. He counted the gifts
wrapped in sackcloth and twine arranged neatly for
Charity, the kinner, and her mamm. He'd enjoy
watching their faces when they opened their gifts,
learned their news, and uncovered his big surprise.

It wouldn't be long before his new family arrived. He grinned from ear to ear. Never would he
have imagined meeting and loving such a beautiful woman, her kind mamm, and her sweet kinner.

Knock, knock. He glanced at the wooden clock. It
was eight.

He grinned and yelled, "Come on in."

Josiah and Beth pushed opened the door, carrying gifts. They said in unison, "Merry Christmas,
Luke!"

Star wagged his tail and barked.

The kinner petted him.

Charity put her basket on the table and gazed at Luke. "Merry Christmas."

Mrs. Vogel followed close behind. "Merry Christmas."

Luke threw a dish towel over his shoulder. "Merry Christmas to all of you."

Beth held up her items. "Where should I put these?"

"Add them to the ones next to the hearth."

Josiah's eyes widened. "Are those for us?"

Beth tapped a finger on her lips. "Which present is mine?"

"Kinner, remember, Christmas isn't about the gifts. We're celebrating Jesus Christ's birthday. Take off your coats, hang them up, and help set the table." Charity shook her head. "They got up at the crack of dawn and have been bouncing on their toes all morning."

"I remember eyeballing the presents next to the hearth as a child. I'm glad they're excited. I am, too." He winked. "Especially this Christmas."

"Me, too."

Mrs. Vogel lifted dishes of potatoes and green beans out of the basket and placed them on the stovetop.

Luke smiled at the kinner's cheerful faces. Christmas this year would be full of excitement having kinner in the haus. The announcement of their news to marry hung on his tongue. He stifled the urge to blurt it out right now. He lifted his Holy Bible from a small table next to his favorite chair. "Are you ready to read the story of Christ's birth?"

Wrinkling his nose, Josiah tugged at Charity's hand. "May we open our presents first?"

"No. This is in celebration of Jesus Christ's birthday. We must honor Him first."

"All right." Josiah gazed at Luke. "Will you read the story, Luke?"

He eyed Charity, smiling at him, and winked. "I'd be happy to." He flipped the pages. "Here's the book of Luke, chapter two." He held it up, then pushed his back into the settee.

Charity and Mrs. Vogel settled into chairs, and the kinner sat close to Luke on the floor. Flames flickered in the fireplace, the air warm.

Luke read the familiar words he'd read so often. He stole glances now and then at the attentive kinner. Their eyes were wide open. Obedient and gut listeners, he loved reading to them. He never tired of reading the story of Jesus' birth.

He finished, and Josiah stood and went to Charity. "May I pray first?"

Charity tousled his hair. "Of course you may."

Josiah returned to the floor next to Beth and bowed his head. "Dear Heavenly Father, forgive me for falling asleep before I finished my prayer last night and for not washing my hands before dinner like Mamm asked. Danki for Mamm, Grossmudder, Luke, Beth, and Star. Danki for Jesus and for our presents. Would You please give us Luke for our daed this year? Beth and I would really, really appreciate it. I love You. Amen."

Luke peeked at Charity when Josiah finished his prayer and winked.

She smiled and shut her eyes.

Luke listened to each of their individual heartfelt prayers to God, and his love grew for each one of them. Then he rubbed his hands together and pointed to a large package on the floor next to the fireplace. "Josiah, this is to you from me. Why don't you open it?"

Josiah untied the twine and burlap covering the gift. He hugged Luke's neck. "Danki, Luke! I love it! I love it!" He lifted the handle and pulled the brand-new, handcrafted pinewood wagon over to Charity. "Isn't it the best wagon you ever laid eyes on, Mamm?"

"Yes, it is, Josiah. Luke spent a lot of time on this for you. You should hug him again."

Josiah scampered over to Luke, and Luke pulled him into his arms. "You're wilkom."

Beth ran her hand along the side of the smooth wood. "Josiah, will you let me take my dolls for a ride in it?"

He puffed out his chest and grinned. "Of course, and you can take me for a ride in it, too."

They laughed.

Luke handed Beth a box. Beth lifted the lid, and her mouth opened wide in surprise. "Mamm, I won't have to ask to use your sewing box anymore!" She kissed his cheek. "Danki, Luke." She held it in her lap and ran her hand over the smooth finish.

He grinned. "Open it."

She lifted the top, then put her hand to her mouth. "Mamm, Luke bought me spools of thread, needles, and brand-new material." She kissed Luke's cheek again. "I love it, Luke."

Charity touched the fabric. "Luke, this is too much."

He shook his head. "I enjoyed buying the presents. I'm glad they like them." He pulled out another large present and pushed it in front of Charity. "Your turn."

She hesitated, then uncovered the present. With a wide grin, she held a hand to her heart. "A treadle sewing machine! Luke, you shouldn't have, but I'll sew twice as many dolls, aprons, and quilts for Sarah and Grace's Sew Shop in half the time using this. Danki." She held his gaze and smiled.

"Mrs. Vogel, open this." Luke passed her a package.

Blushing, Mrs. Vogel peeled away the burlap. "This ink, pen, and parchment paper is perfect for writing my lists of what I need to do and buy at the stores in town. Danki."

Beth placed a present in Luke's lap. "This is from me. I made it."

He peeked inside the clean flour sack and pulled out a navy wool scarf. He wrapped it around his neck. "You did a wonderful job knitting this scarf. It's nice and warm. Danki."

She beamed. "You're wilkom. I'm glad you like it."

Josiah held up his package. "Don't drop it. You don't want them to break. Grossmudder helped me make mine."

Luke lifted the paper box lid. "Yummy! My favorite! Butter cookies!" He pinched off a piece of hard candy on top of one. "Orange is my favorite, too. Danki. Would you like a cookie?"

Beth glanced at Charity. "We can have one before dinner?"

She nodded. "Yes, it's Christmas."

Beth and Josiah each accepted one.

Charity stood and handed him a large soft present.

He opened it and spread the Jacob's Ladder quilt across his lap. He fingered the paper tucked in a small corner pocket. "Should I read this?"

"I make keepsake pocket quilts for Sarah Helmuth's and Grace Blauch's store. I stitched this one for you."

He scanned the letter. *Dear Luke, I tingled from head to toe the first time I met you. I can't wait to start our new life together. My best present is you. I love you with all my heart. Charity.*

"It's perfect. Danki." He held her gaze, glanced at the kinner and Mrs. Vogel, and finding them occupied, mouthed the words *"I love you."*

She patted her heart and grinned.

Mrs. Vogel stood. "I have something for Luke." She crossed the room and passed a gift to him.

He peeled back the white cotton fabric and unfolded the wool afghan. "Mrs. Vogel, this is a generous gift. You must've spent a lot of time on this. Danki."

"You've been a gut friend to Charity and the kinner. I'm grateful to you for taking care of them." She opened her present from Charity, Josiah, and Beth. Her eyes pooled with tears. She unfolded the quilt. "This is beautiful."

Beth pointed. "We tucked a letter in the pocket. Each of us wrote you a note."

Charity's mamm read the notes aloud, tears dripping onto her cheeks. "'Dear Mamm, God blessed me when He gave you to me. My belief in God, guidance to raise my kinner, and the example of being a gut fraa has come from you. I love you and appreciate all you do for me and the kinner. Charity.' Beth and Josiah wrote, 'I love you, Grossmudder,' and signed their names.

"I'll cherish this always." Mrs. Vogel passed Charity, Beth, and Josiah their gifts.

Charity and Beth peeled back the paper at the same time.

Beth held up her scarf. "We have the same one!" She hugged Grossmudder. "Danki."

Charity covered her mamm's hand. "This is perfect."

Josiah pulled the knitted gloves onto his hands. "Look. Grossmudder made me special gloves." He counted from one to nine. He wrapped his arms around her neck. "I love my special present! Danki."

Star sat near the fire, and his head went from side to side to watch them.

Luke petted his head. "Here you go." He handed him a large bone.

Star eagerly accepted his bone and wagged his tail.

Rubbing her stomach, Beth gestured to the kitchen. "I'm hungry."

"I am, too. I'll set the table." Mrs. Vogel stood and stepped to the kitchen. She straightened the utensils and cloth napkins Josiah hurried to put beside the plates, accepted dishes from Charity, and set them on the table, then carried the food and arranged it in the center.

Luke smiled as the women and kinner chose their seats. "Join hands and I'll pray." He bowed his head. "Forgive me of my sins. Danki, God, for Your Son, Jesus. We love You and believe and trust in You. Without You, we would be nothing. Danki for bringing Charity, Josiah, Beth, and Mrs. Vogel into my life. Danki for this food. We love You. Amen."

Josiah scooped potatoes on his plate. "I'm glad you didn't talk to God too long. I'm starved."

Charity covered Josiah's hand. "Josiah, your

words may have made God sad. Talking to God is a privilege, and you shouldn't take it for granted."

He bowed his head. "Dear Heavenly Father, I'm sorry. I really do love You. I'm just hungry. I'll talk to You later. Amen."

Luke stifled a chuckle and passed Charity's mamm the green beans. "Mrs. Vogel, may I pass you anything?"

"No, danki. I'll have trouble finishing what I've put on my plate."

A little while later, Charity and her mamm cleared the table. "Josiah and Beth, you don't have to help do dishes."

They both clapped their hands and grinned.

Luke glanced over his shoulder. "May I help you?"

"Mamm and I will take care of it. Have fun entertaining the kinner."

Holding up a puzzle, Beth gave him a curt nod. "I brought us a puzzle. Come and work it with us."

"I'll find all the outside edge pieces." He joined them on the floor in front of the fire.

A half hour later, Beth snapped in the last piece. "We did it!"

Josiah ran his hand along the finished product. "The birds are orange, purple, and blue. Blue's my favorite color."

Luke stood. "Let's go check on your mamm and grossmudder. Maybe we should help them."

Beth skipped to the kitchen.

Luke and Josiah followed her.

"Are you done yet?"

Mrs. Vogel kissed Beth's nose. "Jah."

Luke said, "I've got one more present for everyone. Get your coats on and follow me."

They shrugged into their coats and hats and padded out the door to the barn. Luke threw back a dark cloth. Their eyes widened.

Charity climbed in. "This sleigh is beautiful!"

"Take us for a ride!"

Mrs. Vogel stood. "Luke, when did you have time to build this?"

"Late at night I snuck out here and worked on it." He helped Mrs. Vogel get in and then hitched the horses to it.

He couldn't contain their special secret any longer. He slid in next to Charity. "Before we go, we should tell them our news. We'll always remember our first Christmas and the sleigh when we reflect on this moment. It will be an easy date to remember."

"You think of everything." She touched his hand. "You tell them."

Josiah leaned in. "Tell us what?"

"I've asked your mamm to marry me. She said jah. What do you say?"

Josiah and Beth clapped their hands and shouted, "Yippee!"

Luke reached for Charity's hand. "We'll talk to the bishop tomorrow and schedule a date."

She grinned and nodded.

Mrs. Vogel wiped a tear and smiled. "This is the best present of all, an unexpected Christmas blessing!"

An Unexpected Christmas Blessing
Glossary

Pennsylvania Dutch / German	English
Ausbund	Amish hymnal with words only
boppli; bopplin	baby; babies
bruder	brother
burnoose	cloak
daed	dad
danki	thank you
dechder	daughters
dochder	daughter
Englischer	non-Amish person
fraa	wife
grossdaadi	grandfather
grossmudder	grandmother
gut	good
haus	house
kapp	covering for Amish woman's hair
kinner	children
kumme	come
maedel	girl
mamm	mother, mom

Ordnung	rules agreed upon by the Amish leaders that must be adhered to by the Amish community
schweschder	sister
wilkom	welcome
jah	yes

This month, look for more comfort and joy in
THE AMISH CHRISTMAS KITCHEN

by

**Kelly Long
Jennifer Beckstrand
Lisa Jones Baker**

A dash of joy brings everything together . . .

*Something's always baking in an Amish oven, and at
Christmastime, all the ingredients for joy are at hand.
Wrap yourself in the warmth of the Amish home—and
the Plain peace of hearts joined by love. Each story
includes a recipe from the author!*

BAKING LOVE ON ICE MOUNTAIN
Kelly Long
Newly married, Clara Mast and Daniel Kauffman
have little to give but love during their first
Christmas season together. But generous hearts
are always willing to be creative in this "Gift of the
Magi" inspired story.

THE CHRISTMAS BAKERY ON
HUCKLEBERRY HILL
Jennifer Beckstrand
When shy Katie Rose Gingerich's *dat* sends her to
Huckleberry Hill to secure a marriage proposal,
she never expects to long for carefree Titus
Helmuth—or to hope that he might want to
spend every Christmas with her . . .

THE SPECIAL CHRISTMAS COOKIE
Lisa Jones Baker

A charity auction, an unexpected friendship, and a stubborn spirit combine in an unusual courtship. But for Emma and Jonathan, overcoming obstacles is just one of the lessons to be learned about special blessings this holiday season.